THE
SILENT
DOLLS

THE SILENT DOLLS

RITA HERRON

bookouture

Published by Bookouture in 2020

An imprint of Storyfire Ltd.
Carmelite House
50 Victoria Embankment
London EC4Y 0DZ

www.bookouture.com

ISBN: 978-1-83888-761-2
eBook ISBN: 978-1-83888-760-5

This series is dedicated to Christina Demosthenous, my fabulous editor who asked for a female detective series just when I had one sitting in my computer waiting! Timing is everything!

PROLOGUE

*Somewhere on the Appalachian Trail, Georgia,
twenty-five years ago*

Tears trickled down her cheeks as she curled up inside the tiny cave-like space.

She rubbed her fingers over the little wooden doll the man had carved. He said he'd made it just for her.

Then he'd told her there were more dolls and a beautiful dollhouse with furniture and fancy clothes to dress them in. All she had to do was crawl through the tunnel.

She hated the dark. But she'd wanted to see the dollhouse so bad she'd wiggled on her belly through the narrow space and followed him.

Now she lay on her side, the darkness all around her. Alone. The ground was cold. Hard. Jagged with rocks. Her fingers touched something wet and sticky. She pulled her hand back, but something brushed her leg. *A spider!* She shrieked, moved as far away from it as she could, but her back hit the wall.

She'd tried clawing her way out, but the dirt and stone was too hard. And she couldn't find the opening. He'd put something in front of it. Maybe a piece of wood? Or some tree limbs?

He'd said he had to leave for a while, but he was coming back. Then they'd play a game. But she didn't want to play a game with him, and she'd told him so.

He'd yelled at her to be quiet. Told her not to cry or scream. Not to be a baby.

But she'd cried and screamed anyway. Her throat was raw, her eyes felt swollen shut.

She wanted her mommy and her daddy. She wanted to go home.

There wasn't a dollhouse in here. Or any more dolls.

He'd lied about that. Had he lied about coming back, too?

CHAPTER ONE

Day 1 Missing

March 1, 4:45 p.m., Crooked Creek, Georgia

Another day. Another criminal to find.

Detective Ellie Reeves crawled beneath the barbed wire fence, gun aimed, eyes scanning the old farmhouse. Smoke billowed from the barn and the scent of chemicals filled the air, a sign that her information was right.

The abandoned barn was being used to cook meth.

Bastards. The mountains had once been safe from crime. Now they offered countless places to hide.

She tugged the barbed wire from her jacket where it had caught, then stood up and ran toward the building, crouching between bushes and weeds as she approached. A beat-up truck and a puke-green sedan were parked beneath a cluster of trees, where the dealers thought they were hidden from sight.

Definite evidence of a meth lab: piles of trash outside; two-liter plastic soda bottles; discarded boxes that had once contained cold pills; windows on the house wide open to release the toxic chemicals.

The acrid, urine-like scent.

She checked her watch. *Should wait for backup.* She'd called it in on her drive here. But there was no time. The cavalry would have to come later. She had to be at her parents for dinner in half an hour.

Her father said it was important. Non-negotiable.

And when Randall Reeves requested her presence, she responded.

Gun drawn, she darted toward the barn door and peered inside. A skanky-looking guy in his twenties with a goatee stood by a smoking pot, a burly older man counting cash into a tin box. Frying pans and a propane tank were in full view. Acetone, pseudoephedrine, coffee filters, and bottles with rubber tubing lined metal shelves. The stench nearly knocked her over.

She braced her Glock, pushed the barrel through the opening of the door and inched closer. A quick visual sweep and she saw a shotgun on the far side of the room on a rickety table.

They'd never reach it in time.

She kicked the door open, gun aimed. "Police. Put your hands up."

The men startled. The burly one grabbed the cash while the scruffy one, as predicted, ran for the shotgun. She fired a bullet that pinged off the ground by his feet, and he screeched and threw his hands up. The other guy ducked and tried to roll, but knocked over the cashbox, bills floating into the meth-infused air like green confetti. He scrambled to retrieve them, but she strode over and slammed her boot on his hand just as he clawed at a hundred-dollar bill.

A siren wailed outside, getting louder by the second. Goatee guy dove for the shotgun, but Ellie nailed him in the knee, and he went down with a loud howl, knocking a tray of chemicals to the floor. Voices and shouts echoed from outside, and one of the Crooked Creek deputies, Heath Landrum, raced inside, gun drawn. Ellie's captain was behind him, his face scowling as he took in the scene.

"Fuck, Detective Reeves," Captain Hale shouted. "You know better than to open fire in a meth lab."

She did, but she couldn't let the jerks escape. Still, she saw what he was upset about. Chemicals had spilled, and the cook pot was beginning to spark.

"Shit. Let's get them out of here." She snagged the one with the goatee and let Deputy Landrum haul the bigger guy outside.

Just as they made it to Landrum's squad car, the place blew up, shooting flames and sparks into the darkening sky.

CHAPTER TWO

After an ass-chewing from her boss, Ellie sped toward her parents' house. She expected another earful for being late from her mother. And another for not stopping to change her clothes. Dirt stained her jeans from crawling on the ground, the barbed wire had ripped her shirt sleeve, and she smelled of sweat and burned plastic from the fire.

Vera Reeves preferred women to *dress* for dinner. She should have given up on Ellie accommodating her a long time ago. Still, she kept nagging and hoping and nagging and hoping that, one day, Ellie would become a girly girl. That she'd finally trade her shield and gun for a wedding ring.

Not going to happen. Ever.

She was a tomboy and police officer through and through.

But tonight, Vera would not rain on Ellie's parade. Her father was planning to announce his retirement, and Ellie expected him to back her in the upcoming sheriff's election. She'd wanted this all her life.

When she was a little girl, she begged him to let her ride along when he went on calls. In high school, when the other girls were primping and infatuated with boys, she'd worked in his office, filing, answering the phone, studying old case files and crime-scene reports. She'd also been obsessed with crime shows and binge-watched *FBI's Most Wanted*.

Gravel spewed from the tires of her Jeep as she spun up the drive to her family homestead. After running a hand over her disheveled ponytail, she dusted off her jeans and t-shirt as she climbed out. She dragged on a denim jacket to cover her holstered gun.

With the steep mountain ridges jutting up in the background, the bare tree branches and dark storm clouds cast an eerie grayness over the land. The national forest was spread out for hundreds of miles, with thick wooded areas, deep gorges, sharp ridges and towering cliffs.

When she was five, she'd gotten lost in the midst of the towering trees and tangled vines and had been terrified. The darkness and cold had closed around her during the night as the hours creeped by, slowly and steadily suffocating her. She still had nightmares where she was struggling to breathe as she crawled through a long, deep cave that smelled of a dead animal.

A cave with no way out.

When her father finally found her the next morning, he'd given her his compass, so she'd never lose her way again. Over the next few months, he'd taught her how to read maps. After that, the Appalachian Trail, the AT as it was known, had become her second home.

Her father had always guided her, protected her. Had never let her down.

He never would.

She noticed a black Range Rover parked to the side of the house. *Damn.* Her father's lead deputy, Bryce Waters, was here.

In elementary school, she'd actually been friends with Bryce. Their fathers fished together, and she and Bryce had tagged along, rowing their own canoe. They'd ridden bicycles all over town, played softball, and built a fort from scrap wood her father kept in the garage.

But once he hit puberty, Bryce changed. Started showing off. Desperate to be popular, a homely tomboy like her had cramped his style.

Then in high school… She shuddered at the memory. Didn't need to think about that right now. It was ancient history.

When she was elected sheriff, she'd make it clear that she wouldn't tolerate his bullshit or drinking on the job, not like her father did.

She didn't give a flip how many women he screwed. She just didn't want to hear about it. And he was definitely the type to kiss and tell.

The gusty March wind whipped through the trees as she climbed the steps to the front porch, a sign that winter was hanging on with a vengeance. The rocking chair creaked back and forth, back and forth, as if someone had just been sitting in it.

Ellie turned, but there was no one there.

Odd, how sometimes the mountains and wilderness offered solace, while other times sinister shadows floated through the dense mass of rocking trees as if they were haunted. Each year attacks on females increased, and the death toll seemed to rise.

It was well-known in these parts that the mountains were home to all sorts. Some folks who sought refuge in the hills and ridges were mentally ill or hiding from the law. Others were simply recluses or eccentrics who balked at society and chose to stay off the grid. Her father called them the Shadow People.

According to Ms. Eula Ann Frampton, the woman on the hill who claimed she talked to the dead, some were pure evil.

Shaking off her morose thoughts, Ellie rapped on the door before opening it. Her heart raced with anticipation, and she expected the scent of her mother's celebratory burgundy beef stew or pork tenderloin to fill the air. Instead, there was nothing but the hint of pine cleaner, indicating her mother's maid had come today. Vera Reeves' house had to be kept as immaculate as she kept herself.

Maybe this was just a family meeting, and dinner wasn't included.

She kicked the worst of the mud from her boots onto the welcome mat before she entered, although nothing but a good scrubbing could remove the Georgia red clay.

Voices rumbled as she headed down the hall toward the living room, where she could hear glasses clinking. Her heart fluttered in anticipation, and she wiped her sweaty palms on her jeans as she stepped through the doorway.

Her mother sat in the velvet wing chair by the floor-to-ceiling brick fireplace, a martini in one hand. Her father held a tumbler of whiskey as he stared into the fire. When he turned, his shoulders were squared, posture rigid. His hair looked mussed, his clothes rumpled, and dark circles rimmed his brown eyes. He didn't quite make eye contact, his lips pressed into a thin line.

She'd seen that look before when he was working a troubling case, one that kept him up late at night, unable to sleep, unable to stop.

Something was wrong.

Had he changed his mind about retiring? Had there been a horrific crime in the town? Was he ill?

Before she could ask, Bryce rushed toward her, a bourbon in his hand, the amber liquid sloshing over the rim of the glass. Tonight, his green eyes glowed with excitement, and he'd combed his wavy sandy-blond hair back from his forehead. He was good looking and he knew it.

She pulled her gaze away. A snake lived under that skin.

"Guess what, Ellie?" he said. "Your dad's going to endorse me for sheriff!"

Ellie went bone still, frozen, as if she'd stepped into the wrong house. Wrong family. Wrong everything.

Bryce's smile suggested he was oblivious to her feelings. Or maybe he wanted to rub the announcement in her face as payback for what she'd done to him years ago.

Probably the latter.

Her father's hands tightened around his highball glass. "Honey, I wanted to talk to you first, but Bryce got here—"

"You're backing him instead of me?" The betrayal made it difficult for Ellie to breathe.

"I thought you'd be happy for me, Ellie," Bryce said, his tone all innocence. An innocence designed for her parents. Bryce was a chameleon. He seamlessly changed skins to suit the occasion and whoever he wanted to impress.

He damn well knew she wouldn't like being thrust aside by her own father, and he was gloating. "You can transfer and work in my office with me," he said with a wink.

Oh, hell, no. She'd never work in the same office as Bryce Waters. He knew that, too.

But that was a conversation for later. Her father was running this show.

"What the hell is going on, Dad? You know I've worked my butt off for this opportunity. And I'm more qualified than Bryce."

"Wait just a minute," Bryce said, feigning hurt. "I'm qualified."

Her mother, dressed in an elegant, green silk pantsuit, swept across the room in a cloud of Chanel No. 5. "Watch your manners, Ellie." She offered her daughter a glass of merlot and patted her stylish brown bob into place, a sign she'd kept her standing appointment at the Beauty Barn today. Gray would never see her hair. "Let's toast the occasion. Bryce is the right candidate. Being sheriff is a man's job."

Ellie pushed the wine glass away. "It is?" she said, barely hanging onto her temper.

"You could always run against me," Bryce suggested with an eyebrow raise. "Except you know I'm pretty popular in these parts."

Ellie shot him a look of disgust. "You may have Dad fooled, Bryce, but I know exactly who you are."

Bryce's eyes narrowed. Curiosity flared on her father's face, and for a moment she thought he might question her comment. But he didn't.

"It's best, Ellie," he said quietly. "Being sheriff is about politics as much as police work. You're constantly in the limelight and under pressure."

Ellie crossed her arms. "You don't think I can cut it because I'm a woman?"

Her mother laid a manicured hand on Ellie's arm. "Honey, elections bring out the ghosts in people's closets. Word might spread about your therapy sessions when you were younger. You know how folks in small towns gossip." She pursed her lips. "You don't want them to find out about your fear of the dark. And the… hallucinations."

Ellie gaped at her in stunned silence. How dare she say that in front of Bryce? And Vera was the one who didn't want anyone to think her daughter was unstable. God forbid a child of Vera Reeves was the hot topic of the rumor mill.

"A sheriff has to instill confidence in the people he represents," Bryce added.

Ellie forced a lethal calm to her voice. "That was years ago. I was only a child, Mother, and traumatized from being lost in the woods that time." Granted, she still slept with the light on—although she wasn't about to admit that…

"It would still come out," her father said. "And you would get hurt, El. Trust me, stick to your job, and let Bryce run the county."

"Are you working the Cornbread Festival in town this week?" her mother chirped. "Tourists are already flocking in. There'll be arts and crafts booths, food trucks, face painting and one of those jumpy houses for the children." She clapped her hands together. "And the Stitchin' Sisters have a special display of their cross-stitch designs and quilts. Bernice at the bakery is even making her homemade fried pies and cinnamon rolls. And there are going to be dozens of varieties of cornbread."

Just what her mother wanted; for her to work small town security details. It seemed strange to Ellie to be celebrating cornbread recipes. But there was an occasion for everything in the mountains. Vera embraced the almost weekly fall and spring festivals which seemed to draw tourists. She insisted they brought in revenue for the fledgling little communities and celebrated the southern way of life.

Ellie, on the other hand, was drawn to mind and word puzzles, maps, and exploring the land. Her father had taken her camping, fishing and hiking and taught her to shoot when she was twelve.

She'd admired her father's toughness and dedication to protecting the residents of Bluff County, which encompassed several small towns along the AT. Stony Gap, where her parents lived, housed the sheriff's office, and Ellie worked at the police department in the neighboring town of Crooked Creek, only fifteen miles away.

Police work was a better fit for her than homemaking. The *only* fit for her.

But if Bryce was sheriff, she'd technically be working for him. She wanted to throw up at the thought.

"But Dad—"

"My decision is made," he replied, his voice curt. "I won't change my mind."

"It is a man's world, Ellie," her mother said. "It's time you accept it."

Sympathy for her mother mingled with bitter disappointment. Her mother actually believed what she said. She'd made a good home for them. She was a supportive wife. But she didn't understand that Ellie was different.

"Not anymore, Mom," Ellie said, her anger bleeding through. "Not anymore."

She removed the compass her father had given her from her pocket and thrust it toward him. "You can have this back now. From now on, I'll find my own way."

Betrayal bubbled inside her as she turned and strode down the hall. The gallery of family photos in the foyer mocked her. All the holiday dinners and celebrations. The trips with her father as they hiked and camped along the AT.

She shoved open the front door, slammed it behind her and jogged down the porch steps. Tears stung her eyes as she climbed into her Jeep, but she brushed them away and floored the engine, more gravel flying as she roared down the driveway.

Damn it.

How could she work under Bryce Waters?

She punched the gas and raced toward the open farmland outside of town. Driving fast had become her tension release. Just as she was reaching eighty and flying toward Haints, the bar overlooking the graveyard where a lot of cops and law enforcement liked to hang, her cell phone buzzed. If it was her father, she'd ignore it.

She glanced at the screen, and saw her boss's name flashing.

Cursing, she pulled over and braced herself for another tirade, fumbled to set up her handsfree, then answered. "Yeah."

"A little girl has gone missing on the trail," Captain Hale said. "Seven years old. Name is Penny Matthews. Ranger McClain is with the family. Get over there pronto."

Ranger McClain—Cord—worked with the Search and Rescue division of FEMA – the Federal Emergency Management Agency – and the National Park Service. The NPS had jurisdiction over the AT, and coordinated with local law enforcement agencies across the 2200-mile trail; fourteen states from Georgia to Maine.

"Copy that."

Ellie's heart hammered. The endless miles of forests, rugged terrain, knife-edge ridges, uneven land, overhangs and steep drop-offs were treacherous. So many places a little girl might fall. So many places she might never be found. There were also wild animals that might prey on a helpless child. Ellie's heart pounded even harder at another thought.

What about human predators?

CHAPTER THREE

The wind picked up, rattling the windows of Ellie's Jeep as she raced toward the park to meet Cord. Noting the storm clouds gathering on the horizon, she flipped on the news.

"*This is Cara Soronto, Eleven Alive meteorologist, with an update on our winter storm advisory. We're now tracking the latest snowstorm along the eastern coast, traveling all the way from New York to Georgia. Folks are calling this one Tempest for its violent winds and bitter cold. Within the next forty-eight hours, expect high winds up to fifty miles per hour and the wind chill to dip into the subzero range. Rain will turn to sleet then heavy snowfall, which could create whiteout conditions.*" She paused. "*Brace yourself, people. We haven't seen anything like this in years.*"

Ellie's stomach knotted. A child was missing, and a vicious storm was on the way? They had to find this little girl fast.

Even without a storm bearing down, the Appalachian Trail was dangerous. Each year at the beginning of March, hundreds of adventure seekers set out to conquer the 2000 miles from Georgia to Maine. But the truth was that most weren't mentally or physically prepared for the unforgiving conditions, isolation, and countless obstacles along the way, never making it to the finish line.

"What time was the child reported missing?" she asked her boss, dragging her thoughts away from the worst possible outcome.

"Timing's a little sketchy, and something you should narrow down," Captain Hale replied. "Parents thought she just wandered off. Looked for some time before they called for help."

"So, it's possible she's been gone for a while." Or that the parents were lying. Covering an accident or a crime, waiting to call because they'd hurt their daughter and needed time to hide the evidence.

Don't go there yet. People get lost on the trail all the time.

"Exactly," Captain Hale said. "Ranger McClain organized a search party as soon as he was alerted. They've been combing the woods ever since, but so far nothing."

Every hour that passed lessened their chance of finding Penny alive. If a predator had abducted her, they could be getting farther away.

Ellie forced the images away. She had to think positive. Cord might be mysterious and a loner, but he was a pro. He knew these woods inside and out. Maybe even better than her father did. She ignored the wrench in her stomach at the thought of his betrayal.

"One more thing, Detective Reeves," Captain Hale said. "The Matthews family live in Crooked Creek, but this happened between us and Stony Gap, so I want you to act as liaison between our two police departments."

Ellie's stomach began to churn. Her gut instinct was to insist she couldn't work with her father or his deputy right now.

But a little girl's life was hanging in the balance.

She'd have to suck it up. Keep it professional. They'd find Penny then go their separate ways.

"I'm issuing an AMBER alert," Captain Hale said. "Let's hope the media can get this in the evening bulletins. The clock's ticking."

Ellie glanced at the clock instinctively. She hung up and pressed the accelerator.

CHAPTER FOUR

Adrenaline spiking, Ellie pulled into the lot for Crooked Creek Park, snagging her camera as she climbed from the Jeep. The chill in the air cut through her, making her pull her coat up around her neck. The dark storm clouds were gathering, rumbling and ominous.

When she'd gotten lost as a child, she'd thought the spiny branches resembled skeletal fingers reaching out to snatch her. She'd seen monsters hiding in between the pines and oaks.

Today that same kind of suffocating fear pressed against her chest.

Except today she wasn't afraid for herself, but for the lost little girl.

Voices drifted from the woods, a woman's anguished cry dragging Ellie back to the present.

Penny's mother.

Sympathy surfaced, but she forced herself to harden. Despite this tragedy, she had a job to do and that meant interrogating the parents. Asking questions they might not want to answer.

But that didn't matter. Getting the truth was the only thing that did.

Through a clearing ahead, she spotted Cord standing near a plaid picnic blanket which he'd roped off and secured while he coordinated with search teams.

The search and rescue dogs were there waiting, two trained handlers gripping their leashes.

A slender brunette, who looked about forty years old, sat on a boulder, sobbing into her hands. A tall man with messy, muddy-colored hair paced in front of her, his jeans and boots dirty, sweat trickling down the side of his face. SAR—search and rescue volunteers who assisted in emergencies—had brought a cooler filled with bottled water. The man she pegged as Penny's father grabbed one and guzzled it.

Cord's smoky gaze skated over her as she approached. He was handsome in a brooding, intense kind of way. Shaggy, unkempt dark brown hair. Strong wide jaw. High cheekbones. A jagged scar ran along his temple and into his hair. His body was honed, muscles galore. Not a man of words, but one of action. His rugged appearance, bronzed skin, North Face jacket, and calloused hands made it obvious that he thrived in the wilderness.

Occasionally she read lust in his eyes, and memories of the one night they'd spent together before she'd left for the academy. Other times he was so brusque she thought he was angry at her, although she didn't have a clue why.

Still, she considered him a friend. No one knew the trail better than Cord. He'd spent his teenage years living in these mountains, even though he refused to talk about that time.

He had no family that she knew of. No sense that he wanted one either.

She didn't have time to ponder those questions now, though. "Have you found anything? Any signs where the little girl might be?" Ellie asked.

Scowling, Cord shook his head.

She gestured toward the parents. "What's your take on them?"

"Verdict's still out. Mother hasn't stopped crying. Father goes from being angry to distraught and back again. He combed the woods for a while before calling for help. By the time I arrived, they were both practically hysterical."

"I'll talk to them then look around." Ellie glanced at the dogs. "Have they been out yet?"

"No, canines just arrived. I asked the mother if she had any clothing or a toy, something of Penny's, that we could let the dogs sniff." He gestured toward the woman, who clutched a pink crocheted blanket to her cheek. "So far, she hasn't wanted to give it up though. Said it's her little girl's lovey."

Children did get attached to things. Not a fan of dolls as a child, Ellie had a stuffed orange fox she'd carried with her everywhere, even on her camping trips. She'd pretended it was real and would ward off a bear attack. Foxy still held a special place on the shelf beside her bed.

"I'll see what I can do," she replied.

Cord pointed toward a wooden board where he'd tacked maps of the mountains. "We've searched a five-mile radius, but we need to expand. Your father's on his way. He can help with that."

A fresh wave of pain washed over Ellie at the mention of her father. But Randall Reeves had worked and lived in Bluff County for over twenty years. As far as knowing the area, he and Cord were their two best assets.

Pushing aside her hurt, she introduced herself to the parents. Mrs. Matthews asked her to call them by first names, Susan and Stan.

"I can't believe this is happening," the mother said in a choked whisper. "We were having such a nice day, and then suddenly… she was just gone."

Was she?

Various scenarios played through Ellie's head like a horror movie. The child had run away. Gotten lost. Was hiding out in the woods.

Then her mind went to the more nefarious possibilities. The little girl had been kidnapped. Sexually assaulted. Killed.

She braced herself to remain objective. Hard to do when a child was involved, but necessary to be effective. Her job was to find Penny Matthews, even if she had to step on a few toes to do so.

"I understand this is a difficult time," Ellie said in a sympathetic tone. "And I know you're frightened. But we're going to do everything in our power to find your daughter."

Fresh tears fell from Susan's eyes. Stan heaved a labored breath. "We've looked everywhere. How far can a little girl go on foot by herself?"

Good question. Another reason they needed to nail down the correct timeline. "Walk me through your day. Tell me everything that happened."

"We've already been through this," Stan snapped.

His wife gently touched his arm. "Honey, she's just trying to help."

"Then she should start looking for Penny!" he bellowed.

Cord's gaze shot to her, silently asking if she needed backup, but she shook her head. She could handle the situation.

"I realize you're frustrated, but please bear with me," Ellie said. "We have teams looking for Penny. It's important I get a clear picture of your day and your family life. Even the smallest detail could be significant."

The father shifted onto the balls of his feet. His wife gave a wary nod.

Ellie adopted a calming tone. Winning the couple's trust was key to convincing them to confide in her. Or to catching them in a lie. "I assure you that Ranger McClain is the most experienced tracker in the area." She gestured toward the baby blanket. "May I give that to the crew now? It's obviously special to you, but it might be helpful in tracking Penny's scent."

Susan wiped at her damp cheeks, then pushed the blanket toward Ellie. "I would like it back though. Please. I crocheted it for her when I was pregnant."

"Of course." Ellie offered her an understanding smile, then motioned to Cord, who carried the blanket to the handlers. One of them knelt, allowing the dogs to sniff it. A second later, the animals put their noses to the ground and set off on the trail.

"Now—" she said, turning back to the couple— "let's start with this morning."

The mother seemed to visibly pull herself together. "Please, Stan," she said, "let's talk to her. Maybe it will help. I… want my little girl home…"

Ellie's heart squeezed. The raw anguish in the woman's voice was real.

Of course, that wasn't proof that the mother didn't know what had happened to her daughter. Or that either of the parents weren't complicit. It simply meant that if there had been an accident or if they had somehow hurt Penny, guilt was setting in.

CHAPTER FIVE

Ellie studied the couple's body language. They sat untouching, barely looking at one another. Was it a telltale sign that they weren't close, or that something had happened, and they were trying to cover their tracks?

"Do you have a photograph of Penny?" Ellie asked the mother.

Susan smiled. "On my phone, but I forgot it and left it at home."

"I have one." The father accessed his photographs and offered his cell to Ellie.

Dozens of candid shots of their daughter filled the screen.

Deja vu struck Ellie. The soft blonde curls and gap-toothed smile reminded her of another child… Mae.

God. Her breath caught. She hadn't thought about Mae in a long time.

"Detective?" Susan's whisper dragged her back to the present, and she studied the pictures. Penny in a princess costume holding a plastic pumpkin full of Halloween candy. Penny at the bus stop on the first day of school with her oversized backpack. Penny climbing a tree. Penny hugging a yellow teddy bear to her as she swung back and forth in a tire swing.

"She's precious." Fear pulsed through Ellie at the thought of what might be happening to the little girl. "What was she wearing today?"

Susan twisted her fingers together. "Her pink t-shirt with the unicorn on it. She got it for Christmas. And she had on black leggings and neon-pink tennis shoes."

"How about a jacket or hat?"

Susan shook her head. "She threw her jacket off and left it over there." She pointed to a bright purple hoodie, then her expression wilted again. Taking her husband's phone, she ran a finger over her daughter's face. "She's my baby. I… can't lose her."

"We'll do everything possible to bring her home," Ellie assured her, carefully avoiding promises she might not be able to keep. "Susan, what happened this morning?"

Penny's mother clutched the phone as if the pictures physically connected her to her daughter. "I made pancakes for breakfast," Susan said softly. "Chocolate chip funny face ones. It's Penny's favorite." Her voice cracked.

Ellie glanced at the husband. "Were you all three together for breakfast?"

A muscle ticked in Stan's jaw. "Yeah. I had a work phone call, but I was home."

"Where do you work?"

"I drive a delivery truck for one of the supermarket chains. But… my boss just laid me off. That's what the call was about."

"That had to have been a blow," Ellie commented.

"Sure as hell was. Sucks when you can't pay your bills." His gaze dropped to his hands, and she noticed scrapes on his knuckles. From a fight? Had he punched something or someone? Or from scouring the woods for his daughter?

Thunder clapped above the treetops, making Susan startle. A reminder they couldn't waste time. "It's not his fault," Penny's mother said. "Stan is a hard worker, always punctual, never takes a sick day. He even worked holidays this year. But the company's done this before, laid off people during slow times."

Being upset over the layoff could go to motive if Stan had hurt his daughter.

She'd explore that line of questioning later.

"What happened after the call?" Ellie asked.

Rain clouds shifted, blocking the fading light and casting shadows across Stan's face. "Penny and Susan were planning a picnic when I came back into the room."

"I encourage her to play outdoors, not to just sit in front of the TV or play video games." Susan gave a small shrug. "We try to be good parents."

Ellie patted her hand. "I'm sure you are, and that she knows you love her."

Stan flexed his hands. "When Penny heard I didn't have to go to work, she begged me to go with them, too. Take my mind off things."

"I packed a picnic lunch, and we drove into the mountains," Susan continued. "Penny played in the playground, then we picnicked here." She indicated the plaid blanket on the ground in front of them. "After we ate, we carried the breadcrumbs to the creek to feed the birds." Susan's chin quivered. "With my allergies, I didn't sleep well last night, so I stretched out to take a nap while Stan and Penny went fishing."

Ellie angled her head toward Stan. "Did you catch anything?"

He frowned. "Naw, fish weren't biting. Penny got bored and wanted to look for nuts and sticks and feathers to make a collage," Stan continued. "She's always collecting stuff."

He paused, and Ellie could see the wheels turning in his mind. Remembering or fabricating a story?

"What happened next?"

He looked down at his hands again. He seemed to be staring at the bloody scrapes on his knuckles without really seeing them. "My leg was throbbing, so I sat down to rest."

"What's wrong with your leg?" Ellie asked.

"Had an accident last year and broke it. Still hurts when it's cold outside or when it rains."

"I'm sorry to hear that," Ellie said.

He shrugged. "Anyway, I told Penny not to go far. I stayed by the creek with the fishing poles while she went digging around."

In her mind, Ellie saw the little girl skipping through the woods gathering sticks, nuts and river rocks just as she'd done when she'd followed her own father as a child. She'd collected arrowheads, framing them and hanging them on her wall.

"A few minutes later, I called out her name and she didn't answer." His voice rose with panic. "I ran all over the place looking for her and couldn't find her."

"His shouting woke me up," Susan cut in. "Then we both started searching."

"Did you phone 911?" Ellie asked.

"I did," Susan said. "That ranger came over with a couple of other men and they started looking. But they couldn't find her either." Raw fear laced Susan's voice. "What if she fell on one of those ridges? Or hit her head? Or what if she slipped in the creek?"

"Ranger McClain and his men will look into all those possibilities," Ellie assured her. "Did you see anyone else in the woods today? Another family maybe? A stranger?"

"No, no one," Stan answered.

"Wait," Susan said. "There was a young couple. They got here after Stan and Penny walked down to the creek."

"Were they hiking the trail?" Ellie asked.

"When they saw me, they decided to take their picnic to the river. They seemed like they wanted to be alone."

Possibly. Or could they have been casing the area for a child to take?

"Anyone else?" Ellie pressed.

"Some teenagers, three boys." Susan pointed toward the trail that led northeast. "They were hiking to the falls."

Stan looked panicked. "Why do you ask? Do you think Penny didn't just wander off? That those boys hurt her?"

Ellie forced a neutral expression, although her mind raced with scenarios. "That's not what I'm saying. If someone else was out here, they may have seen which direction Penny went." Or witnessed what happened to her.

Stan dropped onto the boulder beside his wife and lowered his head into his hands. "What if some monster took my little angel?"

Ellie hesitated for a heartbeat. "Was there anyone—a family member, a brother or uncle, a friend, a neighbor—who showed special interest in Penny?"

"No," Susan cried. "We don't have family close by. But our friends and neighbors and the teachers, they all love Penny, but nothing weird, you know?"

"Stan, how about you? Can you think of anyone?"

He shook his head. "No."

A strained moment passed. Birds chirped and the sound of an animal scavenging for food drifted through the forest. The wind picked up, howling off the ridges.

"Okay… Is there anyone who might want to hurt you by taking Penny? Or someone who thought you had money for a ransom?"

"Heavens, no," Susan replied. "We live paycheck to paycheck."

Stan's eyes darkened, and he grunted. "I had a beef with my boss a while back. But that was because he shorted me in my paycheck. He said it was a mistake and fixed it."

That ruled him out.

Ellie gestured to the scrapes on Stan's hands. "How did you get those?"

He ground his boot into the ground, smashing a pinecone to pieces. Dust fluttered in Ellie's face.

"I… I was so pissed about that call I punched the wall," he admitted. "How's a man supposed to put groceries on the table if he can't work?"

She glanced at his wife for confirmation. "He just lost it for a minute, that's all. What kind of heartless person fires their employees when they have children to feed?"

"I understand your frustration," Ellie said, hoping to form a connection with the couple. "Sometimes hitting something is a good way to let it out." She let the subtext sink in.

Stan pinned her with razor-sharp eyes. "I have a punching bag in the garage. I started using it when our money got tight." He stood and paced, fists clenched by his sides. "But I don't take it out on people. And I'd never hit my little girl. *Never.*"

"We both love Penny," Susan said earnestly. "We had a hard time getting pregnant. Not Stan's fault but mine." She looked down, lips pressing tightly together. "We had to go through IVF. The treatment cost us a fortune."

Stan went ramrod straight. "She's worth every damn cent," he said. "If anyone hurts her, I'll kill them with my bare hands."

CHAPTER SIX

Ellie inhaled a deep breath. If her child was lost or abducted, panic might blind her. She might lash out in rage.

"This is the spot where you picnicked, correct?" Ellie asked, trying to focus on the practicalities.

Stan narrowed his eyes. "Yes. We've already told the ranger all this." He pointed toward the rock bed by the creek. "Then we skipped stones and fished."

"Do you remember anything else? A noise nearby? A car from the parking lot? Voices?"

Stan shook his head. "Just Penny humming. She squealed every now and then when she found a rock or leaf she was excited about. And then it got quiet and… she was gone."

"Did you fall asleep too?" Ellie asked.

A self-deprecating look streaked across Stan's eyes. "No. I just had a lot on my mind. Wondering how we'd make ends meet this month."

Voices drifted from the parking lot, and a minute later, Ellie's father and Bryce appeared in the clearing. Jaw set tight, her father started toward her.

Ellie raised a hand, and he stopped in his tracks. She wasn't ready to talk to him. Yet.

She might never be.

Cord glanced back and forth between them, his brows furrowed, but he didn't question it. Instead he motioned for her father and Bryce to join him at the board where he'd tacked the map and search grids.

"I have to do something," Stan said. "I'm going to look for Penny." He darted toward Cord and her father.

Ellie let him go. She had no real evidence to hold him. And if he was innocent, he was entitled to search for his own child. Although he should be watched, no matter what—if guilt kicked in because he'd hurt Penny, he might even lead them to her.

After her father and Bryce were up to speed, Ellie pulled Cord aside while the men organized themselves into teams.

"The timeline is off. My guess is Dad fell asleep, and Penny was gone long before he realized it."

Cord shifted. "Then Penny would have had time to venture farther away than our original search radius."

Ellie nodded. "Or if someone abducted her, they had time to escape." She tucked an errant strand of hair back into her ponytail. "Also, Susan saw three teenage boys hiking to the falls, and a couple headed toward the river. Pass the word to the teams to look for them. We need to question everyone out here today. Maybe someone saw something."

"I'll fill everyone in and expand the search," Cord said.

"Have them look for signs of an abduction. Drag marks. A scuffle. Blood." Ellie paused. "Also have someone stick with Matthews, just in case he's up to something. I'll stay with Susan. Without her husband by her side, she might open up." Susan's comment about it being her fault they had trouble getting pregnant bothered her. Had Stan been angry with his wife? Had he wanted a child as badly as she had? Had he resented spending the money on IVF?

Cord muttered agreement, then hurried to join the other men.

Wind whipped leaves around Ellie's feet, dark clouds rumbling, casting a grayness everywhere as the last remnants of the sun started to fade. Already she could feel the temperature dropping.

Worse, it would be dark soon. Tree frogs croaked like a band of bandits, crickets joining in the song. Shadows were already hovering and flickering in the deep forest, the sound of a wild animal's howl reverberating off the mountain.

Ellie yanked on latex gloves, removed her camera from her bag, then walked around the area and snapped photographs. The plaid blanket weighed down by rocks, the picnic basket holding plastic cutlery, paper plates and napkins. A trash bag lay on the ground, drawing ants. A cooler sat next to it, empty plastic water bottles by the trash, a plastic container half full of Oreos spilled on the ground. Empty potato chip bags. A chewing gum wrapper. Nothing that stuck out.

Still, she texted the captain and requested an Evidence Response Team, and added:

Have Landrum research the parents' financials. And get warrants for the couple's home, computers and other devices.

Captain Hale simply responded, *On it.*

She circled the picnic area again, searching for blood or signs of a struggle. A torn piece of clothing or a lost button. A rock where Penny might have accidentally fallen and hit her head.

Nothing.

She closed her eyes and formed a mental picture of the family. Penny's blue eyes smiling, pink barrette in her hair, blonde ponytail blowing in the wind. Penny chattering beside her parents, eating lunch, skipping stones across the water's edge. Shrieking with excitement over a tiny stone that looked like a gold nugget.

The creek water rippling softly over the jagged rocks, lulling the mother to sleep. Penny's father tired and frustrated over losing his job. Worried. Angry. Dozing off while something happened to his daughter.

Ellie followed the path to the creek, looking for footprints and disturbed brush, broken twigs and crushed leaves. Anything to tell the story of where the little girl had been. Or signs of someone else at the scene.

Large footprints that could have matched Stan Matthews' stopped at the creek, then they wove in circles and returned to the picnic site. The ERT would cast his footprints for comparison.

Evening shadows flickered across the trail, the sun dropping lower into the horizon beyond the pines, oaks and cypresses. A red, orange and yellow sky streaked the tops of the mountain peaks, disappearing into black as the storm threatened.

With so many search workers, the ground would soon be muddied, the scene compromised with their prints. The wind could already be scattering smaller pieces of evidence.

Ellie surveyed the area. This park served as the base for the AT; it was a popular entry point for hikers beginning their northbound trek and also drew tourists who enjoyed the falls. The closest shelter on the trail was at least eight miles away. The thought of Penny lost and alone sent a shiver right through her. To a seven-year-old, the endless mass of trees and brush would look like a jungle she'd never be able to escape from.

People who set out to tackle the AT saw it as an adventure, a challenge. But most weren't prepared for the grueling steep inclines and the monotonous miles of wilderness. Thick trees hugged each other so tightly light could barely seep in. After a while, the mass of oaks, pines and ash blurred into one another. The trail maps were difficult to read for inexperienced navigators. Hikers got lost and wound up walking in circles. Some disappeared and were never found.

She prayed Penny wouldn't be one of them.

Faced with illness, hunger, fatigue, and plunging temperatures, it was common for hikers to give up, leaving the adventure to return home to the comfort of warm beds, showers and hot meals.

AT shelters—wooden lean-tos with three sides—offered some refuge when conditions turned dangerous, although the buildings were crudely constructed. Worse, rodents infested them, leading to diseases that rendered hikers incapable of continuing.

Then there were those that the mountains hid. Recluses, the homeless, drug addicts, and criminals seeking refuge in the forest. The Shadow People, her father called them. Many of whom didn't want to be found.

A child alone with no provisions didn't stand a chance. At least not for long.

Ellie walked along the creekbank, illuminating the ground with her flashlight. Cord joined her, his expression pensive as he pointed out the men's boot prints, followed by a smaller pair that looked like sneakers. They most likely belonged to Penny.

She snapped more pictures then turned in a wide arc, following Cord toward a giant oak. Moss and lichen covered the ground. Wild mushrooms pushed through the soil.

"Looks like the father rested in this spot," Cord said. A Braves baseball cap lay in the tangled brush; had it fallen when he'd dozed off, and then been forgotten about in his frantic search?

She bagged it to verify it belonged to Stan, before returning her attention to the footprints.

The little girl's prints remained near the creek and disappeared around the curve ahead. The path grew steeper and narrower, threaded with winding tree roots and cobbled with rocks. Dirt and dust swirled around her as the wind intensified, clogging the air.

"She was following the creek," Ellie said.

"It's shallow here, but a couple of miles downstream it reaches a good five feet in depth," Cord pointed out. "If she was a good swimmer, it wouldn't be deep enough for her to drown. Although I can't imagine her wading in the frigid water."

"Unless she had an accident and fell into the creek," Ellie replied. Or someone drowned her. She tried to shake away the thought, but it latched on, ugly and sinister.

The creek grew wider past the hill where they stood, the ground rockier, the drop-offs severe. If Penny slipped and fell in, she could be hurt, hanging on, hoping for someone to save her. "Get a team to follow the creek downstream," Ellie said.

Cord's brows shot up, as if he realized she was right. With night setting in, they had to act quickly.

He made the call while Ellie panned the flashlight to the right. About fifty feet north, something shiny glittered in the weeds. She walked to it, checking the ground as she went, then stooped to pick it up.

An old pocketknife. Plain wood handle. A common brand you could buy at any outfitters' store. Still, she bagged it.

Another few feet ahead, something else was caught in the brush. Ellie crouched down to examine it. She pushed aside the weeds and found a child-sized pink and white friendship bracelet. With gloved hands, she snagged it and turned it over in her hand.

The name Penny was etched on the inside.

CHAPTER SEVEN

The sight of the bracelet made Susan break down. "Yes, that's hers. We made them last week with her little friend." Penny's mother reached for the bagged bracelet, but Ellie shook her head.

"I'm sorry, I need to keep this. At least for now." She gestured toward the Braves cap. "Is this Stan's?"

Susan nodded, then wiped at her eyes. Ellie stowed the evidence bags she'd brought back from the creek, then asked for the parents' phones.

"I'd like to put a trace on them in case someone calls you with information about Penny." Or a ransom call, she thought.

Susan narrowed her eyes but did as she was told. Ellie texted Cord and asked him to confiscate the father's phone as well.

Cord responded: *Scheduled search teams around the clock. Your father is guarding Matthews. He refuses to leave the search.*

Copy that. I'm driving Susan home.

Then she texted Deputy Heath Landrum: *Meet me at the Matthews' house.*

Susan protested about leaving but Ellie insisted on driving her home. By the time they reached the woman's house, Susan looked glassy-eyed and wooden, shock setting in. Heath's dark green Pathfinder was already in the drive.

Thunder boomed in the sky, storm clouds steadily rolling in. As Ellie climbed out, her gaze was drawn to the side yard and the playset. The creak of the empty child's swing echoed in the wind as it swung back and forth, just as ghostly as the rocking chair on her parents' porch.

Behind the fifties ranch house, the North Georgia mountains rose like giant rocky statues. The sharp ridges and cliffs looked even more ominous now that Penny was lost out there in the dark.

Ellie surveyed the property. The yard was neatly kept, the azaleas on the verge of blooming. A child's bike lay overturned near the carport. Trampoline alongside the swing in the side yard. Soccer ball against the fence. No warning signs just yet.

Suddenly a voice called Ellie's name, and high-heeled footsteps clacked on the driveway behind her. "Detective Reeves, it's Angelica Gomez from WRIX Channel 5."

Ellie exhaled sharply. *Gawd.* She'd known the press would pounce—the AMBER alert was supposed to get their attention. She just wasn't ready to face them. And the verdict was still out on whether Angelica Gomez was a vulture or one of the rare good ones.

A slender man with a full beard trailed Angelica, his camera poised to capture the drama.

Heath suddenly appeared by the Jeep, eyes narrowed as he looked at her for direction.

Stepping in front of the reporter and cameraman, Ellie shielded Penny's mother.

"Take Mrs. Matthews inside," she told Heath.

Susan looked startled when the camera's light was switched on, and Ellie cursed. "Get that camera away from her," she shouted. She was tempted to shove it into the leech's face.

The cameraman scowled at her but backed away, and Heath ushered Susan to the front door.

Knowing she couldn't avoid the press entirely, Ellie licked her dry lips and faced the tall, athletic woman. Angelica's hair was black, short and spiked, her skin a golden bronze. Attractive, and judging from the determined look on her face, a go-getter. "You got here quickly."

Angelica gripped the mic with blood-red fingernails. "Actually, we've been waiting for over an hour. We understand a child from Crooked Creek has gone missing?"

Ellie schooled her expression. She couldn't reveal any details. Not yet. "Yes, I'm sorry to say that seven-year-old Penny Matthews disappeared today after a family picnic. At this point, it appears she wandered off and lost her way."

Angelica started to cut in, but Ellie threw up a warning hand. "All of Bluff County law enforcement, including both Crooked Creek and Stony Gap's police departments, are on the case, working alongside Search and Rescue teams to search the woods for the child." She displayed a picture of Penny on her phone, directing it so the cameraman could capture the image. "This is Penny Matthews. She was last seen wearing black leggings, a pink t-shirt with a unicorn on the front, and neon pink sneakers. Anyone with information regarding the child's disappearance should call local police." She gestured toward the mountains beyond the house. "Night is on us and a winter storm is barreling in. We're doing everything possible to find Penny and bring her home before morning."

Angelica thrust the microphone towards Ellie. "Do you suspect foul play?"

The million-dollar question.

Ellie gently eased the microphone away from her face. "At this time, we have no evidence of that, but are considering all possibilities. We ask you to respect the family's privacy during this traumatic time. Now, I need to get to work." Without waiting for a response, she hurried up the sidewalk, her muddy boots pounding the concrete in her haste to avoid the inevitable question on the tip of the reporter's tongue.

CHAPTER EIGHT

Ellie hesitated on the stoop of the Matthews' house. A tattered wreath made of dried leaves, berries and branches hung on the door. So unlike her own mother's designer decorations. Not that her parents were wealthy, but appearances meant everything to Vera Reeves. Score one for Mrs. Matthews indulging her daughter's creativity.

The creak of the swing echoed in the wind and drew her gaze again. For the briefest moment, she thought she saw a little girl sitting in it. Penny with her blonde curls bobbing up and down. Penny home safe, laughing as she pumped her legs, her hair flying in the wind. Her laughter tumbling across the yard as a butterfly flitted around her face.

Before she could ring the doorbell, Heath opened it, his expression troubled. Susan Matthews' tears had probably taxed him to the limits. He was young, late twenties, and a little green, but if he wanted to do police work, he had to grow a pair.

"Where's Susan?" Ellie asked as her gaze swept the entryway into the den.

"In her daughter's room," Heath said with a sigh. "She's in bad shape."

Ellie hissed between her teeth. "It's been a long day." The night ahead would be even longer.

"What did you tell the reporter?" Heath asked.

"The basics." She paused, then handed him Penny's mother's phone. "Working on getting the husband's. See what you can find on here."

He nodded. "On it. I've been looking at their financials. The couple was strapped. So far, no secret accounts, deposits or withdrawals."

Stepping into the living room, Ellie said, "I want to look around the house, see Penny's room." And talk to Susan again. A wife's account of her marriage might change without her husband hovering over her.

"Father admitted they had fertility issues and resorted to IVF. Nearly bankrupted them." As well as fertility treatments being expensive, she'd heard they took an emotional toll on couples. Sometimes even destroying marriages.

"Stan also claims he had an accident last year. See if they owe money for hospital bills or if he's taking pain meds."

The opioid epidemic was rampant. People suffering from long-term injuries often became hooked on prescribed painkillers. As prescriptions ran out, they became desperate, resorting to any lengths to get hold of their next fix.

"Also verify they don't have a trust fund hidden somewhere, or a life insurance policy on Penny."

Heath entered the list on his phone. The deputy was organized to the point of being OCD. He was also tech-savvy. Definitely a helpful skillset in an investigation, and not her strong suit.

Footsteps sounded, and Susan appeared in the doorway from the hall. Her eyes were red-rimmed and swollen. "It's night. Penny hates the dark," she said in a choked whisper.

So did Ellie.

As if to punctuate Susan's concern, thunder clapped outside, and raindrops pinged against the windows. The storm would only make the situation more frightening for a child, and Ellie knew that better than anybody. The growl of bears, mountain lions and wolves reverberated through the black forest, sounding terrifyingly closer than they really were. It was impossible to see your own feet, much less if you were stepping in a hole or off a cliff. As if the wild animals weren't dangerous enough, some claimed there were even man-eating plants hiding among the vegetation.

"I'm sorry, Susan, so sorry." Ellie motioned for the woman to join her in the living room.

Penny's mother collapsed into a big, tattered club chair and began to chew on her fingernails.

While Heath went to do the research, Ellie found two glasses in the cupboard, filled them with water and carried one to Susan.

Dirt and dust from the trail still clogged Ellie's throat, and she gripped her water glass, downing half of it. "Stan mentioned that his leg was hurting. Did he take medication for pain management?"

Susan brushed droplets of perspiration from her forehead. "Just ibuprofen. Nothing stronger." Her eyes widened. "You're not implying he was doing drugs?"

"Just asking routine questions. Remember, it's important that I have a clear picture of everything that happened today."

Susan fidgeted and tapped her foot on the carpeted floor. "I shouldn't have taken a nap. Shouldn't have closed my eyes for a second."

"You thought Stan was watching her," Ellie murmured. "I know Stan was upset about losing his job, and his leg was hurting. Is it possible that Stan nodded off? That the two of you both fell asleep at the same time?"

Susan glanced into her glass as if she might find answers in the clear liquid. "I don't know. I mean, maybe. But Stan is usually so responsible when he watches Penny. He loves that little girl more than anything in the world."

"I'm sure he does," Ellie said. "But if he fell asleep, maybe more time passed than he realized. That could mean that Penny may have been missing longer than you originally believed."

Susan sucked in a deep breath. "I… suppose that's possible."

It meant someone could have taken Penny from right under their noses. But she didn't point that out. Yet.

Now to the touchier matter.

"You mentioned being financially strapped," Ellie carried on. "Did that strain cause problems in your marriage?"

Susan leaned forward, clearly agitated. "Listen to me, we were happy. You're wasting time if you think Stan is to blame for this." She strode to the back door and looked outside into the night. Lightning zigzagged above the treetops, splintering the dark with jagged lines.

Susan's defensive attitude toward her husband could mean they had a loving relationship and family. Although abused women often defended the very men who hurt them.

"I'm sorry if I upset you," Ellie said. "I really am just trying to find your daughter. May I see Penny's room?"

The woman gestured for Ellie to follow her. The house was old, with worn-out beige carpet and fading yellow paint on the walls, but the rooms appeared to be clean, neat, orderly.

A spare bedroom held baseball cards, framed sports posters and a Tom Glavine jersey on the wall, indicating Stan was a serious collector of baseball memorabilia. Passing it by, they reached a cotton-candy-pink room. Dozens of stuffed animals were piled on a white iron bed covered in a pale pink coverlet adorned with dancing fairies. A bulletin board hung above a white wicker desk and held numerous childhood drawings of the sun, rainbows and unicorns. On a bookshelf beside the desk were shoe boxes full of seashells Penny must have collected on family vacations. Another contained pinecones, feathers, rocks and a bird's nest. Penny clearly liked nature.

Much to her mother's consternation, Ellie had similar interests at that age. She'd balked at making hair bows and painting headbands with her mother. Instead, Ellie had brought home arrowheads, frogs and turtles.

Susan scooped up a yellow teddy bear and pressed it to her chest. "Penny wanted to take Toby today, but I wouldn't let her." Her voice broke. "She can't sleep without him and her blankie."

Ellie's chest tightened. Toby was the teddy bear in the picture with Penny.

A wall of sketches caught her attention. Penny's portrayals of fairy tales, princesses, and butterflies were bright and colorful. Odd though that the family picture wasn't quite so cheerful. And in it, Penny's father was standing far away from his daughter. Could mean something, or simply that at her age, she had no perspective of distance.

"Show me where Stan punched the wall."

Susan's eyes flickered with unease again, but she led Ellie to her bedroom. The imprint of the man's fist in the shattered sheetrock looked stark, and dots of blood spattered the plaster. Ellie scanned the room for signs indicating a struggle or fight. A broken lamp or overturned chair. But everything else appeared to be in place.

Still, she had to press while Stan wasn't around. "It's just you and me now," Ellie reminded her. "Be honest, for Penny. Has Stan ever hit you? Or his daughter?"

Anger flashed in Susan's eyes. "No. Stan is not abusive. Stop asking me about him and find Penny."

Susan ran into the bathroom, her sobs drifting through the closed door.

Guilt nagged at Ellie for pushing the woman.

But she had to do her job. If someone had taken the little girl, her room might hold a clue.

Studying it again, she noted children's puzzles, books, toys, and art supplies filling the shelves. No diary or any disturbing drawings. Collages of leaves and pressed flowers hung on another wall. Her closet held only assorted shoes and clothes.

The main bathroom came next. Green child's toothbrush, toothpaste, children's Tylenol, antibiotic ointment, Band-Aids. No prescribed medications. Nothing out of the ordinary.

Returning to the den, she glanced out the front window. Gomez and the cameraman were still there—they were broadcasting or filming a piece to camera, but at least they were keeping their distance.

Ellie stepped out onto the back deck, looking for signs that Stan Matthews was not the loving husband and father he purported to be, or signs someone else could have hidden out back, waiting for the little girl.

Whispers of evil rippled through the forests, trees rattling in the wind. Voices called to Ellie. A child's. Penny crying. Begging to come home.

That creaking swing drew her gaze once again. Only this time it wasn't Penny she saw in it.

It was Mae. Sandy blonde hair, ponytail soaring in the breeze as she pumped her legs. Her big eyes wide with fear.

Ellie's lungs strained for air. *God…* Mae, her imaginary friend. Her childhood therapist said she invented Mae as a substitute for the sister she'd never had.

Medication and hypnosis had helped rid Ellie of the hallucinations and the nightmares. Finally, she'd sent Mae back to the fantasy world where she belonged.

Why was she seeing her now? Because Penny was getting under her skin? Or because Ellie's mother dragged up the past earlier?

Something's wrong with Ellie. She's seeing things that aren't there…

Ellie pressed her hands over her ears to drown out the sound of her mother's disapproving voice.

She sure as hell couldn't allow Mae to come back and haunt her now. Not when she had to prove her father and Bryce Waters wrong.

Determined to stay focused, she pulled her phone from her belt and texted her captain: *Get subpoena for Penny Matthews' medical records. Let's find out if she suffered any suspicious injuries.*

The little girl needed her to be strong.

CHAPTER NINE

Special Agent Derrick Fox was bone tired. Coming off a manhunt where he'd been tracking an escaped felon meant no sleep for days.

Thankfully though, the wife-murdering bastard was on his way back to Hayes Prison, Georgia's maximum-security facility, where he'd spend the next weeks in solitary confinement and finish out his life sentence.

Derrick let himself inside his Decatur condo, desperate for a shower, a pizza, then a much-needed uninterrupted night's sleep. But first he popped the lid on an IPA, carried it to his living room and flipped on the evening news. Just as he'd expected, a recap of the manhunt was playing. His boss, Supervisory Special Agent Aiden McDaniels, stood in front of the camera assuring residents in and around metro Atlanta they were once again safe.

As safe as anyone in a big city like Atlanta could be.

The segment ended, immediately rolling into a breaking story in north Georgia.

Derrick's gut tightened. Just the mere mention of those mountains stirred bad memories and ghosts from his past.

"*A seven-year-old little girl, Penny Matthews, disappeared in Bluff County between Stony Gap and Crooked Creek today around one o'clock,*" reporter Angelica Gomez said. "*Her parents say they were enjoying a family picnic and had been fishing when the little girl wandered off. After an initial search of the area, they called for help. Local law enforcement and search and rescue teams have been combing the area ever since.*"

A photograph of a smiling, gap-toothed little blonde-haired girl appeared on the screen clutching a pink blanket and a yellow teddy bear to her. "*Penny was last seen wearing black leggings, a pink t-shirt with a unicorn on the front and neon pink sneakers. Police are asking anyone with information regarding the missing child to please call law enforcement.*" The numbers for Bluff County sheriff's office and the Crooked Creek police department flashed on the screen.

Derrick sat stone still. His head swam with memories of his own sister disappearing on that trail. Precious Kim, who liked jumping rope and playing hopscotch. Kim, the hula hoop champion in first grade. Kim, who'd just lost her first tooth and broke her toe when she'd kicked a bully at school. Kim, who'd set up a lemonade stand to raise money for the animal rescue shelter.

Kim, who he was supposed to be watching the day she disappeared. Instead, he'd told her to sit on a rock while he waded in the creek. He'd been so engrossed in trying to catch a fish with his bare hands he hadn't realized she'd wandered off.

Vanished without a trace.

She'd never been found.

It was all his fault. He should never have taken his eyes off her.

Concern welled in him as he thought about Penny Matthews. The reporter had mentioned Bluff County. Kim had disappeared near the same area.

His IPA forgotten, he strode to the wall-length whiteboard in his home office. Perspiration beaded his neck as he studied the photographs and the map tacked on the board.

Photographs of more than a dozen other little girls who'd disappeared along the numerous towns and states from north Georgia to Maine. All the families had similar stories. All suffering, laden with guilt, what ifs and horrific images of what might have happened to their precious daughters. Some hanging onto embers of hope that their loved one was still alive. Embers of hope that dwindled as each day passed with no answers.

He'd been tracking the disappearances for the last ten years.

There was a pattern. At least he thought there was. Only he had no proof. No clear profile of the killer or suspect, or where or when they might strike again.

With the girls disappearing hundreds of miles apart in dozens of different jurisdictions, no one else had made the connection.

Penny Matthews' gap-toothed smile flashed behind his eyes. The little girl reminded him of Kim.

He opened his laptop and searched for the name of the police officer in charge of the investigation.

Detective Ellie Reeves.

His pulse jumped. Was she related to Sheriff Randall Reeves?

He quickly ran a background search. Yes. Ellie Reeves was his daughter. Randall Reeves, the sheriff of Bluff County at the time Kim went missing.

The man who'd allowed his little sister's case to go cold.

Maybe it was time he paid the sheriff and his daughter a visit.

If Penny Matthews hadn't simply wandered off, and he was right about the connection between the missing girls, a serial killer was stalking the Appalachian Trail—and had been for over twenty years.

CHAPTER TEN

Crooked Creek

Angelica pushed the microphone at Ellie as soon as she stepped outside the Matthews' house.

"Any updates, Detective Reeves?"

Ellie gritted her teeth. "Not yet. Rest assured we're working diligently to find this missing child before it gets any darker. Again, we ask for anyone with information to phone the authorities." Pulling up her hood to ward off the rain, she elbowed her way past the reporter, dove in her vehicle and hoped the press didn't follow. She had to canvass the neighbors, get their take on the Matthews' family.

The homes in the area all looked to have been built in the fifties, on quarter acre lots, and many had been renovated, although a few still bore the original paint and roofing and sat vacant, needing repairs.

The neighborhood was also near the park in town, and the road leading to Cold Creek Falls, a waterfall which drew tourists and photographers, especially in the fall and spring when white water rafting, canoeing, kayaking, camping, hiking, and exploring the mountains attracted tourists and locals alike.

Ellie spent the next hour and a half knocking on doors, asking about the Matthews family and fending off questions from curious neighbors who were terrified a crime had happened in their own backyards.

Finally, the rain slackened, giving her a momentary reprieve from the pounding downpour.

It turned out the house closest to the Matthews belonged to a woman named Bernice, an acquaintance of Ellie's mother. Bernice was visibly upset when she answered the door. The scent of her homemade cinnamon bread wafted toward Ellie. Her mother had mentioned that Bernice was baking for the festival. Last year Ellie had bought one of her homemade pound cakes and a peach cobbler to support the youth groups' mission trip to Honduras.

"Hey, Ellie, I saw you on the news," Bernice said. "Have you found that precious little girl?"

Ellie sighed. "Not yet, Ma'am. Search parties will be looking around the clock. I'm doing some background work on the family. Do you know Mr. and Mrs. Matthews?"

Bernice fluttered a hand to her chenille robe. "I do, although I know Susan better than the daddy. She and Penny bring me dinner once a week, and I give them free cookies. Penny likes my peanut butter and chocolate chip ones."

"Sounds delicious." Susan was shaping up to be a saint.

"Do Susan and Penny get along?"

"They were so sweet together, it reminded me of my daughter, Lola, when she was little. Although I don't get to see her so much anymore. She moved to California with her husband. He's real uppity and doesn't like the country." She laughed softly. "Thinks just because we talk slow, we're dumb as dirt here. But these hills are my home and I'm proud of it."

"I hear you. Now tell me about the father," Ellie said, steering her back on track. "How was Stan with Penny?"

Bernice's white eyebrows knitted together. "He kicked the soccer ball with her. Taught her how to ride her bike."

"But he was on the road a lot with his job?" Ellie asked.

"Yeah, drove that big rig. Man had a temper, you know. Once he pulled out of the drive so fast, he knocked the trash can over. Another time he sideswiped the mailbox." She tsked. "Good thing that little girl wasn't back there, or he could have run over her."

It could mean nothing. Or it could point to a pattern of violence on Stan Matthews' part.

"Did you ever notice anyone watching Penny? Maybe a stranger or a friend of Stan's? Someone at the bus stop?"

Bernice clacked her teeth. "Not that I recall. Susan always walked Penny to the bus stop and stayed with her until she got on and sat down."

Ellie handed Bernice her business card. "If you think of anything else that might be helpful, please give me a call."

Next, Ellie went across the street. A light was burning in the window, a rusted station wagon in the drive. A hound dog loped up and licked her hand as she approached. She stooped down and gave the dog a back scratch, then made her way to the door. The yard was overgrown, the cement path to the front door cracked, the shutters loose and flapping in the wind.

She scanned the property. No signs of a child.

Everything appeared calm, so she raised her hand and knocked. Footsteps sounded from inside, then a voice shouted, "Yeah, coming."

The wind whistled off the mountain, a clap of thunder echoing in the distance, promising more rain. Ellie clenched her hands by her sides. The clock was ticking. Night had set in fast and furious, the sun obliterated behind gray storm clouds. With winter storm Tempest careening their way, sleet and snow would follow soon and wind chills that could be deadly. If Penny was lost, she prayed she'd found shelter.

The sound of the lock turning echoed from inside, then a moment later, the wooden door screeched open. The scent of cigarette smoke and stale beer hit her so strong that she coughed.

The silver-haired man on the other side made no apology as he puffed on his non-filtered Camel. Slight-framed with stooped shoulders and age-spotted hands, he looked to be in his late seventies. He pushed his wire-rimmed glasses up with a crooked finger as he squinted at her. The dog brushed past Ellie and trotted inside.

She introduced herself, but he cut her off. "I know who you are. Seen you on the news with that reporter."

Of course he had. Everyone else in the county would see it too. She just hoped she didn't let down the people counting on her. "Your name, sir?"

"Lewis Farmer."

"Do you live alone or is there someone else here?"

"Wife passed about thirty years ago. Just me and Gomer now. You found that little girl yet?"

"No, sir, that's the reason I'm here. Have you noticed anything odd around the Matthews' house lately? Perhaps someone watching Penny play outside? A stranger in a car? Maybe someone taking pictures? Walking a pet?"

He knocked the ashes from his cigarette into an aluminum can he held in his gnarled hand. "Naw. Although yesterday Stan had it out with some man in the front yard. Susan yelled at him to calm down, but Stan said no teacher had any right to come to his house and say such things."

"What kind of things?"

"Something about how Stan disciplines her. You know some folks believe spare the rod, spoil the child."

Ellie's breath quickened. "Does Stan believe in corporal punishment?"

"Hell, I don't know. But Stan yelled at the guy to get off his property or else."

CHAPTER ELEVEN

Ellie sat at the kitchen table with Penny's mother again. Susan cradled her daughter's yellow teddy bear in her arms as if it was a baby.

"Susan, one of your neighbors mentioned that Stan had an argument with Penny's teacher."

Susan dumped sugar into her tea and stirred it vigorously. "He did. But it really was nothing."

"Tell me about it," Ellie coaxed.

"Penny drew a family picture at school, and Mr. Zimmerman got the wrong idea."

"What idea was that?"

Susan picked at her cuticles. "She drew Stan with a monster face. But it didn't mean anything. She's a child and was mad because she wanted a pony and Stan said we couldn't afford it." She shook her head as if to dismiss the incident. "Anyway, Mr. Zimmerman stopped by the house and had the gall to accuse Stan of hurting Penny."

Ellie remained silent, hoping Susan would elaborate, but she seemed to be lost in the memory. "Was he?"

"No. For heaven's sake, Mr. Zimmerman overreacted. Stan loves that child."

She paced to the window and Ellie wondered what she saw. Her husband and daughter playing chase in the yard?

Or Penny running scared from her father?

*

Ten minutes later, Ellie flipped on the radio and set out to drive
around Crooked Creek to check out some abandoned properties.
Dark gray clouds still hovered overhead, adding to her anxiety.
Penny was out there alone. Frightened. Cold. Missing her mommy.

Just like Ellie had been that night she was lost.

Her headlights lit on a sign that read BRYCE WATERS FOR SHERIFF,
the first of several he'd plastered along the highway. A visual that
cut through her like a knife.

The weather report drew her back to the overcast skies *"This
is Cara Soronto, Eleven Alive meteorologist, bringing you the latest
breaking news. Winter storm Tempest has already struck New York,
Pennsylvania, and Virginia, causing several deaths and stranding
motorists all along the highways. Major airports are shutting down for
the next forty-eight hours and travelers are advised to stay put, hunker
down and prepare to be snowed in. Residents in North Carolina, Tennessee and Georgia should expect record snowfall, frigid temperatures
dipping into single digits, and a wind chill factor that feels more like
subzero than freezing."*

Ellie shivered and punched the radio off, battling an image of
poor little Penny freezing to death in the woods all alone.

Focus. You're not that scared little girl anymore.

Do your job and find her.

So far, the inclement weather forecast had not deterred tourists.
The Crooked Creek Inn parking lot was full, and in conjunction
with Bluff County, the restaurants and shops had been decorated for
the festival. The committee chairs had marked off spaces for vendors
to set up. There would be arts and crafts booths, antiques, local
produce stalls with jams and jellies, homemade fudge and honey.

Food trucks would park near the stage, which would be show-
casing musicians and entertainment. A chili cookoff between local
business owners was one of the highlights, along with the varieties
of cornbread for tasting. The festival usually marked the beginning
of spring, bringing the first wave of tourists to the mountains. Ellie

had loved it when she was a kid, because she and her father would plan their first whitewater rafting trip of the season for right after. Her heart gave a pang.

As if he sensed she was thinking about him, her phone buzzed and his name appeared on the screen. She let it roll to voicemail and drove past the Stichin' Sisters' Quilt Shop and the Beauty Barn, where the gossip mongers thrived. The owner Maude Hazelnut—Meddlin' Maude Ellie called her—was just locking up, her head bent as if sharing something salacious with Edwina Waters, Bryce's mother.

A second later, her cell rang again. This time it was Cord.

She punched connect. "Please tell me you have good news."

"I wish I could. So far nothing. Randall said he called, and you didn't answer. Where are you?"

"Working. Did you find something?"

"Not yet. By the way, your father stumbled on those teenagers that Matthews spotted. They were setting up camp near the falls. They claim they hadn't seen the little girl. No indication she'd been around their camp or nearby. We've sent them home, with a stern word from the SAR team about respecting mountain weather." Cord paused. He sounded out of breath. "Randall is following up with the parents. We're rotating search teams for the night."

"I'm going to check some of the abandoned buildings around town just in case someone kidnapped Penny and is hiding out. Shondra's doing the same in Stony Gap." She could think of at least two nationally known cases where police chased just one theory without considering another. She wasn't going to make the same mistake.

"Good idea," Cord agreed.

Ending the call, Ellie phoned the owner of Crooked Creek Cottages, then the inn, and asked them to be on the lookout for anyone suspicious, specifically anyone with a child. Kidnappers had been known to disguise a child as the opposite sex, even cutting their hair and dressing them in gender-neutral or opposite-sex clothing.

Next, she phoned Benjamin Fields, the local real estate agent, and asked for a list of any abandoned or vacant properties around the area.

A tense heartbeat passed. "There's a vacant warehouse by the gulley on the edge of town. It was used as storage for factory equipment. And then there's the old Dugan farm. I'll do some research and text you if I find more."

After he gave her the details he had, she ended the call and sped toward the warehouse. Five minutes later, she parked at the end of the alley between a furniture mart and the warehouse, scanning the property.

The furniture mart, which seemed to specialize in handcrafted Amish pieces, was closed for the night, and there were no cars or other signs anyone had stayed behind late. Even so, hiding out inside the vacant warehouse would be difficult with an operating business next door. Still, she pulled her weapon and flashlight, crossing to the boxy metal building. Finding the door chained and locked, she climbed on a dumpster to peer through a grimy window.

Shining her flashlight inside, she saw the entire space had been cleaned out. She couldn't even see a footprint in the dust.

Satisfied Penny wasn't there, she returned to her Jeep, started the engine and headed toward the Dugan farm. The land had access to the approach trail leading to Falcon's Nest, a popular gathering spot to view birds of prey.

The crumbling farmhouse on the property had been deserted for nearly a decade. It would be the perfect place to hide.

CHAPTER TWELVE

Ellie grabbed her flashlight once more, climbed from her Jeep and scanned the farm. Years ago, fall at the Dugans' meant pumpkin picking, hayrides, a corn maze and a booth where visitors could hand-make their own fall and Halloween wreaths.

Now, it looked almost ghost-like. A rusted broken-down truck sat abandoned on the property, its tires missing, windows cracked. The barn was rotting, and the roof needed patching. The mud-smeared windows on the house were boarded up, the porch was sagging, and the wind battered the 'For Sale' sign in the front yard.

The house and barn appeared empty, but Ellie walked toward them anyway, searching for footprints, tire tracks, any sign someone had recently been here.

Nothing stood out, but she kept her senses alert as she approached the barn. Shining the flashlight through the open door, she panned it across the interior. The dirt and hay floor were just as she remembered, but the tables and wreaths were long gone. She eased through the door and scanned the interior. No sign anyone was inside.

She exited the barn then crossed the lawn to the house. After surveying the exterior, and checking the perimeter, she determined the windows and doors were all locked. So was the crawl space. Fields had told her there was a spare key for the back door beneath an old plant pot. She retrieved it and, after turning the stiff lock, she flashed her light inside.

A musty smell assaulted her, and then she noticed trash on the floor. In the kitchen, she found several empty aluminum cans along with a load of bread, moldy food-crusted paper plates, and a plastic jug of water.

Someone had been here. Recently.

A noise sounded behind her.

The whisper of a breath? Or was it the wind?

The floor creaked, and she turned, but a shadow lunged toward her, then something hard slammed across the back of the head. The blow was so sharp that she pitched forward, staggering to stay on her feet. Another sharp crack came before she could reach her gun and stars swam behind her eyes.

She hit the floor face-first then the world went dark.

CHAPTER THIRTEEN

Eula Ann Frampton wrapped her homemade scarf around her wiry gray bun as she stepped onto the rickety porch of her Victorian house. The wind blew off the mountain with a savage sound, swirling the brittle, brown leaves on her lawn into a blinding haze and nearly obliterating her view of her rose garden.

She knew what the folks in town said. She heard the whispers and felt their hateful, frightened stares. "That crazy old Ms. Eula killed her husband Ernie and buried him in her own yard, right there under the roses."

Meddlin' Maude lead the troupe of gossip mongers. "She's a freak."

"Spooky, if you ask me."

"Don't let your children get near her house."

A cackle bubbled in her throat.

Only she and Ernie really knew what had happened. And it would stay between them, where it belonged, just like all good secrets did.

Tonight, though, it wasn't Ernie's throaty whisper that floated to her from the grave.

It was the voices of the little girls.

She hadn't asked to hear from the dead, but the voices broke through the night anyway. It had started when she was just a kid. First, when her granny passed of the awful flu. Then again when Mama went to heaven after being hit by that blasted chicken truck. People still talked about the cages that had come open when the truck crashed, and the hundred chickens that had gone clacking and waddling all across the road. Eula hadn't eaten chicken since.

A snowflake fell, the glossy white crystal landing on the tip of her magnolia tree and reminding her of the next time the voices had come.

The night the first girl had gone missing.

A shiver ruffled Eula's scarf, and tore it from her hair, dragging a strand from her bun as if a spool of thread had come loose. Maybe it was her mind that had come loose when she'd heard that first child's cry.

That first time, after her granny, she'd been terrified. She had run and told her neighbor Birdie, but Birdie said to hush up, not to go around saying such things or folks would show up in white coats and lock her in the loony bin. So she had. But, years later, when she heard the voices after the girl had disappeared, she'd been determined to help. She turned to the sheriff and told him what she'd heard. Thought maybe they could save the child. He was young back then and she thought he was a go-gettter.

But Sheriff Reeves said not to interfere, that no one in Bluff County would believe a woman who they suspected murdered her own sweet husband.

Sweet, her ass. No one knew Ernie, 'cept what he'd wanted them to see.

Still, Sheriff Reeves insisted folks would think she was touched in the head, and they'd take her to a mental ward, and she'd lose her house. Staying here on the mountain was the only way to make sure Ernie stayed put six feet under. And to keep her out of Bluff County Sanitarium.

A coldness washed over her. Once she'd thought the girls' cries were a calling. So she told Preacher but he'd prayed over her and sprinkled her with the anointing water, begging God to save her soul from the illness robbing her mind.

Poppycock. If God *had* intervened, it had been to make the voices cry louder. The only thing that had saved her sanity was to stay at the top of the mountain where she could watch over the trail. Perched on the tip of one of the highest ridges, she was as close to the angels as she could get.

She closed her eyes and welcomed the whispers now. She had to.

Another little girl had been taken. She felt it in the crackle of the wind and the sharp sting of the bitter cold moving in. She heard it in the sound of the forest animals scampering away from the evil, and the river water as it crashed over the jagged rocks, as if God was spitting mad at how dumb and sinful humans could be.

The images of the tiny little faces with their wide, teary eyes floated like pale white shadows in front of her. Some flitted through the thick pines and hemlocks as if running for their lives. One stumbled and fell into the briars, then disappeared into the earth as if the ground opened up and sucked her into its dark abyss.

Another's bony hand clawed through the frozen water, ice snapping and breaking like glass shattering, the cracks snaking along the top of the pond like spiderwebs. Then came the screams begging her to save them from the darkness.

It broke her heart that she could only hear the cries. She was powerless to bring them back from the dead. Or to see them before they were taken.

Why she couldn't have been given *that* gift, so she could help them, she didn't know.

The only gift she had was to listen and offer some comfort to the lost little angels. In one trembling hand she held rose petals. With the other, she plucked them from her palm and tossed them into the wind. The wind lifted the delicate petals into the sky, carrying them across the treetops, then they fluttered down onto the trail, dotting the ground like tiny ruby stones.

The ritual carried her love to the lost ones below.

At the sound of her low voice, the translucent silhouettes of the ghost girls gathered in a circle, small hands clasping one another as if waiting to welcome the latest missing child into their fold.

Clasping her hands in prayer, she began to hum 'Amazing Grace' under her breath as she watched them dance.

CHAPTER FOURTEEN

A sledgehammer was pounding Ellie's skull. Wind banged the loose boards and a tree limb scraped the fog-coated windowpanes.

Disoriented, Ellie roused from unconsciousness and blinked, but the darkness engulfed her, and a rancid odor filled her nostrils. Dear God, she was back in that tunnel. Searching for the light. Crying out for help.

But her cries died in the depth of the long empty space and no one was coming.

Swallowing back nausea, she blinked again, then lifted her hand to her head. Not the tunnel or the nightmare again.

Except this was real, too. She was in a dark space that smelled musty and dank.

Her fingers felt something wet and sticky. Blood.

On the back of her head. Then her temple.

The memory of being attacked resurfaced, and a dizzy spell assaulted her. She was at the old Dugan farm. Someone had been here, and they'd ambushed her from behind.

Were they still inside?

Her hand flew to her holster, and she breathed a sigh of relief that her gun was still there. Why hadn't they taken it? Because they'd been in a hurry to flee?

She remained still for a moment, listening for signs someone was in the house, and allowing the worst of the dizziness to pass. The wind screeched through the eaves of the rotten boards, the bitter cold seeping in, a reminder Tempest was almost upon them.

Sucking in a deep breath to stem the nausea, she rose to her knees, giving her eyes a few moments to adjust to the dark.

She checked her watch – she'd been out less than ten minutes. Glancing around the interior, she raked her hand over the floor for her flashlight, fingers brushing over rotting wood until she snagged it. Another dizzy spell swept over her as she wiped the blood from her hand onto her jeans, and she closed her eyes until it passed.

Then she scanned the kitchen and living area. No one visible. Still, what if Penny had been left inside? She could be hurt or… worse. If Ellie had walked in on the kidnapper, he might have left the little girl and escaped while she was unconscious.

Gritting her teeth against the throbbing in her skull, she pushed to her feet. Still dizzy, she blinked to focus again, then yanked on latex gloves, and checked the kitchen, the cabinets, the pantry, the laundry closet, anywhere a child—or body—might fit. From there, she searched the living room and dining area. The wood floors were dusty and scratched, the walls dingy, paint peeling and pocked with brown spots. The furniture had been cleaned out.

A threadbare blanket that smelled like mildew lay on the floor in one of the three bedrooms, along with an empty pack of cigarettes. The rancid stench grew stronger near the bathroom, making her stomach churn. The toilet looked as if it hadn't been cleaned in a decade, and black mold climbed the wall from a water leak around the tub.

Relief and frustration built inside her chest at the same time. No Penny.

Pushing away the pain in her head, she searched the other rooms, but whoever had been here was gone. Judging from the discarded food containers and trash, they had probably been sheltering here for a couple of weeks.

If Penny had been with them today, it wasn't evident. But a forensic team might find something she hadn't.

Staggering back to the kitchen, she opened the back door and was struck by a blast of air so cold it robbed her of breath. Footprints marred the damp ground—boots. A man's, most likely, given the size.

Even if the man hadn't taken Penny, he'd attacked Ellie for a reason. They needed to track him down.

Judging from the mess in the kitchen, he wasn't meticulous, or hadn't been here, meaning they might find his fingerprints too.

Her phone buzzed and she glanced at it, realizing she'd missed several calls from her captain. She stabbed the button to connect. "Yeah."

"Where are you?" Captain Hale barked.

She quickly explained.

"Christ, Ellie, do you need an ambulance?"

Her fingers brushed over the back of her head and temple again. The blood was drying, and the gash wasn't deep enough for stitches. She didn't have time to waste on a trip to the ER anyway.

Penny's life depended on her.

"No. Just send an Evidence Recovery Team. We might find prints. If we do, we can run them against perpetrators with a history of crimes against children." And maybe they'd get a lead.

"Copy that. I'll dispatch the team right away." Captain Hale sighed. "Listen, Detective, your father is pushing hard to have you removed from this case. What the hell is going on between the two of you?"

Ellie clenched the phone with clammy hands. "Nothing."

"That's a lie, and we both know it," he said. "Whatever you have to do, work it out. And don't let it interfere with this investigation. Do you hear me?"

"Yes, sir." Fury at her father mounted.

"Mayor Waters is breathing down my neck, too," the captain continued. "If we don't find Penny alive, it's going to look bad for our office. The town will want someone to blame, and he'll be looking at you."

Wouldn't Bryce just love that?

A scream of frustration lodged in her throat as the call ended. She'd worked her ass off for the job and sure as hell didn't want to lose it. But right now, finding Penny was her priority.

Fighting off another dizzy spell, she searched the yard again, careful not to step in the muddy footprints by the back door. Tree branches swayed and bowed in the wind, twigs snapping and falling to the ground with a clatter. Leaves swirled across the lawn, while budding trees and wildflowers took a beating from the impending storm.

Shivering, Ellie stepped beneath the cover of the porch to shield herself from the frigid sting of the wind beating through the trees as she waited on the crime team.

CHAPTER FIFTEEN

Cord McClain had seen a lot of storms in his days in the mountains, but his instincts said Tempest might be one of the worst in a decade.

Cursing as the clouds unleashed needle-like rain, he kicked off his mud-soaked boots and stepped inside the rustic log cabin he rented deep in the woods at the edge of the river. The scent of damp earth, the rescue dogs and his own sweat lingered on his skin. Susan's cries echoed in his head.

He covered his ears with his hands to drown out the heinous sound, but it did no good. His head had been filled with screams and cries of shock, death and sorrow ever since he was a little boy living above the mortuary.

Rain began to pound the tin roof like rocks. Shit. In the next day or two the frigid temperatures and wet, frozen ground would create dangerous conditions and could be deadly for hikers. And for the searchers.

Still, the SAR teams would be out all night hunting for the little girl. Memories of the other lost children on the trail traipsed through his mind. The long days of combing the mountains and caves for their little bodies. The endless hours of plunging through weeds and bramble, of wading through icy creek water and crawling into the hollow caverns.

As the night wore on and they hadn't found Penny, the darkness inside him had beckoned. Like a beast, he felt the urges surge through him. The anger and madness that he didn't know if he could control.

The woods usually offered him solace, but Penny was there tonight, and so were the searchers. He had to escape their watchful, curious eyes.

So, he'd come home to lock himself away for the evening.

Shame filled him for who he'd been. What he was. What he could never be.

Ellie had been there, driving the hunt. Ellie with her beautiful golden hair and eyes the color of the sky on a sunny spring morning.

Ellie who he'd allowed himself to have one night with when he was young and more foolish.

Like a savage, he wanted her again. Had dreamed of her in his bed and in his arms. But then, that night, she'd wanted the light on, and he craved the darkness…

Rain pounded the roof, and the wind battered the windows in a deafening roar. He lit the kindling in the woodstove, the only heat in the house, then poured himself a fingerful of bourbon and carried it to his bedroom. Stripping off his dirty clothes, he stared at his mangled body in the mirror.

The jagged scar along his temple was half hidden by his shaggy hair, and his shirt hid the ones on his back. He closed his eyes and remembered the sting of the belt across his bare skin and a deep growl of pain vibrated inside him.

And then there was the branding. The tattoo that represented the evil within him. A reminder of the dark voice who'd put it there.

You have to be punished.

And he had been.

The beatings he could tolerate.

It was the dark hole that had driven him inside his own head. Lying in the small black emptiness with the dirt sifting through his fingers and the rain beating at his face had destroyed the boy inside and turned him into a man with grisly thoughts and visions of death.

The acrid odor of body waste, gas, formaldehyde and chemicals used to embalm the bodies burned his nostrils as if he'd smelled them today on the trail, the only place he could usually escape them. Images of the blood draining from the corpse lying on the cold steel table haunted him.

Needing to purge the rage eating at his insides, he yanked on a sweatshirt, opened his bedside table drawer and removed the key to his work room. A sliver of light seeped into the cold black room, just enough for him to see his collection of knives. Hunting knives, pocketknives, Swiss army knives, a Buck folding knife with woodgrain handle and brass bolsters, a Bush 110 for the outdoors, then an assortment of carving knives and tools.

Piles of scrap wood sat on the floor, ready for his hands to shape them.

He sat down on the stool he'd carved from a tree trunk, chose his favorite jackknife, then ran his fingers over the blade. Holding a rough piece of wood in one hand, he slanted the knife against the edge and began to whistle as he shaved away the imperfections.

CHAPTER SIXTEEN

Day 2 Missing

March 2, 1:00 a.m.

Icy rain slashed Ellie's cheeks, and the wind sifted through her clothes all the way to her bones as she ran from her car to her front door. Her head throbbed and fatigue made her muscles ache as she let herself into her bungalow and shook off her jacket. As predicted, the temperature was dropping quickly, the rain turning to pellets of sleet.

Fear for Penny seized her, and she glanced at the farmhouse clock on the wall. Hours had passed with no clues or leads. And with each one, Penny's chances of survival diminished.

What else should she be doing?

Her stomach growled, but she couldn't face food right now, so she bypassed the breakfast bar and veered toward her desk in the corner of the living room.

A mental checklist ran through her mind. She'd asked the tough questions, interrogated the family and neighbors, and checked two more empty houses. SAR teams were working around the clock, and Penny's face was plastered all over the news and had been circulated to all law enforcement agencies in the state.

Forensics discovered a few loose, short brown hairs in the Dugan house, along with several fingerprints. It was possible they belonged to a hiker, or a homeless person or squatter who'd sought shelter during the cold winter months. Any of those, startled, could be her attacker. Maybe even one of the meth dealers trying to set up shop. But they'd found no pans, chemicals, or supplies to cook the drug.

Everything the ERT had found, including the pocketknife she'd discovered, was on its way to the lab. She'd check in with them tomorrow. She looked again at the clock. *Well, today I guess.*

The wall of maps she kept above her computer mocked her. Trails from Georgia to North Carolina and up into Virginia. All the places she and her father had hiked. All the memories… and the plans.

She flipped through the stack of maps piled on her desk that she'd collected for future excursions.

A fresh wave of hurt washed over her. Those were trips they'd never take. She'd worked so hard to prove she was her father's equal, or as close as she could get, but he'd chosen that narcissistic show-off Bryce over her.

If she'd confided to her father what Bryce had done, would he still have chosen him?

Her cheeks flushed. No… she would never tell him. It didn't matter now anyway. That was years ago.

She was a different woman now. No longer shy and easily intimidated. Now she was strong. Self-sufficient. Independent.

She had to find Penny. Nothing else mattered except that.

Running on adrenaline, she walked into the bathroom to examine her head. One look in the mirror and she realized she looked like pure hell. There was a two-inch gash on her temple at the hairline, blood matted in the strands, and dirt smeared her cheeks. She wet a washcloth and wiped at the dried blood, then leaned forward to assess the injury. Definitely not deep enough for stitches, but it would bruise, turning all kinds of purple and blue. Opening the medicine cabinet, she snagged the aspirin bottle and downed two tablets.

The bottle of anti-depressants/anxiety medicine the therapist had prescribed stared back. She'd stopped taking them years ago. Hadn't had a hallucination of Mae since.

Until today.

But she'd kept this bottle as a reminder of what she'd overcome. The temptation to drown out the fear nagging at her made her start to twist off the cap.

Her hand shook though, and the room blurred. Trembling, she fought the urge, dropped her hand and slammed the medicine cabinet shut. She wasn't that weak, scared little girl or teenager anymore. She could handle this. Besides, she needed a clear head to do her job, and the pills fogged her brain.

Ignoring the stabbing pain in her head, she stripped off her clothes and climbed into the shower to wash away the stench of sweat, dirt and the mustiness of the Dugan house.

When the water cooled, she rinsed off, and stepped from the shower. After drying off, she yanked on a pair of pajama pants and a long-sleeved t-shirt and headed back into the kitchen.

As she passed her dresser, she remembered the sketches she'd drawn with the therapist when she was little. All those memories tucked away. The temptation to look at them washed over her. She picked up the box and ran her finger over the wood grain, and the initial E her father had carved on the lid. Breathing deeply as Mae's voice whispered through her mind, she reached for the lock to open the box. Her fingers trembled again. Her vision grew cloudy. Dark spots danced behind her eyes.

Dizzy again, she blinked and staggered back toward her bed. The back of her knees hit the mattress, and she pressed her hand onto the bed to steady herself. Still, the room was swaying, and suddenly the mountains were swallowing her.

She grabbed a tree branch to keep from diving into a ravine. Then a hand caught her.

The sound of her phone jangling jarred her back to reality.

Her breath panted out, but she reminded herself she was safe. But what had happened? Was she projecting Penny's fears onto herself? Could that have been a memory?

The phone trilled again, and she pushed away the dizziness and hurried to answer it. She checked the number, hoping it was Cord with good news.

No, it was Angelica Gomez. She let it roll to voicemail, then waited to see if the reporter left a message. She did, wanting an update on the case. "Call me, Detective Reeves. I have information for you."

Ellie stewed over the message. Was it just Angelica's attempt to trick her into returning her call? Or could she actually have valuable intel?

Shit. She had to find out, so she called woman's number and poured herself a whiskey while it rang. Swirling the rich, amber liquid in the glass, releasing the scents of vanilla, oak and caramel. She savored the smooth burn of it as the liquid slid down her throat.

She was just about to leave a message when the reporter answered. "Thanks for returning my call, Detective."

Irritation sharpened her voice. "Listen, Miss Gomez. I'm bone tired and need my phone open for leads. If you have something, spill it. I'm not in the mood for games."

"I'm not playing games," Angelica said stiffly. "But I want an exclusive."

Because she thought it was more than a missing person case? "Tell me what you know, and we'll see."

A long pause, then Angelica huffed. "Stan Matthews lied about his marriage. He was having an affair, and his wife knew."

CHAPTER SEVENTEEN

The sound of thunder woke Ellie at 7 a.m. She hadn't meant to fall asleep, but exhaustion had finally claimed her, and she'd collapsed on the sofa somewhere around 2 a.m.

Stan Matthews had lied to her about his marriage. Susan had lied to her about Stan's devotion.

What else had they hidden from her?

She checked her phone, hoping for a text that they'd found Penny. But there was no word. Frustration tightened her muscles. She stood and stretched, and flipped on the radio.

"*This is Cara Soronto with the latest on Winter Storm Tempest. Rain pounded us overnight, and temperatures will quickly drop to the low thirties by this afternoon. We predict sleet and snowfall by night.*" She paused. "*Wind gusts up to fifty-five miles per hour are also expected, with black ice forming on the roads. People, be prepared. Dress warm and stay home if possible.*"

Anxiety knifed through Ellie. No option for her to stay home.

An innocent little girl was trapped out in this mess. She had to get going.

Pulse hammering, she stumbled to the kitchen and made coffee, then showered while it brewed.

The bruise on her forehead looked stark and swollen, but she applied a new bandage, downed a painkiller, then tugged her side bangs over it to cover the wound. She yanked her hair into a ponytail and dabbed powder on her face below her eyes to disguise the purpling bruise.

Muscles aching from fatigue, she poured coffee in her travel mug and headed out to her Jeep. Gray clouds hung heavy above the mountain ridges, the shivering trees sending drops of rain flying down. Ellie pictured a frightened little Penny lost or hurt and her lungs strained for air.

No time to break down, though. That could come later.

She downed her coffee as she drove, but it tasted bitter this morning. Deciding she needed more sustenance, she pulled into the Corner Café and rushed inside. She ordered a sausage biscuit to go.

Gertrude Cunningham, the local librarian, was sitting in a booth near the counter. She waved to Ellie, and it seemed churlish not to say hello. But as she approached, she realized that her mother was also at the table, and Lily Hanover, the head of the Garden Club. Vera beamed at her and gestured toward a mound of fliers printed with Penny's photograph.

"Look, Ellie, we're posting fliers all over Stony Gap and Crooked Creek," Vera chirped. "I'm taking a bunch to church, and Gertie is sending out emails to all the business owners and locals who are on her mailing list for the library."

"Thank you for doing that," Ellie said, and meant it.

Lola Baker, the owner of the café, called Ellie to pick up her order. "Any word on Susan's little girl?"

Ellie clenched her jaw. "Not yet."

A woman hurried by, clinging to her little girl's hand, and two other customers stepped up to order food to go. The man glared at her. "We're getting out of here as quickly as we can. If someone's after our children, we don't want any part of this town."

Ellie had the urge to reassure the people they were safe, but she couldn't do that, she couldn't lie, so she said nothing. Instead, she paid for her food and hurried toward the door.

"Bye, darling," her mother trilled.

Ellie threw up a hand in a dismissive wave, then pushed through the door. Her mother's willingness to ignore the previous evening was infuriating. She'd always deluded herself that she had the perfect family.

Outside, two locals practically accosted her.

"How can you be here eating when Susan and Stan are going crazy with worry?"

"Why haven't you found that little girl?"

"Is there a child snatcher in town?"

"Are you looking for a pedophile?"

Ellie muttered she had to get to work, then dove in her car and peeled from the parking lot. The rain was falling again, and she cranked up her defroster to clear her windshield. Although she saw people starting to open up shops, several cars were already pulling out of the B & B lots.

When she reached the Matthews' home, she saw the Channel 5 news van already parked outside. Angelica Gomez jumped out when she saw the Jeep. Ellie braced herself to direct the cameraman away, but it seemed he was already under orders not to start rolling just yet.

"Did you look into the information I gave you?" Angelica asked, not bothering with pleasantries.

Ellie made a non-committal sound. "I'm working on it."

The reporter grabbed her arm as Ellie attempted to brush past. "You promised me an exclusive. If this cheating bastard hurt his little girl, I want to report it."

Ellie's gaze met hers. Anger radiated in the reporter's eyes, making Ellie wonder why this case was getting under her skin so much.

"Ms. Gomez, we spoke after midnight. It is not yet eight a.m. I'll keep you posted," Ellie said. "Matthews was out all night with the search teams. I need to talk to Susan before he gets home."

Angelica nodded understanding, stepping aside as Ellie passed. Heath let her into the Matthews' house, his hair mussed as if he'd been running his hands through it. His eyes were bloodshot, and he needed a shave.

"Did you get any rest?" she asked.

"Not much. Mother cried herself to sleep. Father called, ranting that we aren't doing enough."

He could join the club. "How about the background information and the couple's phones?"

"No ransom calls. And nothing indicating they planned to get rid of their daughter."

A gasp came from behind her, and Susan appeared in the doorway, her expression horrified.

"How could you suggest such a horrible thing?" Susan shrieked.

"I'm really sorry you heard that," Ellie said. "But it's routine for us to ask questions. It's just procedure." Ellie crossed her arms. "We need to talk, Susan. It's come to our attention that Stan may have been having an affair, and that you were aware of it. Why didn't you tell me?"

Susan clutched the kitchen counter. "Who told you that?"

"Is it true?" Ellie asked.

Penny's mother made a pained sound. "It only happened once," she said in a raw whisper. "And Stan was sorry. He apologized and... we were working through it."

"Then why did you lie about it?" Ellie asked.

"Because I knew it would look bad—make him seem untrustworthy." She swung her hands by her sides. "But he didn't hurt Penny. I keep telling you that."

Ellie pulled her notepad from her pocket and slid it onto the counter. "Write down her name."

Susan's eyes widened in alarm. "You don't think she had something to do with Penny's disappearance, do you?"

Who knew what kind of motive the woman might have? Jealousy can drive a person mad. If she'd fixated on Stan, and wanted him to leave her wife, she could have kidnapped Penny to tear the couple apart.

"Her name," Ellie said bluntly. "And if you talk to Stan, do not let him know that you gave me this information."

Susan's face turned ashen, but she scribbled the woman's name.

Ellie then handed the pad to Heath; he would locate the woman. "Now, Susan," she said tersely. "Don't lie to me again. I need to know everything—the good, the bad, the ugly."

CHAPTER EIGHTEEN

Decatur

Special Agent Derrick had spent half the night reviewing the files on the missing girls.

When he'd finally fallen asleep, Penny Matthews' sweet face haunted him. All the what ifs triggered by the disappearance of a child. The questions, fears and anxiety escalated with every second that passed.

His mother's tormented face, the day his little sister went missing, dogged him now just as much as when he was fourteen. When he'd run to his parents, panicked that he couldn't find Kim.

Kim, his mother's little angel who liked peanut butter cookies, turning cartwheels in the grass, chasing fireflies and collecting them in mayonnaise jars.

Kim, who'd been lost forever on a spring afternoon, just like today. Except today there was no blue sky, no sunshine. The weather was bleak and a deadly storm was on its way. The sheer number of missing children crashed in on Derrick, screaming for him to get justice for them all.

He clenched his fists, watching as the morning news feed spieled onto his computer screen. Yesterday's footage repeated, then an update. Detective Ellie Reeves, entering the Matthews' house.

Her ash-blonde hair was secured in a ponytail, her face heart-shaped. She wore jeans, a white shirt and a denim jacket that revealed the weapon strapped to her belt. The gun looked at odds with the woman's petite frame. She couldn't weigh more than 120 soaking wet.

She was also sporting a bandage on her forehead, and bruising around her eyes the shade of bluebonnets.

Curiosity made him lean forward and study her more closely. That one eye was swollen, but the other one looked puffy, too, a testament to the fact that she'd probably been up most of the night.

No one slept when a child was missing. Either they were working or worrying, causing restless nights and tension you could cut with a knife.

The fact that Penny Matthews hadn't been found was gut-wrenchingly disappointing, but not a total surprise.

He'd been following the string of disappearances ever since the photo of a child resembling Kim had caught his attention ten years ago. She'd gone missing in North Carolina, along the AT.

Whether or not Penny Matthews' disappearance was connected to the other cases was anyone's guess at this point. But he knew damn good and well that Ellie Reeves wouldn't divulge all she knew to the press.

The only way to find out was to talk to her in person.

He also wanted to question the detective about her father. Find out why he let the search for his sister's abductor go cold long before it should have.

God knows his attempts to reach Sheriff Reeves regarding the other cases had failed. Randall Reeves had blown him off, each and every time. Even suggested Derrick needed therapy.

Fuck him.

Derrick packed his notes, the maps of the locations where he'd tracked disappearances and where the girls had come from, and the photographs of each victim into his briefcase, before grabbing his laptop.

He strode into his bedroom and started tossing clothes and his toiletries into a duffel bag. Crooked Creek was only three hours away.

He'd be there by eleven.

CHAPTER NINETEEN

Crooked Creek

The minute Ellie entered the police station she heard her father's voice booming from the captain's office.

He'd damn well better have good news.

"Let someone besides Ellie handle the press on this situation," her father said brusquely. "I don't want her in front of the cameras."

Ellie didn't bother knocking. She burst into the room, blood boiling. "What are you doing, Dad?"

Randall's forehead creased. He looked like a kid who'd been caught stealing money from his mother's purse. His eyes narrowed as he scrutinized her face.

"What the hell happened to you?"

She'd forgotten about her black eye.

Her father locked eyes stubbornly with hers. "Nothing," Ellie said, determined to stay on track.

Captain Hale ran a hand over his bald head. "Are you all right, Detective Reeves?"

Ellie sucked in a sharp breath. "I'm fine." She addressed her father, knowing he was like a dog with a bone. "Someone jumped me from behind last night when I was searching the Dugan farm for Penny. And before you ask, he got away, but hopefully the crime techs found something." She stiffened her spine. "Now let's get back to the elephant in the room. Dealing with the press is part of my job as lead detective." She angled her head toward the captain. "I can handle it and you know it."

Captain Hale's eye twitched. "I know you can."

Her father made a low sound in his throat. "Listen, Rick—"

Ellie balled her hands into fists. Just how chummy were her father and her boss? "May I speak to you in private, Sheriff?"

Her father's brows shot up at the fact she'd used his title. "Of course."

Captain Hale looked confused but threw up his hands in defeat.

Before she left his office, she directed her conversation to the captain. "Let's meet in the conference room for a briefing in half an hour. I texted Cord to stop by so we can regroup. Deputy Landrum should be here, too."

Captain Hale nodded agreement. "I'll call Harley. He's been bored with retirement. Maybe he can babysit the mother while Heath comes in."

Ellie thanked him, then gestured for her father to follow her. They stepped into the conference room next door to the captain's office, her anger mounting as she faced him.

Just as she was on the verge of reaming him out, he lifted a hand toward her cheek as if to comfort her. Ellie backed away. "Don't. I told you I'm fine."

"You don't look fine," he growled. "You look like you had a run-in with someone's pistol. Were you alone, El?"

Ellie gritted her teeth. "Yes. You know we're spread thin with everyone searching for Penny. By the way, where's your deputy?" she asked pointedly.

He raked a hand through his greying hair. He looked tired this morning, the lines beside his eyes even deeper. But she forced herself not to think about the fact that he'd been up all night on the trail with the search teams.

"He… uh… had some things to do."

Ellie made a sarcastic sound. "I see. He's busy tacking up campaign signs while we hunt for a lost little girl." She didn't bother to hide her disdain. "And that's who you chose as your replacement."

A pained look crossed his face. "It's not like that, El."

"It is exactly like that." Bryce had a dick and money. And his father was the mayor. That was all he needed. Her father averted his gaze. All the more reason for her to set boundaries now. "Let's get something clear, Dad. You have no right to come to my work and talk to my boss behind my back."

"But I'm just concerned—"

She lifted a finger to quiet him. "Stop. You may not want me as sheriff of Bluff County, but I've worked hard to earn Captain Hale's respect. And I won't allow you to undermine that."

"That's not what I was doing."

"Yes, it is." Ellie refused to back down. "If you continue to interfere, I'll ask the captain to remove you from the team."

"You can't do that," her father replied. "All law enforcement needs to work together on a case like this. And in case you've forgotten, you work for the sheriff's office just like everyone else in this county does." He punctuated his statement with a fist to his chest. "And that's me."

Ellie felt as if she was six years old and she'd just been admonished. He was right, but the fact that he'd pulled seniority spiked her temper. And when Bryce assumed her father's role as sheriff, she would work for him. He'd definitely play the power card to his advantage.

The urge to vomit seized her.

But she was a fighter and right now she was not going to give in. "That may be true. But that can change. When this is over, I'll transfer to another county far away from here. One where you can't storm in and tell my boss what to do with me."

Her threat shut him up. *Good.* She didn't need this bullshit right now. Her head felt like rocks were rolling around inside it.

Penny Matthews needed her full attention, not for her to be in a pissing contest with her father.

CHAPTER TWENTY

An hour later, Ellie squared her shoulders as everyone filed in for the briefing. The captain, her father, Cord and Heath along with three other deputies from Crooked Creek and Stony Gap turned their attention to her.

She pointed toward Penny's photograph at the top on the board. "This is our missing child, Penny Matthews, age seven, disappeared yesterday around one p.m." She added snapshots of the picnic area, then ones of Penny's sneaker, the friendship bracelet, the Braves hat and the knife she'd found. "These items were collected at the scene and are at the lab now, although we know the hat belonged to Stan Matthews."

She'd marked the white board off into sections labeled "Persons of Interest", "Motives", "Evidence", and "Questions".

A picture of Penny's parents went next. "So far, the parents' story sticks. According to Deputy Landrum's research into the couple's financials and insurance policies, we can rule out ransom as a motive for kidnapping.

"Although last night I learned that Stan Matthews had an affair with a woman named Pauline Shore. His wife insisted it was a one-night fling and they were working through it. We're trying to track down lover girl. So far no luck."

"I'll keep working on that," Heath offered.

Ellie added Stan Matthews' name as a suspect. On another line she wrote Pauline Shore. Beside them she scribbled Motives. *Dad wanted out of the marriage, but saw daughter as an obstacle? Woman was pushing him to leave his wife?*

Ellie tapped the board. "If Pauline wanted Stan to herself, she could have taken Penny to drive the couple apart."

Rumblings of unease spread through the room. "Next, we have allegations of possible child abuse from George Zimmerman, Penny's teacher. But no proof of abuse."

Captain Hale cleared his throat. "I couldn't access her medical records, but her pediatrician indicated that he didn't suspect abuse."

She noted that information on the board, then explained about the incident at the Dugan farm. "There were no signs of a child, but we'll see what forensics turns up."

"We found a torn piece of fabric that looked like a man's jacket near Bald Hill," Cord said. "I sent it to the lab."

He tacked a map detailing the search grids onto the wall. "We've been in and out of every corner within ten miles. We searched heavy areas of brush, the ledges and overhang near the creek, and the AT shelter at Vulture's Point," Cord continued. "Footprints near Bald Hill disappeared into the creek."

An image of the knife-edge ridges near Bald Hill taunted Ellie. The sharp dropout fell over eighty feet, with brush so thick that, if Penny had fallen into it, she might be buried in branches and dirt.

"How about the search dogs?" Ellie asked.

"They crossed over the creek and searched for miles, but no sign of Penny."

She turned to Heath. "Any more on the background checks or financials?"

"Before Zimmerman came to Crooked Creek, he taught at a school in Helen, Georgia. Principal said he was conscientious, but maybe too attentive to the little girls. When he reprimanded him, Zimmerman turned in his notice."

"Keep digging then and talk to the school counselor."

"On it."

"I hate to say this, but it looks more and more like this was a kidnapping, guys. That means Penny could still be in those woods or her abductor could have stashed a car somewhere off the trail, in which case there's no telling how far away they'd be by now."

Her father shifted. "I'll talk to some of the Shadow People and see if any of them saw anything."

Ellie avoided eye contact, simply nodding agreement. Over the years, her father had built up trust among the Shadows.

Captain Hale tapped his pen on the table. "AMBER alert was issued, and all port authorities, train and bus stations and airports are on alert. Penny's picture is everywhere, including NCMEC."

The National Center for Missing & Exploited Children was a vital clearinghouse for information in missing children cases.

"What about that couple Susan saw?" she asked.

Randall shrugged. "Haven't found them yet."

Ellie looked back at the board, worry knotting her insides. If Penny had been abducted, was she still alive?

She clapped her hands. "All right. Let's get back out there. It's been almost twenty-four hours since Penny was last seen. We all know the stats—every hour a child is missing diminishes the chances of finding her alive. And this winter storm will be bearing down on us in a few hours. We have to find this child and bring her home before the wind chill drops and we're covered in snow and ice."

Captain Hale and the others dispersed. Everyone except for Cord, who hung back. "You okay, Ellie?" Concern colored his expression as he gestured toward her eye.

"Yeah. Just worried about Penny."

He gently touched her arm, drawing her gaze to the scars on his thumbs. Scars she'd once asked him about. But he'd never explained. Just as he'd refused to let her into his workroom. Just as he refused to talk about his past.

But there were fresh scars, today. How had he gotten those?

Voices from the front of the station echoed in the hall, and she pulled her arm away.

"Look around in the ravine at Bald Hill. All that brush and the trees that were blown over in the tornado last year…"

"I know," Cord said quietly. "Would be the perfect place to dispose of a body."

CHAPTER TWENTY-ONE

Before Ellie could leave the conference room, Stan Matthews stormed in. His clothes were filthy, his shirt torn, and dirt smeared his face. His knuckles were even more skinned than the day before, as if he'd dug through brush and bramble with his bare hands.

One look at the whiteboard and he exploded. "What the hell? You put my name up there as a suspect?" He pounced toward Ellie, waving his fist. "You think I hurt my baby?" He grabbed her arms and shook her. "I answered all your fucking questions, and I've been out hunting for Penny while you badgered my wife—"

Ellie lifted her hands to push him away, but before she had a chance, someone grabbed Matthews in a chokehold.

"Let the lady go."

Penny's father pulled his fist back, but the stranger threw him to his knees, handcuffing him. Angry that this guy had witnessed Matthews get the better of her, Ellie sucked in a breath.

Stan's eyes shot back to the board and the image of his little girl, and Ellie pulled the screen down to cover it. Then she assessed the man who'd just invaded her conference room.

He was at least six-three, with short-clipped black hair, dark chocolate eyes and broad shoulders. And he wore a suit. *Shit. A fed.*

"Let me go, goddammit!" Stan barked.

"Shut up." The fed kneed Matthews in the back until he howled, his body slumping in surrender.

Ellie planted her hands on her hips. "That was unnecessary. I had the situation under control."

The fed's eyes narrowed to slits as his gaze skated over her face. Her bruise made her look vulnerable, she realized. She couldn't afford that. And the fact that he'd referred to her as "lady" instead of "detective" thoroughly pissed her off.

"Really?" he asked with an eyebrow raise.

"Let me go," Penny's father snarled.

The fed yanked Matthews up and shoved him into a chair. Then he leveled a look at Ellie. "Detective Reeves?"

He had the advantage. He knew who she was.

Then again, her interview with Angelica Gomez was all over the news. Just as the captain warned, if she failed, everyone would blame her. "Yes." She crossed her arms. "And you are?"

"Special Agent Derrick Fox with the local field office in Atlanta. We need to talk." He gestured toward Matthews. "What do we do with him?"

Ellie didn't know whether to feel sorry for Stan or throw his ass in jail. If he was innocent, his wife needed him. If he was guilty, he deserved to rot in prison. Either way, if he'd hurt Penny, she needed him to confess, and she had to question him about Pauline Shore.

"I assume you're here about our missing child case," Ellie said to the fed. "This is Stan Matthews, Penny Matthews' father."

The agent went bone still, his expression vacillating between anger, suspicion, and sympathy.

"Mr. Matthews has been out searching for his daughter all night." She gave Stan a sympathetic look. "You're probably physically and emotionally exhausted, aren't you, Stan?"

Penny's father's eyes filled with tears, and he mumbled a yes. "Take my name off that board," he muttered, his voice weak. "I didn't hurt my daughter. I told you that."

Ellie adopted a calming tone. "Yes, but you didn't mention your affair, Stan."

Stan's face blanched.

Ellie planted her fists on her hips. "Why did you lie to me about your marriage?"

His eyes shifted back and forth as he debated how to answer.

"Did you have an affair?" Ellie asked.

"It was just one stupid night," he muttered. "I was upset, got drunk and hooked up with some woman at a bar. It meant nothing."

"It meant something to your wife, I'm sure," Ellie said bluntly.

Guilt flashed across his face. "I know, I know. But it only happened once, and she forgave me."

"Really, Stan?"

His gaze shot to hers. "Yeah. We were having a rough time then. The money was gone, and she was busy with the kid and—"

Ellie saw red. "So, while she was busy raising your child, you, who were feeling so put upon, decided to have some fun, huh?"

"That's not what I meant," Stan snapped.

Ellie thumped her boot on the floor and waited.

"I felt bad, okay. I swore it wouldn't happen again." His voice quivered. "And it didn't. I never saw the woman again."

"No phone calls? Secret rendezvous?"

"No." Anger hardened his voice.

"Are you sure she didn't want more? Maybe she wanted you to leave your wife and be with her?"

"Hell, no," Stan barked. "She probably screws a different guy every night."

Ellie arched a brow. "So, if we look into your phone records and your computer, we won't find any correspondence with her?"

"No. Now what does this have to do with finding my little girl?"

"Time is of the essence here, Stan," Ellie said bluntly. "When you lie to me, it wastes my time. Is that what you want?"

"No…" His voice warbled. "I want you to find my daughter."

"Then you can't hold things back from me. Do you understand?"

Stan's face crumpled, and he nodded.

"Maybe he needs to sit in lockup for a while to think about it," Agent Fox suggested.

Ellie considered that option. "I think what Mr. Matthews needs to do is to go home, shower, eat something and get some rest." She kept her expression cool. "Your wife needs you right now, Stan. Do you think you can pull it together if we let you go?"

Emotions played across the man's face as he studied her. Finally, he murmured yes.

She gripped him by the collar before the agent uncuffed him. "If I find out you're lying, or that you know where Penny is and didn't tell me, I'll throw the book at you. Do you get what I'm saying?"

He glared at her but gave a small nod.

"Uncuff him," she told the agent.

His thick black brows furrowed. "Are you sure? He assaulted you."

"He's upset and terrified for his child," Ellie said. "I can forgive that."

Gratitude softened the anger in Stan's expression.

The agent pulled a key from his pocket and unlocked the cuffs. "If it happens again, I'll throw you in a cell myself."

Stan lurched up shakily, then lumbered from the room.

Ellie turned to the agent and stared him down. "For the record, Special Agent Fox, I can take care of myself. This is my case, and no one is going to interfere."

Fox squared his shoulders. "Actually, Detective Reeves, I have important information that may shed new light on the investigation." A challenge lit his eyes. "Or are you too stubborn to accept help when it's needed?"

CHAPTER TWENTY-TWO

Ellie's first instinct was to throw the agent out of the conference room. His arrogance pissed her off.

"Which is it, Detective?" he said. "Pride or the case?"

"We're looking for a missing child," she said, impatience edging her voice. "This is not a game or a rivalry between law enforcement agencies. And just because I'm a small-town detective and from the South, don't make the mistake of thinking that I'm stupid."

One brow shot up. "I would never do that."

"That precious child has been out in the elements—lost, hurt, and in danger. So, if you have information, then cut the attitude and spill it."

He studied her for a moment, tension building. A small smile tugged at his mouth, which irritated her even more, because it drew her attention to the fact that he was handsome.

She did not have time for handsome.

"Can we talk in private? I don't want any interruptions."

"Of course. Do you want coffee?"

"Thank you, that would be nice."

He set his briefcase on the table and began to pull out files. Needing a minute to compose herself, Ellie left the room, poured two mugs of coffee and carried them back to the conference room. Closing the door, she set the coffee on the table and situated herself in the chair facing him.

"Did Captain Hale request your help?"

The agent shook his head. "I'm here because I saw your news broadcast."

"And you have information about Penny?" she asked bluntly.

He let a beat pass. "Maybe," he finally said. "Tell me what you've got first."

Ellie stepped to the whiteboard, uncovering it and filling him in. He remained stiff-postured, silent, assessing. "Your turn now."

The agent released a weary sigh. "If this isn't an isolated case where the child wandered off and got lost, or if the parents aren't involved, it's possible it's related to other cases I've been working on."

Judging from the seriousness of his tone, Ellie sensed she wasn't going to like what he had to say. "What are you talking about?"

He removed a picture of a blonde-haired child about Penny's age. "This little girl's name was Kim. She disappeared from the AT twenty-five years ago and was never found."

"Twenty-five years ago. How could that case be related to Penny Matthews?"

From the file, he took out photographs of a dozen little girls around the same age and spread them on the table. Although the hair color varied and some were from single family homes versus two parent families, the story he told her about each child was similar. Her horror mounted with each account.

Families camping, hiking, picnicking, vacationing—someone turned their back or simply looked the other way, and then their daughter was just… gone.

"Oh, my god, are you saying what I think you're saying?"

Special Agent Derrick Fox nodded grimly. "I think someone has been preying on little girls along the AT for over two decades."

CHAPTER TWENTY-THREE

Ellie scrutinized one photograph after another, nerves setting in.

If Special Agent Fox was correct, this case was a lot bigger than she'd imagined. The AT fell under federal jurisdiction, and utilized the National Park Services and local law enforcement from various towns in the fourteen states along the trail. That was a lot of gaps for information to slip through.

Still, denial shot through her. A serial killer was not hiding out in her mountains. No way. Her father would have picked up on it before now.

"I've lived in this area all of my life," she said when she finally found her voice. "And my father has been sheriff for over twenty years. If there's a serial killer stalking the trail, why is this the first I'm hearing about it?"

The agent's jaw tightened. "For one, there's no definitive pattern, no specific time of year or month that indicates a trigger for the abductions. Also, the timing is inconsistent. Sometimes the children went missing a few months apart. Other times, it was a year or more. And in two instances, the children weren't reported missing for weeks because of parental issues and custody battles. At least three victims disappeared from foster homes, which also delayed reporting."

Ellie rubbed her temple. Her head was starting to throb again. "Show me. Put the victims on the board in order of when they disappeared and from where."

Special Agent Fox gathered the photographs and tacked them on a second whiteboard, jotting down the girls' names, their hometowns, the date and place they were reported missing. He started with the most recent.

"Penny Matthews, age seven. Crooked Creek, Georgia."

He added a question mark beside her name, before continuing.

"Millie Purcell, age six, Springer Mountain, Georgia."

Springer Mountain was the beginning of the trail in Georgia and an hour from Ellijay, a popular destination. It was also the southern terminus of the AT, and a summit of 3782 feet. Hikers often went to the visitor's center at Amnicola Falls, another tourist hotspot, and took the approach trail to begin their trek.

He continued pinning up the photos.

Sandy Baines, age five, Smoky Mountains, North Carolina.

Brenna Hart, age seven, Charlottesville, Virginia.

Dara Jackel, age six, Blue Ridge Parkway, Virginia.

Lois Clinton, age five, Gatlinburg, Tennessee.

Joy Lewis, age seven, Bristol, North Carolina.

Phyllis Elliot, age six, Pigeon Forge, North Carolina.

Ginger Williams, age five, Hot Springs, North Carolina.

Ansley Paulson, age six, Jasper, Georgia.

Casey Little, age, six, Dahlonega, Georgia.

With each name, Ellie's anxiety spiked. The faces of the little girls were haunting in their innocent beauty.

Last, he added the little blonde-haired girl that resembled Penny Matthews. Twelve names.

"And this is Kim Fox, age five, Hiawassee, Georgia." His voice cracked when he said the girl's name. "She disappeared twenty-five years ago. I believe she was his first victim."

The truth dawned in sickening clarity. This wasn't just a case he'd caught wind of. It was personal. "Kim… she was related to you?" Ellie asked.

"Yes. She was my little sister."

CHAPTER TWENTY-FOUR

Somewhere on the AT

They called him the Watcher.

He lived in the shadows of the forest, slipping from one dark corner to another. Searching. He'd been searching for a long time.

For answers. For the truth. For the bones.

He carried his burlap bag with him over his shoulder, his eyes trained on the rocky, nearly frozen ground. On the sounds around him. Squirrels foraging for food. Frogs croaking. The river water crashing onto the bank. A snake hissing somewhere in the woods.

Sometimes his pain weighed him down. But today, he shoved it to distant parts of his mind. His job was to watch over the forest. Protect the innocents.

Except once again he had failed.

Another search party had been in the woods last night. Calling a little girl's name. Dogs sniffing and chasing her scent. People frantic to find her before night set in and the cold enveloped her.

Before the big storm struck like a cannonball.

Just when folks thought spring was going to show its face, Tempest had decided to spin toward the South and wreak havoc. Locals and tourists were not prepared. Roads would turn to black ice. Temperatures would be frigid. Some wouldn't heed warnings, certain the weathermen were just creating hype.

But he felt the brutal chill robbing the warmth from the air and feared for the lost little child.

She was still missing. Hidden somewhere in the cracks and crevices of the mountain. If she cried out for help, the searchers wouldn't hear her pleas for the roar of the wind.

He trudged for miles and miles up into the hills to a place called Bloody Rock. Locals claimed a brutal battle between the Native Americans and white men happened here years ago. Rain and snow had weathered the rock over the years, but the crimson stain remained as a reminder that the world could be a dark and ugly place.

A reminder that some who entered the woods never came out. At least not alive.

He hiked over tree roots so gnarled and embedded in the ground they snaked for miles. Tree branches held hands in the wilderness, blocking out light, trapping the lost inside until they spun in circles and lost their minds.

Some might say he was one of them.

Others… well, it didn't matter.

His foot brushed something hard, another jagged steep incline that jutted over the mountainside. A beam of sunlight slanted across the thick mass of tree limbs, dead leaves, vines and crumbling rock below.

He suddenly halted, his gaze drawn to the deep brush to the right. A tiny sliver of alabaster. Bone.

Pulse pounding at the possibility he'd discovered a body, he shoved aside tree limbs and brush, hacking them away with his pocketknife. Sweat trickled down the back of his neck, the icy rain turning the strands of his beard into brittle-like straw.

He lost his footing, tripped over a stump, nearly plunging over the side of the ridge. Grabbing a root, he pulled himself back up. Panting for a breath, he got to his feet and skidded down the treacherous path.

Finally, he reached the bottom. Yanking on gloves, he treaded carefully through the sticks, debris and foliage until he reached the spot where he'd seen the bone.

He knelt to examine the area, then slowly dislodged the bone from where it was caught in a cluster of twigs.

It definitely was a bone. A human one. A child's.

His fingers brushed over something smooth, wood. A tiny little wooden doll. He gently scraped away the rotten leaves and mud around the toy, and saw it was nestled in the skeletal remains of a hand.

He bowed his head and choked back a cry. For a brief moment, he mourned the little person to whom the bones belonged.

But if there was one bone, there would be more. With his gloved hands, he began digging.

Sorrow and regret welled inside him, emotion choking his throat.

But he couldn't report what he'd found. Then he'd have to join the world again. Face the questions. They'd accuse him of the crime.

He found the skull, gently lifted it and ran his fingers over the delicate bones. Bones that were brittle now and crumbling. The alabaster was darkening, fragile, thin, clean of hair and skin. How long had she been here?

He wondered what the little girl's name was. Who had lost her. If she'd suffered before she died.

Using his knife, he carefully uncovered the remaining fragments of the body, collecting and placing them carefully in his bag. Finally, when his search unearthed no more, he tied the sack closed.

Satisfied there had just been one set of remains, he carried the bag back up the steep incline. The sound of the creek water crashing over rocks mingled with his labored breathing.

When he reached a small clearing covered in emerald green moss and lichen, he paused. Tucked beneath a cluster of live oaks and facing the water, it was shielded from the elements and animals. He set his sack down, retrieved his trowel and began to dig a grave. Inch by inch, he tossed the dirt aside until he made a safe place for the bones, gently laying them inside.

He covered them back up, making sure the grave was deep enough that an animal foraging for food wouldn't disturb the small body's final resting place.

He wanted her to be found, though. Not to lie here in eternity without her family knowing where she was or wondering if she might ever come home. With no place to visit her and whisper how much they loved her, how sorry they were she was gone.

He found a large rock, and a branch that had fallen in a storm, and crafted a small headstone for the bones. He lay the wood in a cross, then used his pocketknife to carve a number into the wood.

Number one.

She was the first one he'd found. But he'd lived in these mountains for years now. He knew there were more.

CHAPTER TWENTY-FIVE

Crooked Creek

Derrick clenched his jaw to control his emotions. He hadn't come here for sympathy. He wanted answers.

"I'm sorry, Special Agent Fox," Detective Reeves said, her voice softer than before. "I can't imagine what you and your family have been through."

"It was a difficult time. Still is." He averted his eyes. "And if we're going to work together, call me Derrick."

She nodded. "All right. I'm Ellie." She walked over to the board and studied the faces. "None of the little girls were ever found?"

He shook his head. "Local authorities investigated each case just as you've been doing. Parents were questioned, family members, neighbors, friends, teachers. Search parties combed the woods and mountains for days. No evidence pointing to a specific suspect." Although her father was on his list. And another name had cropped up in more than one investigator's report. Cord McClain—the ranger who'd helped with the search teams. His partner was digging for more information on the man now.

Derrick had been mentally composing a profile of the killer. The perp had to know the trail, the entry points, where to hide. He might live in the mountains or even on the trail or a neighboring town.

Who would know that better than a ranger?

Ellie cleared her throat. "The parents were cleared?"

"Yes. Each story was slightly different, but similar. The families were on vacation, hiking, fishing, swimming, camping. Two different foster kids disappeared from a field trip, a year apart. In each case, the girls just vanished."

"Were the fosters from the same family?" Ellie asked.

He shook his head. "No connection between any of the families or the agencies they were affiliated with."

"So, he's choosing the girls at random. An opportunist."

"Looks that way. Although he only chooses females."

The fact that the victims were all female twisted at Derrick's gut. He prayed every day that they weren't dealing with a sexual predator. Without a body to autopsy, they couldn't be sure of that.

Ellie began sticking pushpins on the wall map in the various locations where the girls had vanished.

"Let's say you're right," she said, standing back to follow the trail of pins. "You believe your sister was his first victim. She disappeared near Stony Gap. The next two girls also disappeared in Georgia. Then he moved onto North Carolina where he took three more. After that he went to Gatlinburg, Tennessee where he took another. Then Virginia where he took two more. Then he came back to the Smokies and Georgia, taking two more girls. And now Penny Matthews here in Georgia again."

Derrick studied the detective as she analyzed the information. He hadn't known what to expect from her.

But he'd done his homework before coming. Not only was she Randall Reeves' daughter and a looker, she'd graduated top at the police academy. Had been cleaning up meth labs around the area. Earned her detective shield two years ago. No blemishes on her record, just glowing reports. Although she was young. Thirty maybe? How much experience could she have had?

Her whiteboard was impressive, and it appeared she was following protocol, asking the right questions, open to all the possible scenarios. She'd even expressed compassion for Stan Matthews. Derrick felt the same mixed emotion.

His family had been put through the ringer when Kim went missing. His parents treated like persons of interest. The police also interrogated *him* as if he'd done something to Kim.

He'd never forget Randall Reeves' harsh voice as he'd grilled him. *Little sisters can be annoying. Does your sister bug you? Are you jealous of her? Maybe it was an accident, the two of you got in a fight and you shoved her, and she fell off a ledge?*

As an adult agent, he understood the man had been doing his job. Only recently, he'd reviewed the sheriff's initial reports on the investigation.

But something felt off.

Not that Reeves hadn't asked questions, interviewed locals, sent out search parties looking for Kim, but… his notes had inconsistencies. At first, the sheriff had been adamant that he wouldn't give up until he found Derrick's baby sister.

Then suddenly he'd closed the case.

Derrick's mother had plunged downhill into depression. And his father… he'd been enraged one minute, despondent the next. Being accused of hurting his child had torn him apart. The press had made it worse, plastering their pictures everywhere. Some friends and neighbors supported them and had sympathy. Others gossiped and looked at them with suspicion and fear. Derrick's friends' parents had suddenly stopped them from seeing him.

Weighed down by grief and fear and the accusations, his father had run his truck off a cliff. The truck exploded on impact, and his body had never been found. He still remembered his mother's anguished sob when the police had showed up to deliver the news.

Derrick released a heavy breath. Within months, his sister and his father were both gone.

Bitter anger bled through him. If Randall Reeves hadn't given up so easily, maybe they would have found Kim. And his father would still be alive.

CHAPTER TWENTY-SIX

Ellie studied the timing of the disappearances. Derrick was right. The lapse between them varied by months, sometimes more than a year.

It was odd for a serial killer to lay dormant for long periods, although it happened. Sometimes they found a family, friend or job that made them content for a while, before something happened to trigger their need to hunt again. Another possibility was that they could have been ill or even incarcerated.

That is, if they were dealing with one perpetrator. Child kidnapping and human trafficking rings were a growing problem. The thought made her ill, but she couldn't dismiss it.

"You checked prison records and psychiatric hospitals for a possible suspect?" Ellie asked.

"Of course," Derrick said. "I've considered that there may be more victims than the ones I've identified. During those time lapses, he could have still been hunting, but no one reported the child missing or the name got lost in the system."

"How could a person not report a missing child?" Even as she asked the question, the dark answers nagged at her. "Wait. Don't answer that. I know. Foster parents who didn't want to lose their monthly paycheck."

Derrick gave a grim nod. "Parents in custody battles or with drug or alcohol problems. Possibly illegals. For now, we should focus on the victims we know about. Those old cases might give us a lead."

Ellie thought out loud. "A serial predator's first is usually significant. Someone who meant something to the perpetrator."

"True." A muscle ticked in his strong jaw. "But trust me, my family was dissected like bugs under a microscope."

"Could someone have been watching or stalking your sister? A neighbor or relative?"

"Not that we'd noticed, although my parents considered that theory," Derrick said, his voice terse. "By the time the sheriff stopped pointing the finger at my family, the kidnapper was long gone."

"How old were you at the time?"

"Fourteen," Derrick replied. "I was supposed to be watching her, but I told her to sit by the rocks while I waded in the creek. When I looked up later, she was gone."

Ellie's heart gave a pang. "I can't imagine how scary that was."

His jaw tightened, and a heartbeat passed before she pushed her emotions aside. "If you're right, we have to broaden our investigation." Which meant she needed to review the old cases herself. "Tourist season is just beginning," Ellie continued. "People are pouring in for the festival and to begin their trek northward. Whoever took Penny could easily be hiding in plain sight."

The date his sister went missing suddenly struck Ellie. Kim had been six. About the same age as Ellie when they'd moved to Stony Gap.

"Derrick, who was the lead investigator on your sister's case?"

His body went still, tension radiating from him. "Sheriff Randall Reeves."

A strained silence stretched between them. That was the reason he'd come to her first.

"You know he's my father?"

He gave a clipped nod. "I tried to discuss my theory with him before, but he wouldn't listen," Derrick said. "When I saw you were heading up the Matthews case, I drove straight here."

Ellie folded her arms. "I don't understand. Presented with this information, how could he not have listened?"

"He said I was seeing things that weren't there. That I should talk to a shrink." Derrick cursed. "But I think he closed the case long before he should have. There are also discrepancies in the interviews he conducted."

His accusation took her off guard. Her father was respected and admired in Bluff County. For over twenty years, he'd protected the residents and was instrumental in helping rescues on the trail. He wouldn't have made mistakes in a missing child case. "What kind of discrepancies?"

"A couple of months ago, I talked to two of the locals he interviewed. Their stories don't match your father's notes."

"After two decades, people forget details," Ellie pointed out. "They confuse memories, get the days mixed up."

"My memory is clear," Derrick said. "I recall your father grilling my parents and me. He thought we hurt Kim."

Ellie's chest clenched. "As a federal agent, you know it's necessary to treat everyone as a person of interest until they're ruled out."

"I do know that now," Derrick said. "But something wasn't right about the investigation. My gut's telling me. And I intend to figure out what it was."

He was right. If that case was connected to the Matthews girl, she couldn't ignore the evidence Derrick had presented.

She had a child to find.

CHAPTER TWENTY-SEVEN

"Let me see those files," Ellie told Derrick. "Then we'll talk."

He gave a quick nod, then unpocketed his phone. "I need to make a call. Take all the time you need."

As soon as he closed the door, Ellie checked in with Cord. It was past noon.

"We've covered over ten miles now," Cord said. "No sign of Penny or anyone else. But the storm is coming, El. The wind has picked up and it feels more like twenty than thirty-five. The sleet will start any minute."

He sounded bone tired and worried. "No footprints?" There had to be something.

"If there were, the rain last night washed them away," Cord replied.

"Are there security cameras in the parking lot at the park?"

"Afraid not. But when this is over, I'm going to push the NPS to install them."

"Good. What about the dogs?"

"They followed downstream but lost the scent. Workers searched the creek and park for miles. No sign of Penny."

Frustration overcame Ellie, and she glanced at the faces on the whiteboard with a growing sense of horror.

"Focus on the shelters or caves in the woods now," Ellie said. "If Penny was abducted and her kidnapper didn't leave via car, he found a place to hide out."

"Copy that."

She hung up, grabbed another cup of coffee, then skimmed her father's notes.

Derrick's father, Gerrard Fox, was a pathologist who'd worked in a research lab. According to Randall, both parents were distraught.

During the weekend camping trip, Mr. Fox left for a couple of hours to meet a colleague. Colleague and wife confirmed his alibi. The mother, Margaret Fox, a florist, had set off to gather wildflowers for an upcoming wedding and left the son in charge of Kim.

Ellie's gut tightened.

Father blamed himself for not staying at the camp. Mother blamed herself for not keeping Kim with her. Derrick blamed himself because he was supposed to be watching his little sister.

Except for his mother's coworker, who hinted the couple had marital problems, there was no evidence indicating they weren't happy.

Her father had grilled Derrick. *Had he gotten sick of his sister bugging him? Had they fought? Had he pushed her, and she'd fallen?*

According to the sheriff, Derrick had been sullen and angry, and denied the accusation.

If there was any truth to her father's suspicions, Derrick wouldn't be here now driving this investigation, would he?

Derrick seemed adamant that a serial predator had taken Kim, that she was his very first victim. If that was true, Kim couldn't still be alive.

So, what had the killer done with her body? And with the other children's?

CHAPTER TWENTY-EIGHT

Ellie thumped her fingers on the table as Derrick reentered the conference room. "You mentioned discrepancies?"

"In some of the statements," Derrick pointed out. "According to your father's notes, our neighbor Ned Hanline claims he saw Dad spanking Kim. But my father never laid a hand on us. Ever. And when I questioned Hanline, he denied making that statement." Derrick rubbed his hand over the back of his neck. "Also, my mother's assistant supposedly said Mom mentioned marital problems. Tammy insists that statement was false, that she told your father my parents were happy."

Ellie frowned. That didn't make sense.

"What bothered me most is a conversation one of his deputies had with a youth group camping nearby," Derrick continued. "One of the boys claimed he saw a little girl with another teenage boy about a mile from our camp. The girl looked lost and was crying, but the bigger boy dragged her along. At the time, the kid thought they were brother and sister, but when he heard about Kim, he thought he might have been wrong." Derrick hesitated. "But your father didn't release that information. Instead, he focused on my dad."

"Have you spoken with the teens in that youth group?"

Derrick shook his head. "No. Their contact information wasn't taken down properly."

Ellie flattened her hands on the table. "I'm sure that was just an oversight." Although at the very least, he should have followed up with the group.

There had to be an explanation.

She stood, collected the notes and handed them back to Derrick.

His jaw tightened. "You're not even going to consider that I'm right? How can you dismiss the evidence in front of you?"

"I'm not dismissing it." Ellie gestured toward the door. "We're going to have a talk with my father."

Surprise flashed on his face, followed by a look of relief.

She thought her father might be in the woods searching for Penny, so she texted him and asked where they could meet.

He replied straight away: *Home now. Come on over.*

Hurrying into her office, she snagged her jacket and keys. Derrick followed, a gust of wind rocking the traffic light in the center of town as they stepped outside. As predicted, the rain had turned to a light sleet, pinging off the store roofs and sidewalks, the skies ominous and dreary.

She pointed to her Jeep. "I'll drive."

Derrick climbed in the passenger side without comment. BRYCE WATERS FOR SHERIFF signs were dotted around as they drove through town, each boasting a picture of Bryce's smiling face.

Nausea threatened, but she tamped it down. Bryce was the least of her worries right now.

The Jeep hit an icy patch, causing her to skid slightly as she turned onto the road leading to her parents' house. Just yesterday, she'd driven this same way with high hopes for her father's announcement.

Today she was heading there with a knot in the pit of her stomach and accusations screaming in her head. A little girl had been missing now for twenty-four hours. Another little girl had gone missing twenty-five years ago in a similar manner, and her father had failed to mention it.

If Derrick Fox had made a connection between the two, why the hell hadn't her father?

CHAPTER TWENTY-NINE

Stony Gap

The blustery wind tossed debris across her parents' lawn as Ellie threw the Jeep into park. The cold made her skin tingle. A loose shutter flapped, and sleet slashed the windows. Wet earth sucked at her boots as she climbed from the vehicle and the bitter breeze blasted her in the face. It was too cold for Penny to be exposed in the elements. Hypothermia was far more dangerous than the wild animals on the trail.

Derrick stuffed his hands in the pockets of his coat and followed her up to the door, his eyes scanning the property as they made their way up the porch steps.

Ellie's mother was just coming down the staircase when Ellie stepped inside.

"Honey, I'm glad you decided to drop by."

Ellie gestured to Derrick, who'd paused behind her. "This is about the case, Mom. I texted Dad."

Disappointment flitted in her mother's hazel eyes. "All right then. But he's tired. He was out all night trying to find that child."

Ellie brushed past her. "That's the reason I'm here. This is Special Agent Derrick Fox. He may have insight into the case."

Her mother's face paled slightly, then she stepped aside, and Ellie led Derrick into her father's study.

Like so many times before, he stood in front of one of his maps, studying it as if it held the answers to the world. Maybe it did.

Maybe it could tell them where Penny Matthews was.

He turned at the sound of their footsteps, then his breath hitched when he saw them.

CHAPTER THIRTY

Derrick had been waiting for this day for a long time.

He should have come to see Sheriff Reeves sooner. But his theory had been shot down so many times when he'd spoken with local law enforcement on the other cases, and Randall's quick dismissal over the phone had held him back. He'd wanted concrete evidence to connect them all before proceeding.

They didn't bother with pleasantries. He wasn't in a cordial mood.

"Dad," Ellie said. "You remember Derrick Fox?"

"Of course." The sheriff gestured toward the two wing chairs facing his desk. "Remind me which agency you're working with now."

"The FBI."

Sheriff Reeves exhaled. "I didn't realize you'd brought in the feds, Ellie."

"Actually, she didn't call me, sir. I came on my own." Derrick set the folder containing duplicate photographs of the girls and his notes on the desk. "Ten years ago, when I joined the Bureau, I reviewed my sister's case. I hoped to find some new evidence or something you'd missed that might help me learn what happened to her."

The sheriff crossed his arms. "Did you?"

"I found discrepancies in your notes. Statements that contradict each other. I also searched for other similar cases, and as I stated when I tried to discuss my theory with you before, I found some."

Irritation snapped in Randall Reeves eyes. "Go on."

Derrick opened the folder and spread the pictures across the sheriff's desk. "All of these girls are between the ages of five and seven. All disappeared somewhere along the AT."

Randall sank into his desk chair and thumbed through the pictures, his throat muscles working as he swallowed.

Derrick studied the man's reaction. Not surprise. Not recognition. Confusion? Wariness?

Finally, the sheriff lifted his head, a frown marring his face. "None of these cases have been solved?"

Derrick shook his head. "Local law enforcement investigated, but as in my sister's disappearance, they cleared the parents, never pinned the crime on anyone, never found the girls, and the cases went cold."

"And you believe they're connected," Sheriff Reeves said. Not a question, but an observation.

"I do. And I think Penny Matthews may be another victim."

Ellie's father rustled through the notes again, a vein throbbing in his neck as he skimmed the information. Ellie sighed. "Dad, missing children's cases make national news. Didn't you see the news about any of these girls and wonder if they were taken by the same person?"

The sheriff's look turned to annoyance. "Of course. I even talked with a few of the investigators. But no one saw a connection. The families weren't related, the girls disappeared in several jurisdictions and there was no consistency with the timing." He aimed his look at Derrick. "Why would a perpetrator kidnap one child and then wait another year before taking another?"

CHAPTER THIRTY-ONE

"I asked the same question," Ellie said. "But there could be reasons. Maybe there are more victims that we don't know about. Or he was incarcerated, or something happened in his life to make him stop for a while, then he started up again."

Her father's expression flattened. "If the same person abducted each of these girls and kept them hostage, someone would have seen him with one of them by now."

"Not if he lives in isolation or off the grid," Derrick pointed out.

Or if he killed them and left their bodies somewhere they wouldn't be found. Ellie's stomach churned.

"I have two agents working this angle, specifically looking at human trafficking rings, which is probably the likeliest link. But some small towns have antiquated systems and others fail to report in a timely manner. Others lost reports, one office had a natural disaster that destroyed all their files, and a couple of families refused to cooperate. They'd had enough of being treated like suspects."

"So, the alleged abductions occurred in different jurisdictions and with no time pattern. Have you at least found a potential person of interest who was in all those places? Either someone acting alone or with links to an organized ring?" Randall asked.

Derrick shifted, as if he had an idea but didn't want to say. "None that could have been in every single location."

Ellie twisted her mouth in thought. "Perhaps one of the crimes was personal, and the killer took the other girls to throw off the investigation."

"That might happen with one or two, but it would be far-fetched to kidnap a string of girls to cover the abduction or murder of one," Randall said matter-of-factly. "An organized crime ring is more probable. If it's an individual, he'd likely have been in his twenties or thirties when the first girl disappeared—that's when most serial killers start their sprees. Although some start in their teens." He shot Derrick a challenging stare.

A muscle ticked in Derrick's jaw. "I'm here because I know I didn't hurt my sister, and I want justice."

"Which raises the question about that youth group your team talked to when Kim disappeared, Dad," Ellie interjected. "Why didn't you track down their contact information and follow up?"

Randall's lips thinned. "There was no need. The boys had nothing to do with Kim's disappearance." He aimed a questioning look toward Derrick. "Have you shared this theory with your father?"

A coldness washed over Derrick's face. "My father killed himself nine months after you closed Kim's case."

Ellie sucked in a breath.

But her father showed no reaction. "Are you certain he's dead? I heard his body was never found."

Derrick clenched his hands into fists. "It wasn't, but he left a suicide note."

"In that note, he said he couldn't live with the guilt, didn't he?" Ellie's father asked.

"You knew?" Surprise and anger hardened Derrick's voice.

"I did. A serial killer's first victim is usually significant. Since you're tossing around the theory that the same person abducted all these little girls, and that it started with your sister, maybe you need to ask yourself if that person could be your father."

CHAPTER THIRTY-TWO

Ellie stared at her father for a heated moment as Derrick stalked from the room.

At the sound of the front door slamming behind him, she folded her arms, torn between trusting her father and questioning him. Derrick seemed so convinced Randall had messed up. "Do you really think Derrick's father did something to Kim?"

The vein in his neck throbbed the way it always did when he was angry. "I never found proof, but as you know, I had to interrogate him. His suicide made me wonder if he took his own life out of guilt."

Ellie wasn't quite ready to believe her father's theory. "At the time of his suicide, did you look into the possibility that he could have faked his death?"

Her father shook his head. "Not then. But Derrick is the one connecting the cases. I simply pointed out one possibility. Derrick blamed himself back then. He could have accidentally hurt his sister, then the family covered it up."

Ellie didn't want to believe that either, although what did she really know about Derrick Fox? She'd read about cases where a cop or rescue worker was actually the perpetrator. "If that was true, why would he bring attention to the other missing girls?"

"If you knew anything about serial killers, sometimes they escalate because deep down they want to get caught."

His condescending tone irked her. She didn't see Derrick as a killer.

And she'd never seen her father so unsympathetic toward a victim's family. To hell with his suspicions. She didn't understand anything her father had done lately. He was becoming more and more of a stranger.

Her phone buzzed on her hip. The captain. "I have to take this."

"I'm going to join the search teams." Her father reached for his keys, anger radiating off him in the stiff set of his shoulders.

On her way out, Ellie nearly ran into her mother, realizing she'd been listening to their conversation.

Ignoring her disapproving look, Ellie answered the phone and stepped outside.

"Tell me you've got something," Captain Hale barked.

Fox was already in the Jeep, so she stayed sheltered from the worst of the stinging rain on the porch. She needed to talk to the captain alone.

"Ellie?" he snapped.

"I'm here. And… yeah, I may have something." She explained about Derrick showing up and his theory.

"Son of a bitch," Captain Hale muttered. "We can't have a serial killer in our county."

"I hope not," Ellie said. "But I've seen the files, and he could be right. Which means Stan Matthews is innocent."

A tense silence passed, the captain's breathing filling the awkward quiet.

"Work the angle," he said in a commanding tone. "And by the way, not sure if it's the same couple Matthews saw, but a man and woman checked in two days ago at the Crooked Creek Inn and left yesterday. I ran their tag and got a pop at a Quick Mart near Dahlonega. Local deputy said the couple claim they saw a man with a little girl that could have been Penny."

Ellie headed toward her Jeep, where Derrick sat looking into the mountains. "Where was that?"

"Near Rattlesnake Ridge."

Gray tornado-looking clouds moved across the sky, and sleet was starting to fall, slivers of ice hammering down.

They had to hurry. They needed to find Penny before Tempest unleashed the worst of her fury.

"And Ellie," Captain Hale said. "I think you're right about Matthews. The officer showed the couple a picture of the father. The man they saw with the little girl was not him."

"Did they describe him?"

"They didn't see his face. Said he was tall, dragged one leg slightly, wore an old tattered coat, gloves and a ski cap."

She needed more. "I'm on my way."

It looked like Derrick was right. A serial killer might be stalking the AT right in her own backyard.

CHAPTER THIRTY-THREE

Penny scooted as far away from the doorway of the cave as she could. But the space was so tiny and dark she couldn't see very far.

Goosebumps skated up her arms. It smelled bad in here, like rotten bananas when they turned brown and slimy and the fruit flies swarmed around them.

The ground was hard and damp. And the sharp edge of the rocks jabbed at her back.

She clutched the little wooden doll in one hand and hugged it to her. He'd carved it just for her, he'd said. A treasure she could add to her other dolls. Only she didn't have many dolls, mostly rocks and stones and things she found outside.

But she had thought it was cool when he said he'd made the doll out of wood from a fallen tree. Stuck here in the black hole, she wanted to trade it for Toby, her yellow squishy teddy bear with the soft fur and fluffy ears. When she whispered her secrets to Toby, he listened. And sometimes he whispered back.

But this doll said nothing. It just stared up at her with its hollow empty eyes.

She'd been a bad girl. She had wandered off from the picnic site. Had been mad at her daddy because he didn't want to play with her.

So she'd snuck off on her own. That was stupid.

Where was Mama now? Was she awake? Would she come looking for her?

The sound of water trickling down the rocky wall echoed nearby. Something skittered across her arm. A spider? Rat?

Tears filled her eyes. But she blinked them back. She couldn't let him see she was scared. Then he'd get mad like before. She didn't like it when he was mad. His eyes got big and scary like the monsters that peered at her from her closet at night.

The grating sound of his knife against the wood made her shiver. She pictured the knife piercing her skin. Blood dripping down. Red on the floor. Dots and dots of it like paint splattering.

A cry lodged in her throat.

Don't be a crybaby, he'd said.

Pressing her fist to her mouth, she pulled her knees up and wrapped her arms around them. She tried to remember what had happened. She'd stumbled, twisted her ankle. Her foot slid over the edge. She was falling. Dropping further and further. But then he'd jerked her up and saved her.

He'd said she had to learn a lesson. Had to be punished.

She'd been punished before, and she didn't like it. Not one bit.

She closed her eyes and tried to think happy thoughts like Mama taught her to when Daddy was in one of his moods. In her mind, she felt Mama's hand stroking her hair. Wiping away her tears. Singing softly a silly song she made up about chasing puppies in the backyard.

Rocking herself back and forth, she tried to think of sunshine and rainbows and unicorns, but she couldn't see them in the dark. She wanted to go home to Mama. Feel her arms around her. Sniff the strawberry bodywash she used when she took her bath.

Her body shook as the tears spilled over. She tried to hold back a sob, but it screeched from her throat and came out like a balloon popping.

The knife went still. He stopped carving. He was listening.

She buried her head in her arms and squeezed her eyes shut. But she heard his footsteps and knew he was coming for her.

CHAPTER THIRTY-FOUR

Crooked Creek

"What's wrong?" Derrick asked once he and Ellie were back on the road. Wind banged Bryce's campaign signs back and forth. Posters with Penny's picture on them covered the store fronts and light posts, although the wind tore at them, ripping one into shreds and tossing it across the ground.

Others advertised the upcoming Cornbread Festival. Even with the storm threatening, vendors were erecting booths and some tourists remained, wandering the quaint stores, hunched in their coats and hats, faces shielded by thick wool scarves.

Ellie relayed her conversation with her boss.

"I'll tell Cord to direct the search toward Rattlesnake Ridge. I can drop you at your car."

"No, I'm going with you."

"Are you sure about that? A city boy like you might have a hard time on the trail."

His eyebrow rose, eyes flashing with irritation, and she almost smiled. "Don't worry about me," he said darkly. "I'll keep up."

"Your call," she said with a shrug. She gestured toward his dress slacks and shoes. "Do you have hiking boots or winter gear with you?"

He frowned. "Yeah, I have boots, insulated pants, gloves and a jacket in my car."

"Then we'll swing by and get them. I'll grab us something to eat while you change."

Her phone buzzed—Deputy Landrum. "What's up, Heath?"

"I ran down Pauline Shore. She confirms Stan Matthews' story about the one-night stand. In fact, she moved to Atlanta a couple of weeks after they hooked up."

"So that eliminates her, and Stan's motive of wanting to leave his wife."

"Yeah, and I can't find anything on Zimmerman to point to him. In fact, he was coaching a little league game when Penny went missing. And everyone I talked to said he had an exemplary record."

Now Derrick had arrived, Ellie felt safe dismissing Zimmerman as well.

"What now?" Heath asked.

She explained the information Derrick had presented. "Right now, it's just a theory, Heath. So keep it between us."

"Copy that. And let me know what else I can do."

She murmured she would, then ended the call. Ten minutes later, she parked at the station and Derrick retrieved his duffel bag from the trunk of his vehicle. After he quickly changed inside the building and she grabbed them sandwiches, they got back on the road, the thick gray clouds overhead threatening more ice and snow, trees shivering, the wind howling. Ellie drove north, about fifteen miles from the park where the Matthews had picnicked. When they'd arrived, she radioed Cord, who said he'd meet them at the ridge with Wilson, the SAR dog he worked with.

She retrieved her backpack, which held a sleeping bag, extra compass, her own hand-drawn maps of various sections of the trail, flashlights and other necessary supplies. Then she and Derrick donned jackets, ski hats, and gloves, and she yanked on her hiking boots.

Derrick looked somber as he scanned the mountains ahead. She guessed he was reliving the trauma of losing his sister in the hills.

The memory of her own ordeal flashed back, making her break out in a sweat. One night alone in the woods had traumatized her. What would it do to Penny?

Derrick's gruff voice interrupted her thoughts. "Which way?"

"Northeast," she said, then gestured toward the trail. "Rattle-snake Ridge is about six miles from here."

Wind gusts whipped through the trees, gaining momentum, the temperature dropping by the hour. "Let's go."

She took the lead, the two of them weaving through the overgrown brush and endless trees. Even though it was only mid-afternoon, daylight was waning, the dark clouds casting shadows and robbing what little sunlight remained. The fragrance of southern balsam and Fraser fir filled the air, a reminder of the holiday that had passed, when her family had gathered to celebrate, and she'd been hopeful about her future at the sheriff's office.

Though Ellie was no botanist, her father had taught her enough to avoid the thick patches of poison ivy growing in the woods and along the riverbank, where the water rippled and gurgled, slashing the jagged rocks that led to the falls.

Ellie used the makeshift bridge someone had erected across the water where it overflowed the bank, then veered around a cluster of hemlocks and froze. For a second, she thought she saw a wisp of a child peering from behind the rocks ahead.

Blonde hair like Penny's.

Big blue eyes, tormented-looking as they peered at her through the foliage.

Mae.

Her stomach clenched, and she blinked away the image. But the sound of Mae's cry lingered in her head.

"Ellie?"

Derrick's deep voice jerked her attention back to the present, and she sucked in a sharp breath.

"What's wrong?" Derrick asked.

"I… thought I saw something, but it was nothing," she said, grateful her voice sounded steady when her heart was pounding.

Was she starting to hallucinate again?

God, no. It was just this case. It was getting to her. Making her see ghosts.

She gestured toward a thicket ahead. "Come on, let's keep moving." One foot in front of the other, they maneuvered their way up the steep hill toward the ridge. Tree roots, vines, brush and broken limbs impeded their trek, and they hiked without talking.

Tension thickened between them as the chill in the air intensified, dead brown leaves raining down on them, mingling with the icy precipitation. She wanted to reach the ridge and find Penny before the snow started falling and blurred her vision. Wind beat at her, and her boots sank into the wet moss and mud. She pushed through the thicket, scanning every turn for signs of Penny or footprints indicating where the man had taken her.

After several miles, night descended, the lone howl of a wolf shattering the deafening silence. The acrid scent of decay led them to a dead deer and a campfire that had been snuffed out. Using her flashlight, she searched for footprints, a man's or child's, but if they'd come this way, the rain of the last twenty-four hours had obscured the tracks.

Rattlesnake Ridge stood tall and ominous, with a steep drop of over eighty feet, and was known to be a hotbed of snakes. When they reached it, they divided to search the surrounding area.

No AT shelter here, but Ellie discovered a small cave.

Branches had been piled in front of the opening. She quickly began to pull them aside. Somewhere in the distance a coyote howled. Thunder clapped. Rain beat down like drums, mingling with pellets of ice.

Yanking away the limbs, Ellie aimed her flashlight into the dark opening and was assaulted with the strong smell of something rotten.

Heart pounding, she stooped down and peered inside. But an icy fear immobilized her.

Terrifying memories of crawling into a dark hole when she was little paralyzed her. A tunnel. Like the one in her nightmare. She'd thought it led… where? Dammit, she couldn't remember.

Help me.

A child's cry whispered to her in the darkness.

"I'll go," Derrick said, as if he sensed her resistance.

Cold sweat beaded the back of her neck. Her stomach lurched. Nausea rose to her throat.

She had to fight it. Save Penny.

Summoning her courage, she called Penny's name and crawled into the dank, black interior.

CHAPTER THIRTY-FIVE

Rattlesnake Ridge

Halfway into the cavernous opening, Ellie suddenly felt a viselike grip around her neck.

She hoped she'd outgrow her fear of the dark, but her phobia lingered, the suffocating sensation wrapping its tentacles around her throat and squeezing hard, cutting into her windpipe.

Stop it, don't be a baby. Penny might be in here. She needs you.

Forcing herself to breathe through her nose, she closed her eyes and meditated for several seconds. *Think of your safe place*, the therapist had taught her. The treehouse daddy had built for her. It was nestled between the oaks, high above ground so she could see across the backyard. High enough the wild animals couldn't reach her if they roamed on the property from the woods beyond. Foxy was there, too, cuddled in her arms, listening as she whispered secrets in his ears.

Then she was tucked in her iron bed with her grammy's quilt covering her, snuggling her just like Grammy's arms used to do before she died. So many times, she'd watched her plump body bent over the scraps of fabric squares, nimble hands shifting and arranging the different prints into a beautiful design like pieces of a puzzle.

Slowly the terror subsided, and she opened her eyes and released a calming breath. "Penny, are you in here?"

Dead silence met her call.

The musty scent of damp earth, moss and decay filled her nostrils as she belly-crawled a few feet in. One inch at a time. *Find Penny. That's all that matters.*

Finally, the ceiling of the cave grew taller, the opening wider, and she pushed up on her hands and knees, then stood. Her head almost brushed the ceiling, but at least there was more air.

"Penny, are you here, honey?" She scanned the interior of the space and saw footprints ahead. A man's. Adrenaline churning through her, she hurried forward, examining the floor for a button or garment, an indication Penny had been inside.

More prints lay ahead, and she moved toward them, discovering a set of smaller ones. Definitely a man and a child.

Penny and whoever had taken her *had* been here.

Scrambling ahead, she followed the tunnel as it wound into a small clearing. Water trickled down the interior wall, pooling on the ground. Damp moss dotted the rock. Slimy mud collected on her boots.

But no one was inside.

Still, someone had been here. She scanned the widest section, and her flashlight beam fell on something in the dirt.

Pulse pounding, she crossed to it and illuminated the rocky floor. It was a small piece of wood. With gloved hands, she dislodged it from where it was half-buried in the dirt and held it up to the light.

It was smooth, hand-carved, carefully crafted. A tiny wooden doll like something a child would play with.

Déjà vu struck her, and for a second, the world turned black and tilted. She felt dizzy again. Her vision blurred. The doll with the little round head and thin arms and big eyes carved deep into the wood… it seemed familiar, as if she'd seen a figure like this before.

She shook her head, but she couldn't place where she might have seen it.

Susan hadn't mentioned that her daughter had a doll with her, had she? Was it Penny's? Or something her abductor had given to her?

Knowing it needed to be analyzed, she removed a baggie from her pocket and stowed the toy inside to send to the lab. If they found prints matching Penny's, she'd know the little girl had been here. And if her abductor had given it to her, they might lift his prints, too.

Hope fueled her. Maybe they were getting close.

She searched the area again and noticed a section of leaves piled together. They looked crushed, as if someone had used them as a pillow.

After snapping a photograph of the pile, she crawled back through the tunnel, holding her breath the whole way. The sound of the wind whistling assaulted her as she pushed through the opening, and sleet pelted her, stinging her cheeks.

Gripping the doll, she stood and brushed dirt and debris from her pants. "Derrick, where are you?"

"Over here!"

When he broke through the clearing, his dark gaze latched onto hers.

"Did you find anything outside?" Ellie asked.

He shook his head. "Some broken tree limbs a few feet ahead. Footprints, but they disappeared into the creek." He glanced at the cave opening. "What's that?"

"A hand-carved wooden doll I found in the cave. I think Penny and her kidnapper were here."

Hope flickered across his face. "So, she might still be alive."

Ellie nodded hopefully, then texted to request an ERT to the cave pronto. Her phone buzzed just as she sent the message.

Cord. She punched connect and put it on speaker.

"Ellie, you need to get over here."

Ellie's heart thundered. "What's wrong?"

A tense heartbeat passed, then Cord's deep baritone voice filled the silence. "I found something. It looks like a grave. A small one."

Fear pulsed through Ellie. Derrick staggered slightly, his face ashen.

They both began to run toward the river.

CHAPTER THIRTY-SIX

Falling leaves mixed with the sleet as the wind gusts picked up. Ellie spotted Cord stooped beside a mound of dirt a few feet from the water's edge.

As she and Derrick approached, her pulse quickened at the sight of a wooden cross and oval river rock.

Grim-faced, his flashlight in his hand, Cord gestured toward the freshly turned ground. "I almost stumbled over it."

Ellie swallowed hard, using her own torch to illuminate the area. Fresh leaves and wildflowers covered the dirt, as if whoever dug this grave had cared about the person who'd died.

The length and width of the mound was the size of a large animal. *Or a child*, she thought grimly.

Was it Penny? Had her father hurt her accidentally and then buried her, spreading flowers on her grave because he loved her? Or was her disappearance related to the other missing girls?

"This is Special Agent Derrick Fox from the FBI," Ellie said. "Derrick, Ranger Cord McClain has been leading the teams searching for Penny Matthews."

The men exchanged a short hello.

Ellie noticed Derrick narrowing his eyes at Cord, his body going rigid. "How did you say you found the grave?"

Cord patted the SAR dog, who stood guard by the stone. "Wilson led me here."

"Wilson is an air scent dog," Ellie explained. "If he picked up Penny's scent, she might be in that grave."

"I didn't see a child's footprints," Cord said. "There was a partial man's boot print by the river, but whoever it was brushed over the rest of the prints to cover his tracks." His sleeve rode up and she noticed a bandage on his arm—a hazard of the job. He was always covered in them.

Emotions crowded Ellie's chest. A little girl's footprints had been inside the cave. Which meant Penny might have been carried here. Had the kidnapper killed her in the cave, then brought her body out here to bury her? Why not leave her in the cave where she might not have been found? The thoughts swirled in her head.

"I'll call another Evidence Recovery Team and the ME." Ellie pulled her phone and made the call.

When she hung up, she began to snap pictures of the scene, searching for forensics to help identity the person who'd dug the grave.

Derrick knelt and studied the small mound with a reverent expression. Then he aimed a dark look at Cord, making Ellie wonder what exactly he was thinking. "This was dug within the last few hours. The flowers are still fresh."

"Matthews?" Cord asked. "But he was with the search teams this morning, then we sent him home."

Ellie frowned and filled him in on her conversation with her captain. "We think Penny was abducted."

Cord's smoky eyes narrowed to slits. "Abducted?"

"Yes. And there may be others," Ellie said, the truth sinking in.

"Look at this." Derrick pointed to markings on the stone, and Ellie lowered herself to study them. They were crude, scratched into the shape of an angel.

She snapped a photo of it, then leaned closer to analyze the details.

"That's the Roman numeral one on the cross," she murmured beneath her breath. Her gaze jerked to Derrick's.

"A one for his first victim," Derrick said in a husky tone.

Their gazes locked. Ellie swallowed hard. "A one, as in there are more."

CHAPTER THIRTY-SEVEN

Derrick struggled not to react to the sight of the small grave. Or to the unbidden image of his sister being buried here.

Files from the cases where Cord was mentioned teased his mind. From those, he'd been compiling a profile of the killer. And the ranger fit.

He was tempted to jerk Cord by the collar and demand to know if he'd put the body here.

But first he had to gather the facts.

Find out if Kim was in that grave. His mother had kept her pictures all over the house. She'd left his sister's room exactly the same as when Kim had been alive. Her white four-poster bed still held the pale green comforter with the yellow tulips on it. Shelves still housed her favorite dolls, stuffed animals, and the books she'd read over and over until she'd memorized them. Kim had liked to bake with her mother, but she'd also enjoyed kicking the soccer ball with their father.

She would have liked Ellie. She was feminine, but comfortable in the outdoors, and seemed like a woman who didn't back down from a fight.

Would Ellie cover for Randall if he'd screwed up? Or Cord?

The ranger had been mentioned in more than one police report in the missing girls' files. He could slip through the woods virtually unnoticed. He also knew the area. And he'd been first on scene to search for Penny.

Was it a coincidence that he'd been on duty in more than one of the disappearances?

The Roman numeral on the marker made Derrick's stomach clench but fit with his theory.

According to Derrick's count, there would be ten more bodies, a dozen counting Penny. And he was no closer to finding the psycho than he'd been before.

The ranger stooped down, intently studying the tombstone marker. The fact that he'd found the body raised Derrick's suspicions even more. Had McClain put it there to make himself look like a hero?

"How long have you worked SAR?" he asked the man.

McClain's thick brows bunched together in a frown. "I've been with FEMA and the NPS for about ten years."

About the same time Derrick became attuned to the possibility that the cases were connected. "In this area?" Derrick asked.

Cord gave a short nod. "I grew up hiking the trails. It was a natural fit."

Again, although McClain would have been a young teen at the time of Kim's death, he fit the profile. And it was possible he'd started a violent streak early on. It was more rare, but it happened.

But he needed something concrete before he tossed around accusations or shared his theory with Ellie.

"How did you get into SAR?" Derrick asked.

Cord jammed his hands in the pockets of his work jacket. But not before Derrick noticed dirt beneath his fingernails. His clothes were filthy, too, his boots mired in mud. A serious hunting knife hung on his belt.

"Volunteered once on a search team and realized I was good at it. Sheriff Reeves suggested I make it a career."

The realization that he was tight with Randall Reeves was enough to make Derrick cautious about what he said around the man.

A gust of wind swept through the trees, tearing pine needles and cones from the trees and scattering the wildflowers across the ground. Ellie caught them and put them back on the grave, as if she couldn't stand to see it bare.

Leaves rustled, trees dipping and bending beneath the force of the strong winds, limbs cracking and splintering. The scent of damp moss and a dead animal wafted toward them, followed by the sound of voices.

A moment later, two teams of investigators arrived to work the scene. Ellie sent one team to the cave. Then she introduced Derrick to Dr. Laney Whitefeather, Bluff County's medical examiner.

The ME stooped by the grave to take a look, and Ellie stepped back while the ERT began to process the scene. Two of the crime techs combed the area looking for forensics while the other two photographed the gravesite, then began to gently dig up the grave.

"How long have you known McClain?" Derrick asked Ellie. Anything to distract him from the nauseating fear that they might be uncovering his sister's bones.

"Since I was a teenager," Ellie said. "Met him when I volunteered to help on a search and rescue mission for a lost boy."

"What's his story?"

Ellie pushed a strand of hair from her cheek. "He's good at what he does. He's rescued countless lost hikers and injured ones over the past twenty years."

"What about family?"

Ellie shook her head. "None that I know of, at least none that he's ever talked about. He's pretty much a loner and keeps to himself." She furrowed her brows. "Why are you asking about Cord?"

"He found the grave," Derrick said. "Could have stumbled on it, or he could have put it there."

"That's a stretch." Disbelief flickered in Ellie's eyes. "Cord may be the brooding silent type, but he's not a killer."

"Are you sure? How did he know that body was buried here?"

"You heard him. Wilson led him to the grave." Now her tone sounded annoyed. Maybe she and the ranger had a thing.

Hell, he didn't care. Nothing would stop him from finding out the truth about what had happened to his baby sister.

Ellie looked as if she was going to say more, but voices cut her off.

One of the investigators tapped his shovel against a rock. "We found bones."

CHAPTER THIRTY-EIGHT

For a brief moment, the ground in front of Ellie blurred into a fog.

She was seven years old, wandering the graveyard alone. Night had fallen and the wind blew dead leaves across the brittle grass. The silk roses and fresh flowers that had been left on the graves by loved ones stirred and fluttered over the mounds, like multi-colored fireflies. Whispers of the dead called to her.

"I'm here. Find me."

She turned in a wide arc and searched the desolate cemetery. Shadows floated in a haze, the ghostly images of the dead rising in the misty rain.

"I'm scared, Ellie. Help me."

A shiver ripped through her, and she staggered through the rows of graves, careful not to step on them. Bony hands snaked through the dirt mounds, reaching for her feet. Faces of the ones who'd passed drifted in front of her, hands locked, hollowed eye sockets dark with pain, mouths opened wide in silent screams.

She paused to read the names on the grave markers. One by one, she searched. A shadow moved by the statue of the angel and waterfall. Mae?

Suddenly, her mother snatched her arm. "Ellie, what are you doing out here?"

Then her father. "Are you okay, honey?"

Ellie lifted her hand to show them where Mae was standing, but suddenly she was gone. Faded into the distance again, her wispy silhouette glowing in a white light as she ran through the cemetery.

Her father clasped her hand in his. "Come on, let's get you home."

"This obsession with Mae has to stop," her mother cried. "Randall, we have to get her help."

Another voice dragged her from the memory. Cord's. "You okay, El?"

The world shifted back into focus, and she gave a little nod. Although she wasn't okay. Nothing about Penny Matthews' disappearance or a serial killer on the trail was okay.

The sight before her was gruesome. The dirt mount, hand-carved marker. The tiny grave, maybe four feet long...

Ellie held her breath as the ERT investigator brushed away soil from the remains.

Bones.

Not Penny Matthews. Her body wouldn't have decomposed to this extent. These bones were old. Crumbling. Fragile. Void of hair and skin and muscle tissue.

Which meant the child had been dead for some time. The ME would have to determine approximately how long.

Derrick's erratic breathing turned into a pained sigh.

"Poor baby," Dr. Whitefeather murmured. "We're going to find out who did this to you."

"Damn right we are." Ellie explained they might be dealing with a serial killer, and that Derrick's sister might have been among the victims.

Laney's expression turned to sympathy.

Derrick cleared his throat. "Can you tell if the remains are male or female?"

Dr. Whitefeather yanked on latex gloves, headgear and lamp, then brushed away enough dirt to see the skull, chest and pelvic area.

"A girl," she said, her tone somber. "But I'll call in a forensic anthropologist to perform the autopsy."

"I'll have my sister's dental and medical records sent to your office." Derrick's voice emerged as a whisper.

Compassion filled Laney's eyes. "I'll take good care of her."

"Whoever left her here must have cared for her," Ellie offered. "Or else why the flowers?"

Cord knocked dirt from his hands onto his work pants, but he remained silent.

Derrick's dark gaze settled on the ranger. "The grave is fresh. The perp must have killed her somewhere else and kept her, then moved her here recently."

Her father's accusation echoed in Ellie's head. Was it possible Mr. Fox had done something to his daughter, then faked his death? That he was the killer they were looking for? That he'd buried Kim here for Derrick to find?

"Let's get her to the morgue." Dr. Whitefeather stood. "Then you can figure out who's to blame."

Derrick walked by the river while the team began to carefully excavate the bones from the ground. One by one they laid them on the tarp to recreate the child's body.

"Look at this," Laney said, glancing up at Ellie.

Ellie crouched down beside Laney as she pulled an object from the damp earth.

Ellie's breath caught. It was a hand-carved wooden doll just like the one she'd found in the cave.

A doll that the killer must have made and given to the girls.

CHAPTER THIRTY-NINE

Somewhere on the AT

He hadn't wanted to move the little girl.

But those damn dogs and the law were all over the mountain, sniffing and digging and getting way too close.

He'd had to wait until they headed in another direction, then he'd scooped up the child, hauled her to the ATV and zipped through the woods off the trail, the storm swallowing the sound of the engine.

"Shh, don't make a sound," he'd warned her when he'd tied a scarf around her mouth.

Tears leaked from her eyes.

"Don't be a crybaby," he'd hissed.

She'd cried anyway.

The cold blustery wind felt good on his cheeks as he'd put distance between him and the law. The weather wouldn't slow him down. He thrived here in the wilderness, as if he was born to it.

Loud barking boomeranged off the ridges. Those fucking dogs were smarter than the humans, nipping and chasing his scent.

They wouldn't find him though. They never did.

He knew the ins and outs of this mountain because he'd lived here most of his life. If you'd call what he was doing living.

Sleeping in the woods and the AT shelters. Making a bed out of leaves and vines. Stealing food from campers. Hiding in the shadows. Living like a ghost.

Watching. Searching.

Finally, he reached his destination and carried the little girl inside. She kicked and beat at his chest, but she was so tiny he barely felt her fingers digging at him through his winter coat.

"This is going to be your new playhouse," he told her as he set her in the special box he'd built just for her. He laid a blanket on the floor and scattered little wooden dolls across it.

She looked up at him with big teary eyes, as if he was a monster.

But he wasn't. He was just like her. He'd wanted a mommy and a daddy to love him. But they hadn't. No one had.

Not like the pretty little girls they'd doted on.

"I'll be back," he whispered.

She screamed and he considered gagging her again.

But there was no one to hear her. Let her scream her little heart out.

He closed and locked the door, and she beat at the wooden slats as if they were prison bars. A chuckle rumbled from him at the fact that she had fight in her.

Once he'd had that same kind of grit, until it had been beaten out of him. He'd had to learn his lesson, the fosters said. That's when they'd locked him in the cage in the dark basement.

Remembering the search teams, he hurried back outside and parked the ATV deep between some trees. Wind bit at him as he dragged branches and vines over the vehicle to shield it from sight. Not that the search workers would come this way. They'd stay close to the trail, as if they expected him to leave breadcrumbs for them to follow.

Idiots.

He gathered wood for a fire, then crawled inside the home he'd carved himself in the mountain. The old mine shaft made a perfect escape and safe haven during the worst of the bad weather.

The little girl cowered against the wall of the big dollhouse he'd made for her, her knees drawn up to her chest, her arms around them. Her head was bowed, and her body jerking with sobs.

Fear clouded her angelic little face. "I want Mama," she whined.

He cracked the door just enough to shove a cup of water and some crackers toward her. Her hand shook as she snatched them and wolfed them down. Then she turned up the water and sucked it down, spilling half of it down her face. It dripped off her quivering chin like raindrops, splattering her pink t-shirt.

He stooped down in front of her and brushed her hair from her face.

Her eyes widened, big saucers in her tiny oval face. She reminded him so much of the first one he'd taken.

The one who'd gotten away.

The one he still wanted.

CHAPTER FORTY

Crooked Creek

The wind pounded Ellie's Jeep, forcing her to clench the steering wheel in a white-knuckled grip to keep it on the road. Rain splattered the windshield, a thick fog blurring her vision as if it was a premonition of what was to come.

Fear engulfed her, sending her back to the night she'd been lost. A storm had brewed that night, too. She'd curled into a ball and listened to the wind rip branches from the trees. Part of the dirt roof above her had been shaken loose and rained down on her face.

The chime of her phone dragged her back to the present. Seeing her boss's name on the screen, she pictured him pacing his office and running a handkerchief over his sweaty bald head. She answered and quickly filled him in on what she'd found.

"Is it Penny?" he asked.

"No," Ellie said. "These remains have totally decayed. The girl has been dead for a long time."

"Jesus Christ," Captain Hale bellowed. "The mayor is going to go apeshit over this. And the town will be in a complete uproar."

They had a reason to be.

"Matthews has not been out of sight," Captain Hale said. "Do you think he did this?"

"No. I think Special Agent Fox is right. We've got a serial predator." Which meant they were back to square one, with no suspect.

She was snapped out of her thoughts as the Jeep skidded on the asphalt. Remembering to turn into the skid instead of fighting it, she managed to maneuver the vehicle back between the lines. Water spewed from her tires, falling pinecones hitting her windshield.

The sound of paper ripping echoed over the line, and Ellie imagined her boss opening up another pack of mints and popping one in his mouth. Ever since he'd decided to quit smoking, he'd been chain-eating them. "So what's the next move?" Captain Hale asked.

"I left investigators combing the woods nearby for forensics, and another team is working the cave. Identifying the victim should enable us to notify the family and nail down the timeline of how long the child has been missing." She described the dolls and relayed that she was on her way to the Matthews' house. "Maybe we'll get lucky and he left a print on it."

"You'd better hope so," he said, clearly agitated. A hesitation. "Shit, Mayor Waters is calling. I have to put out fires now. Keep me posted."

Derrick remained silent as she ended the call, a deep-seated pain seemed to be simmering just below the surface of his calm. At one point, he closed his eyes and laid his head back against the seat, and she thought he might have fallen asleep.

How many times had he and his mother raised their hopes only to have them crushed? Had Mrs. Fox imagined bringing her daughter home and watching her grow up? Picking out homecoming dresses and comforting Kim over break-ups with boys? Planning her wedding?

How many times had she imagined burying her daughter?

The family wanted closure, but every parent of a missing child held out some grain of hope they'd find their loved one alive.

As sympathy flared through Ellie, her phone buzzed. Her boss again.

She braced herself for another blessing out as she connected.

"Ellie," Captain Hale said, his voice shrill. "Did you talk to Angelica Gomez?"

Ellie turned the wipers up full force. "Not recently. Why?"

"I'm sending you a news clip. Just watch."

Anxiety slithered through Ellie and she pulled to the shoulder of the road. She tapped the link Hale had sent and a news clip appeared on screen.

"*This is Angelica Gomez reporting to you from the edge of the Appalachian Trail only a few miles from where Penny Matthews disappeared. Although the search continues for the missing little girl, this evening search workers discovered the remains of a child buried near Rattlesnake Ridge. The identity of the child has yet to be determined, but rest assured, I'll be bringing you the answers as soon as police release the information.*" Angelica's soft voice was appropriately solemn, the earnestness in her eyes almost touching.

Ellie wanted to scream.

Fuck. If Stan and Sue Matthews saw this before she had a chance to talk to them, there'd be a shitstorm.

She clicked back to the captain. "That information did not come from me, sir."

"Then who the hell fed her the story?"

Ellie's mind raced. "Did you tell my father?"

"Of course. I had to. He's the sheriff, for crying out loud. The search teams needed to know to look for more graves."

Ellie dropped her head into her hands with a groan.

"Had to be Bryce Waters. He's in campaign mode now."

"Son of a bitch," Captain Hale muttered. "I'll call Randall and tell him to get his deputy under control or I'll lock the little fuckwad up myself," he said, hanging up.

Ellie ground her molars, grateful her boss had seen through Bryce.

Derrick opened his eyes and looked up at her. "What's wrong?"

She handed him the phone and let him watch for himself as she pulled back onto the road.

A litany of curse words spewed from his mouth. "This is why I hate dealing with small town cops and the press."

She wanted to defend small town law enforcement but bit her tongue. She was pissed herself.

Heaving a breath, she turned the corner to the Matthews' neighborhood. The last thing she wanted was for the couple to hear a body had been found and to believe it was Penny.

As soon as she turned onto their street, she spotted a news van parked in front of the house. Rage boiled her blood as she parked and climbed out. If Angelica had told the Matthewses, she might just kill her.

The reporter and the cameraman ran toward her, mic extended. "Detective Reeves, have you identified the remains of the child you found today?"

Ellie shot the woman a venomous look. Did she have no compassion for the family inside that house? "As I've said before, I cannot divulge details of an ongoing investigation. I will issue a statement when I have more to share."

"But don't you think people in this area need to be warned that a predator is stalking their children?"

Yes, she did.

Had Bryce told Angelica about Derrick's theory? If he had, she was going to have the bastard's head on a platter. "When and if that is determined, I will address the public," she said, keeping an even keel to her voice. "Now get out of my way so I can talk to Penny's family." *And undo the damage you've done.*

Angelica spun toward Derrick. "Special Agent Fox, is it true your sister disappeared in the same manner as Penny Matthews? That you believe the cases are connected?"

Derrick pushed the camera away from his face with a steely look. "No comment. Now, let us do our jobs."

Ellie and Derrick rushed to the front door, and Susan let them in, slamming it behind them.

She looked haggard, pale-faced with swollen eyes, and she was still wearing her pajama pants and a stained t-shirt, as if she hadn't had the energy to get dressed all day. Stan was pacing behind her, a desperate recklessness in his agitated movements. "Was that Penny you found today?"

CHAPTER FORTY-ONE

Ellie gritted her teeth. "No, we're still looking for Penny, and have reason to think she's alive. I found a child's footprints in a cave."

The couple clutched each other and visibly sagged in relief.

"Then where is she?" Susan asked, her voice hoarse.

"The search teams are working around the clock and are focusing on the area where I found the footprints."

"But you found another little girl's body?" Stan's eyes looked glassy with fear.

Ellie knew this was hard for Derrick, but she couldn't lie to the couple. "Yes, but the child has been deceased for some time, so it may not be related to Penny's disappearance."

Susan made a strangled sound.

"But it could be," Stan barked.

"Mr. Matthews," Derrick cut in. "Don't jump to conclusions."

Ellie felt the pain and worry emanating from Derrick. "Please, let's sit down." She guided the couple to the family room and waited until they situated themselves on the sofa. Then she removed the evidence bag with the wooden doll from her pocket. "Does this little doll look familiar?"

Susan immediately shook her head. "No, that's not Penny's. Why?"

"I found it on the trail." Along with another one in a small grave. But she refrained from mentioning that.

Derrick cleared his throat. "It would be helpful if you could give us something with Penny's DNA on it so we can compare it to what we find on the doll. A toothbrush or comb would do."

"Of course." Susan ran into the bathroom, returning a moment later with a pink hairbrush and child's toothbrush. Derrick bagged the items and promised to return them once they were finished.

"I have an idea," Ellie said. One to satisfy the nosy reporter and make her work for them for once. "That is, if you're willing to do it."

Susan clutched Ellie's arm. "What? Tell us. We'll do anything to get Penny back."

"I want you to go on TV and make a personal plea for Penny," Ellie said.

Susan and Stan exchanged looks, then they both spoke at once, agreeing immediately.

"Good. I'll go talk to Ms. Gomez."

Derrick cornered her by the door before she went outside. "Do you think this is a good idea? What if Angelica tells them a serial killer has their daughter?"

"Let me handle her," Ellie said. "At least this way we control the media, and we might get a helpful tip."

Derrick didn't look convinced. "Sometimes public pleas draw out false confessions from attention seekers. And we're bound to waste time chasing false leads."

"At this point we need all the help we can get," Ellie said. "The clock is ticking, Derrick. We don't want Penny to end up like that little girl in the grave."

Ellie regretted the words the minute they slipped out of her mouth. Derrick's tormented look said it all.

But the best way to find this predator was to tackle the situation head on, and that meant using every resource available to them.

Angelica Gomez was one. She would report the story anyway, and Ellie preferred to guide the dialogue in the direction she wanted. She stepped outside and motioned Angelica to the porch while Derrick made a phone call.

"I'm going to shoot you straight, Angelica," she said in a no-nonsense tone. "We are not going to mention the word serial predator or killer. We want to find Penny alive, and we don't want to glorify this kidnapper by making him famous. We don't even want him to know that we suspect he may have done this before. Do you understand me?"

"You promise me an exclusive?"

"You have my word." Ellie gestured toward the cameraman. "He'd better keep this under wraps as well. The two of you don't want to be responsible for getting a little girl killed, do you?"

Angelica's eyes blazed. "Of course not." She gestured toward her partner. "And don't worry about him. He'll do whatever I say."

Ellie hoped so. She had enough loose tongues to worry about with Bryce Waters.

"I've set up a tip line for anyone calling with information," Derrick announced. "When the segment ends, be sure to flash the number on the screen."

Angelia agreed, then entered the house and offered the couple a sympathetic smile. "I'm so sorry to hear about your daughter," she said. "Hopefully seeing how much you love her will bring some helpful information."

They set the couple up in the living room, and the cameraman adjusted the lighting while Angelica suggested the couple showcase a photograph of Penny. Susan clutched Penny's teddy bear in her arms as they began. With his big button eyes and worn ears, the soft yellow furry bear looked well-loved.

The couple painted the picture of a loving couple terrified for their daughter, exactly the image Ellie wanted them to portray as they begged the kidnapper to return their daughter.

"This is Toby, Penny's bear," Susan said. "My little girl is afraid of the dark and can't sleep without him."

"She's so tiny and sweet and all we have," Stan said. "Look at her innocent face." Stan's voice broke. "We'll do anything to bring her home."

"Last week she donated her piggy bank money to the nature center to save a turtle who'd been injured." Susan gulped back tears.

"She likes to make artwork out of nature items. And she wants to be an artist when she grows up." Her voice broke. "Last week she painted a picture of the sunshine. I… just want her to see it again…"

"Please don't hurt her," Stan pleaded. "Please."

Ellie's heart wrenched as Stan and Susan broke down and cried, cradling each other.

The reporter once again recited the number for the tip line, then the interview came to an end. Now, they had to wait.

Ellie walked Angelica and the cameraman to the door.

"People around here need to be alerted if some maniac is hunting their children," Angelica said in a low whisper. "Twenty-four hours, Detective Reeves, then I will run with the serial killer angle, with or without your approval."

CHAPTER FORTY-TWO

Somewhere on the AT

He lined the little dolls up in a row, naming them after each of the girls he had taken.

But the first one was special. He traced his finger over the smooth wood, the little round head, the tiny little legs and arms, and smiled. She had been so pretty.

All he'd wanted to do was play with her.

He'd watched her for days. Seen her singing 'Skip to My Lou' as she did cartwheels in the yard. Watched her and her daddy toss sticks into the creek and dig for worms. Watched her mother dote on her, giving her candy and taking her to the park, and baking cookies in the kitchen that smelled like heaven.

Watched her play with dolls. She'd combed their hair and dressed them in fancy clothes and had tea parties where she set out real cookies and pretend tea.

He'd wanted to be part of a family, too. Had wanted a little sister to play with. So, he'd started making the dolls. He'd known if she saw them, she would follow him.

Then one day she'd wandered away from her parents, just like he'd hoped. He'd snuck up and shown her the dolls he'd made and lured her to his secret hiding place. But once she was inside, he'd heard her parents coming and he'd run.

Couldn't get caught or they'd be mad, just like the fosters were when he pulled the other girls' hair or threw toads on them to hear them scream.

Laughter caught in his throat. He liked to hear them scream and watch their little faces turn horrid-looking with fear. Then they weren't so perfect and pretty anymore.

The mommies and daddies who'd come looking for children to take home hadn't wanted him. Said he was too big. Too old. Too awkward. Too withdrawn. Too weird. One of his eyes twitched. He walked with a limp.

But everyone loved the pretty little girls. The mommies said they were angels. Like sweet little dolls.

They took them home and gave them pretty, fancy rooms and warm beds and toys. While he stayed at the orphanage, slept on a ratty cot and played with sticks and wore hand-me-down rags that the rich kids tossed out.

He crawled back into his dark place and stared at the little girl. It had been a while since he'd taken one. Over a year.

But she'd just been there playing all alone. Hunting treasures. Her parents were both sleeping like lazy pigs while she wandered along the creek bank and ventured onto the ridge.

She'd slipped and almost fallen over. But he'd saved her.

Then the little witch had bit him.

He rubbed at his forearm where it still stung. She would be sorry for that. She had to be punished.

CHAPTER FORTY-THREE

Crooked Creek

It was near 9 p.m., and Derrick wanted a drink bad.

Those bones had gotten to him. And that tiny little grave… *God help them.*

Children were not supposed to end up dead.

The realization that he might have found Kim today made it hard to breathe. He envisioned his mother's face. Having to tell her about the bones they'd uncovered in a plain dirt grave. How this would have torn his father apart.

His phone dinged with his mother's ringtone. Inhaling a deep breath, he answered. "Hello, Mom."

"I saw the news, Derrick." Her voice quivered with emotions. "Was Kim in that grave?"

He squeezed his eyes closed at the pain in her words. He knew she'd try to be brave. But they'd both been dreading this forever. "I don't know yet, Mom, and won't until the autopsy is complete. I'm sending Kim's medical and dental records to the ME's office."

Ellie's soft sigh reeked of sympathy, but he couldn't look at her. He'd rather have talked in private, but the Jeep wasn't roomy enough for that.

"You won't lie to me, son," his mother said. "Neither of us want this, but we will deal with it. At this point, I just want to find her and bring her home."

Grief, guilt and anguish flooded Derrick's throat, and it took him a minute to gather himself enough to answer. "I promise I'll let you know as soon as I do." He paused, haunted by the memory of the way she'd collapsed when she'd learned Kim had been abducted. "Is there anyone there with you?"

"Lou Ann, from next door," she said softly. "She insisted on staying tonight."

"Good. I don't want you to be alone."

"You're such a good son, Derrick." Her voice cracked again. "Just be careful. I can't lose another child."

Derrick forced a calm to his voice although his heart clenched. "Don't worry. I'll be fine."

They said goodbye, and he stared out the window at the thickening fog of clouds and precipitation. A dark night made darker.

"If you need some time tonight, leave me with those notes and videos and I'll look over them," Ellie said gently.

Derrick shook his head. Now they'd found one body, he was even more determined to uncover the truth.

"No, if we divide up the case files, it'll go faster."

"My office then? Or we can grab some food and then go to my house?"

He didn't feel like eating, but his stomach growled. "Food, yeah. Then your office." Going to Ellie's house was too personal.

And he had no business getting personal with her, not when he was so vulnerable right now. Not when he suspected her friend Cord might be involved.

Not when he believed her father had been negligent. Maybe even incompetent.

Or... had Randall cast suspicion on him and his father because he himself was the killer?

You're grasping.

Still, the moment the idea occurred to him, he couldn't let it go. Considering that Kim, this predator's first victim, disappeared on the trail under Randall's jurisdiction, and now the kidnapper had returned to the area, it was logical to assume he might have lived nearby. He'd started in the area and returned to taunt the police with the fact that he was clever enough to have gotten away all this time.

Who knew the mountains, where to hide, and *how* to hide evidence, better than Sheriff Reeves? He'd lived in Bluff County when Kim disappeared. He could have traveled up and down the trail using it as his hunting ground and no one would have questioned or suspected him.

His mind circled back to Ranger Cord McClain, another possibility. He'd grown up in the mountains. Like Randall, people trusted him. He was a loner. Could snatch a little girl without anyone even noticing it.

He'd found the first body, too, when dozens of SAR teams had been searching the mountain.

That alone warranted running a background check on the mysterious man.

"Why is your name not in the hat for sheriff?" Derrick asked as they passed sign after sign boasting BRYCE WATERS FOR SHERIFF.

Ellie pressed her lips into a tight line.

He'd hit a nerve.

"After the police academy, I planned to work with my dad. But my parents thought it was too dangerous for a woman."

"You seem like you can handle it," he said.

She cut her eyes toward him. "Thanks. A lot of men in the South still think they're superior. All the muscle and brawn." But good detective work took mental toughness and brains as much as all that muscle. And one look around the station house would show you that supposed muscle seemed to have settled around more than one officer's waistline.

"Maybe your folks just wanted to protect you."

"So they said." She lifted her chin. "I can protect myself."

He didn't comment. Had a feeling whatever he said would piss her off. Besides, he was still working the theory about her father.

Maybe Randall knew Ellie was smart and might see through his incompetence if she took office?

Ellie pulled into the parking lot for a place called Soulfood Barbecue and cut the engine. The rain and sleet had eased for now, but heavy gray clouds hung low in the sky, promising to spill their guts overnight. A giant metal pig stood in front of the restaurant's long wooden porch and smoke billowed from the twin smokers to the side. The aroma of smoking pork and beef brisket filled the air, and people sat inside devouring their dinner.

As if she was still ticked at their earlier conversation, Ellie opened the car door, got out and slammed it behind her. Following her into the diner, the smoky aroma of the barbecue and earthy smell of collard greens made his stomach growl.

A TV hung above the bar, the news footage of the Matthews couple's plea playing. Voices grew hushed and curious looks turned their way as they entered.

Ellie murmured a greeting to two older women who were passing out fliers with Penny's picture on them. Other patrons shifted restlessly, looking frightened as they watched the news. A pencil-thin older lady with a gray bun sat alone at a table, her fingers running over the flier. The other customers seemed to be giving her a wide berth.

"Who's that?" he murmured to Ellie.

"Eula Ann Frampton," Ellie said softly. "She claims she talks to the dead. Some folks around here are scared of her. Others come to her wanting her to commune with their lost loved ones."

His gut tightened. His mother had been so desperate that she'd once visited a medium after Kim disappeared. The woman had been a charlatan, cheating grieving people out of their money.

Still, some people believed.

The two ladies handing out fliers passed Eula's table, then one of them stopped and glared down at her.

"Do you know where Penny is, Ms. Eula? Is she still alive?"

Pain clouded Ms. Eula's eyes as she looked up at the women. "I… can't say."

"Can't or won't?" one of the women hissed, before they both hurried off.

The hair on the back of Derrick's neck prickled. The town was riddled with panic. Tension was mounting between neighbors as locals began to fear there might be a killer living among them.

How would they react when they realized almost a dozen girls had died at the hands of this monster?

CHAPTER FORTY-FOUR

Eula Ann slipped the flier into her crocheted bag, set a five on the table to pay for her tea, and tottered from the diner. Whispers and stares followed her.

Some wanted to believe. Others thought she was crazy. Even those condemned her, as her secrets weren't hers to keep. As if she was cruel enough to lie about seeing Penny's spirit pass. As if she was hiding a killer.

That Ellie Reeves girl gave her a sad smile, her eyes full of the horror of what she was just learning. That there were more little bodies out there.

That neither one of them could stop it from happening.

CHAPTER FORTY-FIVE

Ellie's heart tugged for Ms. Eula. She lived alone on the mountain, away from the stares and ugly whispers. Because no one understood her, some feared her.

Or was it because she'd murdered her husband, like the rumors claimed?

It didn't matter. That was ancient history. She had a child killer to find.

The sound of a male voice rumbled from the bar, and she pivoted. Dammit, if Bryce wasn't there with a beer in hand, wolfing down a pulled pork sandwich.

She caught his eye as she crossed the room to place a to-go order. She and Derrick ordered barbecue plates with coleslaw, Hoppin' John and collards. A drink would be nice, but she had too much work to do right now, so chose sweet tea instead.

Feeling Bryce's eyes on her, she decided to confront him. Derrick stood by her, solemn and stoic.

"You leaked information to Angelica Gomez, didn't you?" she snapped.

Bryce's lips twitched as if fighting a smile, then he wiped barbecue sauce from the corner of his mouth with a napkin. "I was just doing my job," he said. "Besides, Randall asked me to handle the press. Said you were busy."

Anger hardened her tone. Her father again. "Using this missing little girl to make your campaign is low even for you, Bryce."

Anger flashed in his eyes. Then something else. Regret? A second later, it was gone. He slanted an irritated look toward Derrick.

"Your daddy mentioned a feebie was in town. I didn't realize you'd called for help."

"She didn't," Derrick said, his voice lethally calm. "Don't screw up this case with your political agenda, Deputy. There's more at stake than you know."

Bryce's eyes seethed with fury. "Then why don't we work together, and you share information with me?"

Ellie stabbed him in the chest with her finger. "Because I know you like to talk. Now stay out of my way, Bryce."

Derrick took a half-step closer. "Do what she says, or Detective Reeves will be the least of your problems. We'll let you get back to your beer. We have police work to do."

As the waitress brought their food, Ellie reached for her wallet. Derrick stepped away from Bryce, shook his head and paid the bill. "You got lunch."

Ellie snatched up the bag, anxious to get away from Bryce.

"That guy's an asshole," Derrick said as they climbed back into the Jeep.

Yes, he is, thought Ellie. *Always has been.* Back in high school, Bryce had spread a rumor he'd screwed her behind the bleachers. After that, she'd had to fend off horny teenagers thinking she was easy. "Didn't take you long to figure that out." Yet her father was still backing him. Go figure.

Body taut with tension, she peeled from the parking lot and raced toward the station. Captain Hale was gone when they arrived, and Heath was monitoring incoming calls for the tip line. She spread the food on the table in the conference room, and Derrick organized his files. The pictures of the little girls taunted Ellie from the white board. Blonde, brunette, auburn hair. Blue eyes, hazel, brown. This stalker didn't have a type.

Except for the age. He liked them young.

That thought sent a shudder through her, and she prayed Laney wouldn't find evidence of sexual abuse.

Tracing her finger over the pictures, she murmured each girls' name, determined to see them as people, not just victims. She could practically hear their cries for help. Begging for justice.

Did the bones they'd found today belong to one of them?

Derrick stood in front of the board studying the photographs, lingering in front of his sister's. Her chest constricted at the anguish in his expression.

Finally pulling himself away, Derrick booted up his computer and opened the interviews he'd copied onto his hard drive, and they ate while they reviewed them. Ellie barely tasted the smoky, sweet barbecue, or the hot sauce she added to her greens, although her stomach thanked her as she washed the meal down with sweet tea.

Some of the film was old, grainy and poor quality, but the situations were all similar. A law enforcement officer sat in a room questioning the missing girls' loved ones.

By the third interview, the stories grew increasingly more difficult to watch. It was heart-wrenching to see mothers and fathers crying, begging the police to find their children, their fear turning to anger when the officer suggested the parent might be responsible. Neighbors, teachers, relatives, coaches were interrogated.

All ended without a lead.

"Most of the mothers mentioned a toy or clothing the child had with them when they disappeared. A key chain, pop bead necklace, a rag doll," Ellie said. "Were any of those items ever found?"

Derrick shook his head. "No. Kim was wearing a locket my mom gave her as a birthday present. But searchers never located it."

Ellie's heart squeezed. Serial predators often kept souvenirs from their victims. Had this man kept the little girls' personal items to remember them by?

She continued to skim the files, her heart stuttering when she saw Cord's name appear on one of the reports. Three videos later, and another mother mentioned Cord. "He was close by and heard us calling her name," the father said.

Ellie grew more uncomfortable with each interview.

By the time she'd watched the last video, nausea threatened. She didn't like the ugly thoughts crowding her head. Why hadn't Cord mentioned working the other missing children cases?

"Where's my father's interview with your parents?" Ellie asked.

Derrick's expression darkened. "There wasn't one."

Ellie tapped her boot on the floor. "I guess it was so long ago, it wasn't common practice."

"No," Derrick said. "My mother said he taped them, but I was told the tape was missing. So were some of his notes. Apparently, they were lost in an office fire."

Ellie combed through her memory banks. She didn't ever recall a fire in her father's office.

CHAPTER FORTY-SIX

Somewhere on the AT

They were yelling the little girl's name all over the mountain. He'd hidden on the ridge above the park where he'd found her and watched the panic as the parents ran around looking for her. Then they'd called the rescue workers.

The same woman who'd been talking to the mama that first day had been on the news, too. Detective Ellie Reeves.

That golden hair. Eyes the color of a robin's egg. Skin pale and milky.

She looked just like she had as a child. He'd been looking for her for years. A giddy feeling stole through him. And now here she was, back on the mountain looking for him!

The little girl's cries from inside the mine shaft drifted to him, a reminder that she was crying for her mama.

Mama should have been watching her daughter better though. So should the daddy. But they hadn't, and now she was his.

He piled branches in front of the shaft opening, then hunkered down to whittle by the fire.

More dolls. So many dolls.

He hated the silly little things. But the girls liked them. And when he told them he'd hand-carved them, they wanted to hold them. Play pretend. Give them made-up names and a beautiful princess life.

Caught up in their fantasy world, they followed him to see his dollhouse. The three-story mansion with the pretty pink shutters and the twirling lights on top.

Maybe one day he'd build it.

Laughter bubbled in his chest.

Then again, maybe not.

There was no need for a dollhouse. Why should the wooden creatures have luxuries he didn't have? The dolls could sleep on the ground like him.

He picked up another piece of wood and traced his finger over the grain. Then he slanted the edge of the knife blade and cut into it. The wood began to splinter in his hands, and he repeated the motion a dozen times. But the images of that detective flashed behind his eyes, and his finger slipped, slicing into the tip of his thumb.

He raised his hand and watched the blood drip onto the ground, the color blurring as the urge to see Ellie Reeves up close built inside him.

It wasn't time yet. He'd play the game a little longer. Lead her deeper into the woods, watch her squirm and hunt.

He wrapped a handkerchief around his bloody thumb, then collected three of the little dolls and put them in the coffin he'd carved to hold them. Then he put out the fire and set out down the mountain.

He'd leave Ellie Reeves a present for when she got home tonight. Some of his precious little dolls to remind her that he wasn't finished.

CHAPTER FORTY-SEVEN

Crooked Creek

Ellie and Derrick jotted down anything remotely similar in the cases in an attempt to pinpoint a common suspect in all of the disappearances.

The trail was their only clue.

As much as Ellie hated to admit it, her father and Cord were the only two people who'd been involved in multiple cases.

Except her father had made a note that he'd questioned more than one Shadow person. Someone he hadn't named had mentioned seeing a man in dark clothing running from the area where Kim went missing. But the man had disappeared and no one in the mountains knew who he was. Or if he was dangerous.

Was it possible the killer was one of them?

According to her father, the Shadows had a secret method of communicating and passing messages among themselves. But they didn't share it with anyone. Especially the law.

Maybe one of them had seen something in the woods.

An email from the ME pinged on her phone. "Laney says the forensic anthropologist will be here in the morning," she told Derrick after reading it. "Hopefully, tomorrow we'll have answers about the victim's identity, cause of death and more about the timing."

A muscle ticked in Derrick's jaw. This was personal for him. Painful.

Ignoring the temptation to comfort him, she pulled up the photos she'd taken at the gravesite and scrolled through them, searching for some indicator of who'd buried the little girl. Zeroing in on the tombstone marker and the etching, she wondered about the significance.

Something niggled at the back of her mind. Cord again… she was sure he had a collection of books on the history of grave markers and tombstones in his house. When she'd spent the night with him, she'd noticed a shelf of books by the fireplace, but when she'd started to look at one, he'd yanked it away from her. Then he'd become brusque and distant.

"The cross was carved by someone who's an expert," Derrick commented.

Ellie's pulse jumped. Her father whittled, said it relaxed him. He even sold his decoy ducks at the festivals in town.

No… she couldn't allow Derrick to make her suspicious of her own father. She might be angry with him, but he'd always been her hero. He'd rescued countless individuals and families over the years. Countless children.

"Look at the angel," she said. "Her finger is pointing north. There's a tiny marking above it."

"What do you think it means?"

"The angel may be trying to tell us something." Ellie enlarged the photo. Recognition hit her as she studied the image etched above the angel. "It's a hemlock tree."

Derrick scraped his hand over his stubble. "You're sure?"

Ellie nodded. "There's a place called Hemlock Holler on the trail." Ellie stood and stretched her aching shoulders. Her body teemed with the need to follow the clue tonight. But a glance at the clock, the pounding rain outside and common sense told her it was too late. "First thing in the morning, I'm hiking up to take a look. There may be another body buried there."

"Or the killer could be leading you into a trap," Derrick said as he snagged his keys from his pocket.

True. She caught him at the door. "Listen, Derrick, I know you want this guy and it's personal, but don't go up there by yourself. I don't have time to hunt your ass down when you get lost."

One brow slid upward. "You assume I'll get lost?"

She gave a half-crooked smile. "More seasoned hikers than you have. We'll go together first thing."

Tension filled the silence, as if he was trying to decide whether or not to trust her.

But he had no choice. She was right and he knew it.

Ellie was leading this investigation. And she knew these mountains better than he did.

"All right. I'll be up early," he replied. "Text me when you're ready to go."

As soon as the door closed behind him, Ellie texted Cord. *Need to see you. Your house?*

Seconds passed. Just when she thought he wasn't going to reply, he responded and told her to come over.

Yanking on her coat, ski cap and gloves, she headed out to her SUV, the sleet and cold battering her. She'd only been to Cord's cabin a couple of times, once after a long search and rescue before she joined the academy. The cabin sat on a ridge deep in the mountain, isolated from town. He said he liked it that way. At the time, she'd thought it odd, but then Cord was mysterious and not the social type. Truthfully, she wasn't either, so it had never bothered her. Except that he kept his house pitch-dark. Didn't like lights on.

And she had to have light.

Memories of the night they'd shared resurfaced. Infatuated with her father's work and determined to follow in his footsteps, she'd volunteered to help on search and rescue missions. The fact that Cord had worked with her father made the volunteer work even more appealing. At sixteen, as a tomboy teen, she'd been drawn to

Cord's tough, brooding exterior. Her father bragged about Cord's instincts and his knowledge of nature.

The fact that he didn't want to discuss his upbringing had intrigued her even more. The summer after graduation, right before she'd left for the police academy, she'd dogged him in the hunt for a lost teen.

Exhausted and half frozen from a two-day search and after rescuing the boy from a mudslide, she'd wound up spending the night at Cord's.

Running on adrenaline from the harrowing rescue, they'd ripped each other's clothes off and had fast, hot sex. Intense sex.

But that's all it had been. When she'd wanted to know more, why he insisted on pitching the room in total darkness while they'd slept together, he clammed up. Wouldn't answer her questions about his past or the scar on his forehead.

The next morning, he'd been dressed when she woke up and had ushered her to the door, his voice holding a mountain of regret. Embarrassed but telling herself it was for the best, that she was starting a new life, she left the next morning without looking back.

Still, sometimes when she looked at him, or on a cold lonely night, her skin tingled at the memory of their night together.

But it didn't pay to get involved with the men she worked with.

Muddied everything. She wanted their respect more than she wanted them in her bed.

Besides, she'd pegged him as a bad boy with too many issues, who'd break her heart if she gave in.

Forcing herself into the present, the starless night engulfed Ellie in its eeriness as she turned off the main highway and wove around the sharp switchbacks. Thunder rumbled again, more rain hammering her car. The wind had pulled off a loose branch and tossed it into the road, and she had to veer around it. The sky was hidden by the thick forest, the spiny branches intertwined like braided rope.

Hopefully, Stony Gap would get at least one day of the festival in before Storm Tempest brought life to a halt.

She slowed and turned onto a narrow one-lane drive that disappeared into the woods. Cord's rustic cabin sat at the end, with the river running behind it. Pines and oaks shrouded the house, which looked as if it had been built on the very edge of the ridge, into the mountain itself. She remembered looking out the sliding glass doors and getting dizzy at the sight of the holler so far below.

There were no other houses or cabins for miles and miles. No one to watch. No one to hear.

A lone light glowed from the side porch. Otherwise, darkness bathed the property, making it look almost spooky.

She parked, ducking against the elements as she picked her way along the stone walkway then climbed the steps, the sound of the river echoing in the quiet of the night.

He opened the door before she knocked, his five o'clock shadow thick and dark, adding to the dangerous edge of his chiseled features. Dark circles rimmed his smoky eyes, and the scar on his forehead looked more stark in the sliver of firelight coming from the wood stove.

"We have to talk." She pushed past him. Without the lights on, the house felt almost cave-like, making her shiver with the frightening memory of being lost all those years ago.

Even though she'd had nightmares the night she'd stayed with him, Cord insisted on keeping the light off when they were in bed. When she'd flipped on the lamp, he'd gone cold all over and had immediately switched it off.

Then he'd reached for his clothes, and any intimacy between them had been suddenly ended.

He closed the door behind her now, questions filling his eyes. Her gaze fell to that bandage on his arm, and he tugged his sleeve over it.

Cord cleared his throat. "Did the ME identify the body?"

"Not yet. Hopefully tomorrow."

Not bothering to wait for an invitation, she crossed into the living room, grateful for the wood stove's warmth. Cord's house was minimalist. A reddish-brown leather couch and a chair with a bearskin rug on the floor. A battered wooden table with straight back wooden chairs. No pictures or personal items. No cozy blankets or warm homey scents.

Taxidermy animals sat on the shelf on the far wall. A wild cat. An odd-looking black cat. A mountain lion's head hung above them. He'd added those since she'd been here last.

Unease made her heart skip a beat. "I didn't know you were into taxidermy."

He made a low sound in his throat, then shrugged.

The way the animals' lifeless eyes pierced her made the hair on the nape of her neck prickle. Desperate for light, she flipped on the lamp by the coffee table that had been carved from a tree trunk. Cord tensed for a moment, but he didn't move to extinguish it.

A large brown book was open, sketches of ancient tombstones on the pages. Another book on the table held a collection of photographs of mausoleums. Another depicted ancient religious symbols associated with death.

She gestured toward a volume on angels. "You didn't mention your interest in this when we found that grave marker today."

His already serious eyes darkened, and he glanced down at his scarred thumbs. "I've had those books for years, but barely looked at them. Finding the grave made me remember them. Someone gave them to me."

Ellie raised a brow. "Family?"

He shrugged but didn't respond.

Ellie's pulse clamored as something fell from his pocket. At the sight of the object, she swallowed back a gasp. Not a wooden doll, but a crudely carved angel.

"You carve, too?" she said in a raw whisper.

A strained minute passed. His breath wheezed in the air. "A little." Curling his fingers around the angel, he tucked it in his palm. "Is that why you're here, Ellie?" A tinge of venom laced his voice, anger she'd sensed lay just below the surface. "You think I made those little dolls and killed those girls?"

Ellie's emotions pinged all over the place. "I… no. But I do have some questions." She struggled to regain her composure. She didn't want to be afraid of Cord. Once she'd thought they were friends. "Why didn't you tell me you'd worked on three of the other missing children's cases? Little girls about the same age as Penny?"

Heat flared in his eyes. "It was a while back. I didn't think it mattered."

Ellie frowned. She didn't quite believe him. "Every detail in a homicide investigation matters. Those cases might be connected to Penny's disappearance."

Cord walked over to the bar in the corner of the room, set the angel figurine on it, and poured himself a whiskey. He offered one to her with a gesture, but she declined. With her nerves already frayed, booze and Cord might play havoc with her common sense.

"You think the body we found today has something to do with Penny and with this Fox guy's sister?"

"I do. There are more, Cord," she said softly. "And if we don't stop this madman, Penny might not be the last. So, if you're withholding information, please tell me."

He swirled the whiskey in his glass. "If you want to know about the angel carving, the angel represents innocence, purity."

Like the little girls. "Was there anything you saw, or someone you suspected in those other cases? Someone who was at all the crime scenes?"

A bitter look slashed his angular face. "You mean other than me?"

She released a weary breath. "I'm just searching for the truth. Cord. I want to find Penny," she said softly.

"I get it now. Because I worked the rescues, that fed has filled your ears with doubts about me, hasn't he?"

"This has nothing to do with him," Ellie said, sweat beading on her forehead. "When I asked you about your past, you shut down. I know you have secrets, things you don't want to talk about. And all those books there, and the taxidermy, and you practically live in the dark. It's disturbing, Cord."

His eyes narrowed to slits. "You're one to talk. You have secrets, too."

"What are you talking about?"

"Your childhood. Your fear of the dark."

Ellie licked her dry lips. "How do you know about that?"

"You told me. Don't you remember waking up screaming the night you stayed here, then you jumped up and turned all the lights on? You yelled out for someone named Mae, but when I asked you about her, you ran onto the deck."

Humiliation washed over her. She'd never told anyone about Mae and her therapy sessions. Didn't want people to look at her like they did Ms. Eula.

Cord's hand tightened around his glass. "If you don't trust me by now, El, then get the hell out."

Razor-like tension stretched between them. Cord didn't speak again. He walked to the sliding glass doors leading to his back deck, stepped outside with his drink, and left Ellie standing there alone.

Was he challenging her? *I'll share my secrets if you share yours?*

That was not going to happen today.

She had come for answers. Hoped he'd confide in her. Instead, he'd turned the tables on her, then ordered her to leave.

Fuming and confused, she spun around and strode through the front door. The wind rattled leaves and shook the trees, then the dark clouds above boomed with thunder, and began to unleash their fury, rain turning to sleet.

She dove inside her SUV and sat inside with the wipers working to clear the windshield. She'd thought she and Cord were friends.

But she'd been wrong.

Like it or not, she would find out what he was hiding from her. Then she'd know if she could trust him. Or if he'd been lying to her all along.

CHAPTER FORTY-EIGHT

Penny shivered and drew her knees up to her chest, then chewed on her fingernails to keep from crying again.

He didn't like it when she cried.

But it was getting harder and harder. She missed her warm bed. Her pink comforter. Her sheets with the little pink flowers on them.

And Toby. Her plush, squishy sweet yellow teddy bear. At night he kept her safe. She whispered to him when she was afraid. Told him all her secrets.

The little wooden dolls were not the same. They were slick and hard, not soft and cuddly. They didn't have real eyes or smiles. Toby's big button eyes looked at her like he loved her back. And she liked to rub his fluffy ears when falling asleep. When she rubbed one of the little dolls, a splinter pricked her finger.

The mean man reminded her of a Big Foot like she'd seen in the scary movies her friend's brother liked to watch. With one hairy arm, he dropped a pile of sticks in front of her. "Here, build a dollhouse with these."

She kicked at the pile of twigs as he shuffled from the creepy black space. She didn't want to build a dollhouse. Or play with the stupid dolls.

She wanted to go home and sleep with Toby and her princess pillow and listen to her mommy sing to her while she fell asleep.

CHAPTER FORTY-NINE

Crooked Creek

On her drive back to her bungalow, Ellie tuned into the news, anything to drown out the voice in her head whispering that Cord might have a sinister side to him.

Or that he knew more than he was saying about the disappearance of the little girls.

"*In spite of Tempest expected to blow in late tomorrow, Mayor Waters has announced that the Cornbread Festival will proceed with its annual parade and festivities,*" the radio announcer said. "*Although due to heavy winds and freezing temperatures, many of the activities will be held indoors. Check our website for details to follow.*"

Ellie rolled her eyes. How could people possibly celebrate when they hadn't found Penny?

Battling her own fear as sleet drizzled down, she parked and battled the elements as she hurried up her porch steps. Just as she reached for the doorknob, her foot hit something on the mat. Cursing herself for forgetting to leave her outside light on, she used her phone flashlight and discovered a small carved wooden box with a thin piece of rope tied around it.

A chill slithered through her, and she startled at the sound of brush crackling and tree limbs groaning. Pulling her gun, she gripped it and spun in a wide arc, surveying her property for whoever had left the box. Shadows moved and danced as the trees bowed against the force of the wind. The sleet was falling faster now, thicker, the pellets almost bullet sized.

If someone was out there, he'd disappeared into the thick foliage. Suddenly freezing and desperate for the warmth of her home, she unlocked the door, picked up the box in her coatsleeve and carried it inside, flipping on lights as she went.

Keeping her gun at the ready, she placed the box on the kitchen table, then quickly moved from one room to the next, searching. After clearing the house, she returned to the kitchen, lay her weapon on the table, then yanked on latex gloves.

Fear pressing against her chest, she held it to her ear and listened. Nothing. Carefully, she examined the box, but there was no card indicating who'd left it.

Growing more uneasy with every second, she slowly untied the cord, then lifted the lid, trembling when she saw the contents.

Three tiny wooden dolls, just like the one she'd found in the grave, lay in the middle of the box on a piece of red velvet cloth.

CHAPTER FIFTY

Somewhere on the AT

Even through the deluge of ice and snow, the Watcher had been hunting bones all night. Once he'd stumbled on the first set, he'd found four other bodies nearby in the brush. All discarded, as if the little ones were nothing.

But they meant everything to the families who'd lost them. Everything.

Their suffering drove him to scavenge the forest in search of other innocents taken before their time.

The SAR team had found the first grave. He'd stood on a ridge, perched beneath the awning of the cypress and oak trees, taking cover from the storm as he waited. Thankfully, they'd found her.

Now they could take her home so her family could honor her in death.

Although the fear of not knowing what had happened to their daughters would be replaced by the reality that they'd been murdered and left for the animals to ravage.

He'd carefully found a resting place for three sets of the bones and gently laid them in the ground. Another gravestone and cross for the precious angels, a temporary placeholder until they received a proper burial with prayers and gospel hymns and their families there to mourn.

He came across a bear print, and the thought of the animal roaming through the woods, its teeth gnashing, big paws smashing brush and the forest floor, made his pulse quicken. He had to hurry. Didn't want to tangle with the big black animal.

Or let it destroy the bones.

He listened, trying to work out if the bear was still nearby. Nothing.

Still, the roaring wind carried voices. More SAR workers.

He couldn't let them find him. Or know what he'd done.

Gripping the bag of bones over his shoulder, he stealthily moved in the opposite direction, fighting exhaustion. He'd barely slept in two days.

Icy rain thrashed through the trees, the cold pellets pummeling him, sharp and slick as the river stones. He pulled his hood over his head and wove around a bend, searching for a holler to take shelter in. The damp slushy ground felt like quicksand, but he picked up his pace. The storm would slow the SAR workers down.

But not him.

The trail was his home. It could be bitter. The wind freezing cold. The terrain unforgiving.

But he welcomed the pain. It was the only thing that made him feel alive.

Until he'd found the bones and buried them.

Uncovering the girls' remains had finally given him purpose.

CHAPTER FIFTY-ONE

Crooked Creek

The dolls stared up at Ellie with sightless eyes. Their stiff wooden bodies were unbendable, the shapes of the mouths macabre, like wooden puppets. Tiny indentations that resembled tears trailed down the dolls' cheeks.

Cold fear gripped her. The box was their coffin.

Was the number three significant? Did that mean he planned to take three more victims?

Shaking all over, she rushed to the bathroom and ripped open the medicine cabinet. The anxiety medication sat waiting. One pill, two, could calm her nerves.

But… no buts. If she succumbed to her need for medication, she'd become dependent on the pills again. Sure, they'd calm her anxiety. But her mind would blur, become foggy. And she'd sleep like the dead.

She didn't have time for that. She had to focus.

This sadistic son of a bitch had to be stopped.

He was toying with her. Taunting her. Playing a game.

Rage festered inside her at the idea of him using the children in his demented plans.

She slammed the cabinet door shut and returned to the kitchen. The dolls and that box needed to go to the lab. Not that she expected to find DNA on it, but maybe a partial print?

Her hands shook as she stored the box inside a bag. First thing in the morning, she'd send it to forensics.

Pouring herself a vodka, she phoned Derrick, breathing out a sigh when she heard his gruff voice.

"The killer was here." She swirled the clear liquid in her glass, inhaling the crisp citrus scent. "At my place."

Tension reverberated over the line. "What? When?"

"I don't know. But he left me a present. Three of those little wooden dolls in a box." She swallowed hard. "It's a message, Derrick."

"I'll be right over."

"No," she said a little too quickly. She didn't want him to see her fear. She had to be strong.

"Don't be stubborn." Impatience tinged his voice. "He may have left evidence."

She dropped her head into her hands. "I'll look around."

"Not alone," he said gruffly. "He knows where you live, and he's been there. He could be outside hiding, waiting to ambush you."

If he'd wanted to hurt her tonight, he could have done so when she'd found the dolls.

"I'm at the inn in town. I'll be there ASAP."

Realizing the futility in arguing, she texted him the address and hung up. While she waited, she walked to the French doors in back and looked into the woods. Like stepping stones, the ridges were stacked, rising toward the sky and jutting above the deep hollows. Grainy clouds scudded across the tops of the peaks, the natural corridors filled with dogwoods, elms, hemlocks, balsam firs and red spruces.

Was he there now? Watching and laughing?

The rustle of snowy limbs catapulted her back in time.

She was running and playing hide and seek with Mae while her father pitched the tent by the creek.

As night fell and the moon glowed like a giant orange ball in the inky sky, she and Mae had chased fireflies into the woods. They'd lined up the rocks in the shape of a heart and drawn their names with sticks.

She pounded her head with her fist.

Stop thinking about Mae. Penny needs you to be strong.

A knock jerked her back to the present, then Derrick's voice. Struggling to remain calm, she let him in. His face turned ashen at the sight of the wooden box.

"The unsub built a fucking coffin," Derrick muttered.

She nodded, her emotions ping-ponging between outrage and fear, and anger at herself that he'd outsmarted her.

For a moment, their gazes locked. Seeing Ellie tremble, he reached out and pulled her to him. For the briefest of seconds, she allowed him to hold her. She was shaking harder than she ever had in her life. Even more than the dreadful night she'd spent alone and lost in the woods as a child.

"We'll find him," Derrick murmured.

She nodded against him, grateful for his warmth. She hadn't realized how cold she was until she felt his body next to hers, his arms around her.

A second later, they both pulled away. Derrick glanced back at the box, then yanked a flashlight from inside his jacket. "I'm going to search outside. Maybe he left footprints or something behind."

Ellie doubted it. This man had evaded police for over twenty years. He hadn't been caught because he was smart.

The only thing he'd left behind was what he'd wanted her to find.

CHAPTER FIFTY-TWO

Day 3 Missing

March 3, 12:10 a.m., Somewhere on the AT

After leaving Ellie the dolls, he'd hurried back to Penny. Couldn't let anyone find her until he was ready. She'd cried all day, begged him to let her go. She didn't want the dolls. She wanted her mommy.

An idea stole through his mind though as he'd ventured into town. In spite of the sick-ass storm careening toward the mountains, tourists had flocked in like birds flying South for the winter. All for that stupid Cornbread Festival.

A smile teased at his lips, and he yanked his ski cap tight over his ears. There were all kinds of strangers in Bluff County now. Families with kids.

Pretty little girls for the taking.

Maybe he'd get a playmate for Penny.

"Hush little baby, don't say a word, Mama's gonna buy you a mockingbird…"

Hating the lullaby that chimed in his ears like a broken record, he pressed his fist to his mouth to stop the hideous words from coming out. That song… one of his foster mothers used to sing it to the new little girl who'd come to live with them. She'd petted her and rocked her when she cried and planted sweet kisses on her forehead as she cradled her close like she was her own child.

But when he'd cried, she'd hit him and yelled, "Hush. Big boys don't cry."

But he had cried. And it had been bad.

Now it was bad for the little girls.

CHAPTER FIFTY-THREE

Not knowing how long they'd be on the trail, Ellie had packed her backpack with enough supplies to last through the day and into the night. If there was one more grave, there might be another.

She wouldn't rest until she found them all. And hopefully they might lead to a clue as to where Penny was.

After searching the outside of her house and finding a partial footprint, Derrick had taken photos and sent them to his partner, then he'd slept on her couch. She'd balked at first, but he insisted on staying in case the killer returned.

Truthfully, she probably wouldn't have slept at all if he hadn't. But she'd never admit it. Anxious to get to work, he'd left at dawn to shower and prepare for the hike, and they were meeting at the police station.

She set the wooden box on the seat beside her, then flipped on the weather report as she drove.

"*Folks, this is meteorologist Cara Soronto. Last night's heavy thunderstorm may have passed, dumping at least two inches of rain and some sleet in the Appalachian area. But the worst is yet to come. In the next few hours, temperatures will drop at an exceedingly fast pace. By later afternoon, the mountains will be a winter wonderland. With temperatures in the single digits and wind chills below zero in the mountainous areas, it's not safe to be on the roads or outdoors. Residents are urged to stay home and hunker down as winter storm Tempest reaches blizzard conditions.*"

Ellie clenched the steering wheel in a white-knuckled grip. Bitter, dangerous winds, and accumulation of snow in the mountains would make finding Penny—and the graves—difficult. Maybe impossible. If whiteout conditions occurred, they'd have to call off SAR teams or risk more lives.

Could she justify endangering others to save one little girl?

Maybe not. But she wouldn't give up herself.

Irritated, she stabbed the radio off and sped into town.

When she arrived at the police station, Derrick was parked and waiting. Today he was dressed for what lay ahead, in a warm jacket, insulated pants, snow cap, gloves and boots. An army-green backpack was slung over his shoulder.

Shadows darkened his chocolate brown eyes, and worry lines creased his forehead. He acknowledged her with a low grunt.

Not a man of words. That was fine with her. She'd gotten too close to him the night before. It couldn't happen again.

Gathering the box with the dolls, she went to drop it off inside. She'd already texted her captain, and he would forward it to the lab. After leaving it in his office with the paperwork for chain of custody, she hurried back outside. Derrick was waiting by her Jeep, his coat pulled up against the biting wind.

When they settled in her vehicle, he handed her a folder. "Thought you might be interested in this."

"What is it?"

"Take a look."

A mixture of emotions slammed into Ellie as she realized he'd run a background check on Cord.

"Did you find something gritty?" she asked, instinctively angry.

"You tell me."

She'd considered running a background check, but she'd wanted him to come clean with her about whatever he was hiding without betraying his trust.

But he hadn't. He'd thrown her out.

Inhaling a deep breath, she skimmed the contents. There wasn't much about his young years, nothing about his parents or where he was born, or what had happened to them. Just that he'd been placed in the system.

Foster homes. Some were decent enough, but others were notoriously misguided, and reports of abuse abounded. Kids felt unloved and deserted. They were bounced from one home to another. Suffered from attachment disorders. Sometimes acted out their pain with aggression.

Pain wrenched her heart as she imagined Cord as a little boy hauling his belongings in a trash bag when he was shipped from one stranger's house to another.

Some children acted out because of the system. Others got passed from home to home because of their behavior. Social workers were paid diddly squat and their heavy workloads allowed little time to make the necessary home visits and follow-ups.

The report had little specifics on the homes Cord had been shuffled to, only that there was almost a dozen by the time he was ten. God… what was it like not to have a home or a family? Had he gotten the scar on his forehead from one of the foster parents who was supposed to protect him?

Her pulse jumped as she zeroed in on number eleven. The family lived in an apartment above a mortuary. The foster father was a mortician who ran the family business. Funerals were held in the parlor downstairs, the preparation of the body in the basement.

Jesus. She'd attended enough autopsies to know that once the scent of death and the pungent pickle-like odor of formaldehyde got under your skin, it was hard to get rid of it. The process of embalming a body was gruesome, and her brain was filled with images of bloated corpses, draining blood and preparing the body for viewing.

A shiver ruffled the fine hairs on the back of Ellie's neck. Had he witnessed the mortician at work? Watched the man stuff the nose and throat with cotton, then sew the mouth shut?

Was that where he'd gotten those books on tombstones and grave symbols?

Skimming further, she found no details on what went on in the house. Instead, the report picked up when Cord was arrested for assaulting another kid as a young teen.

Ellie jerked her head up and saw Derrick watching her.

"You didn't know?" he asked in a gruff voice.

She shook her head. "Why are you giving this to me?"

"Because he fits the profile of our killer," Derrick said bluntly. "And if you want to stop this madman and find Penny Matthews alive, you have to face the fact that your friend might be the monster we're looking for."

CHAPTER FIFTY-FOUR

Hemlock Holler

Ellie struggled to wrangle her troubled emotions as she parked at the entry point near Hemlock Holler. She didn't want to believe anything bad about Cord. His history of foster care was disturbing, but it also roused sympathy in her heart for the little boy who'd been tossed around with no stable home.

A gust of wind startled her. In a few hours, three full days would have passed since Penny was last seen. Even without the bad weather, could Penny still be alive? Did she have food or water? Had her abductor already killed her?

Derrick's voice came out hard. "Aren't you going to say anything about Ranger McClain?"

The accusations in his eyes fired her temper. "Just because he grew up in the system and was arrested as a juvenile doesn't make him a serial killer. A lot of foster kids, even teens who aren't fosters, get in trouble." She didn't know why she was standing up for him after how he'd treated her.

"But it proves he's prone to violence," Derrick pointed out. "And the fact that he lived above a mortuary could mean he knows a lot about the symbols on tombstones and their meanings."

She had seen those books… and he did have a bandage on his arm. Could he have been injured when he abducted Penny? Had she fought back?

Ellie scanned her memories of Cord. Sure, he was mysterious and brooding. Had dark secrets in his eyes. He was also stubborn.

She'd seen him drive himself for days to find someone lost on the trail. He'd punished his body by hiking miles and miles with no rest, stopping at nothing to find a lost hiker.

Yet each time, just as she thought they were getting closer, becoming real friends, he disappeared without an explanation. Sometimes for days. Even a week or more.

"I know Cord," she finally said. "Trust me, he isn't preying on children." Although even as she defended him, doubts crept in. She'd thought she'd known her father, too.

Derrick's eyes blazed with suspicion. "How do I know you're not covering for him because you're in love with him?"

Rage bled through every cell in Ellie's body. In love with Cord? Covering for a killer preying on little girls? "Because I want the truth, and I want to save Penny, and I have integrity." Ellie stabbed at him with her finger. "And if you don't trust me, then let's split up. I don't need you tagging along."

She felt like she was breathing fire as she climbed from the Jeep and retrieved her pack. He followed, pulling on his own bag, his expression tight. But at least he kept his mouth shut.

Maybe she'd lose the asshole in the woods, and he could find his own damn way out. Let him have to call Cord to rescue his butt and then he'd learn what kind of man her friend—or supposed friend—was.

Pulling her personal map from her pack, she studied it, memorizing the twists and turns and ridges that lay ahead. Four miles to Hemlock Holler, where a cluster of hemlock trees conjoined in the center of a twenty-foot drop off. Local folklore claimed the holler was full of poisonous plants and vines that curled around a person's neck and strangled them. Some said the flowers on the ridge grew as God's way to honor the deadly trap below.

It was an oxymoron—stunning beauty in one of the deadliest, most desolate places in the woods.

Mud and wet leaves dragged her boots down as she led the way through the winding trail. The temperature was dropping, the cold air freezing the precipitation on her cheeks into ice crystals. Wind rippled through the leaves in a ghostlike whisper, birds cawed and somewhere in the distance vultures swarmed, diving into a clearing to feast.

Derrick remained silent, close on her heels, as she slashed through the thick brush and patchy weeds, clearing a path. She climbed over rotting tree stumps and roots wound so thickly together they resembled a bed of snakes. Twigs snapped and cracked, and thin limbs that had broken off in the wind occasionally impeded their path.

The sound of her knife whacking at the overgrown brush to clear a path mingled with the sounds of raw nature. Insects buzzed and hummed, vultures grunted, frogs croaked. With gloved hands, Derrick pushed vines and brush aside and they forged on. Up hills, over steep inclines and between trees so tall and thick that it was hard to see anything beyond the trunks.

Derrick's breathing sounded behind her, but he kept up. He was in good shape. Not that she cared, but she sure as hell didn't want to have to haul him miles and miles in the woods if he collapsed.

She paused after mile three for water, and Derrick followed, his dark eyes searching ahead. "How much farther?"

"About a mile," she said, then recapped her water bottle and trudged off again.

The wind grew more bitter, raging as it tore at the trees and leaves. The wildflowers dancing in the wind had savored the rain the night before, but tonight's snow and ice would bury them beneath a blanket of white.

Ellie's pulse quickened as she led Derrick across a narrow ledge toward the wildflowers. The rocks were loose and crumbled and scattered beneath her feet. Derrick cursed as he lost his footing. Then she heard a louder crack, and a cry.

Spinning, Ellie saw Derrick slip over the ledge, clawing at a tree root to try and stop himself going over. She shouted his name, raced to the ledge, dropped to her knees and reached for his hand. But his fingers slid through hers, and he went slipping down the slope toward the ravine.

CHAPTER FIFTY-FIVE

Horror seized Ellie, and time stood still. Derrick flailed, struggling to latch onto the moss-covered wall.

His fingers clawed at the damp earth, and somehow he grabbed a vine, slowing his fall. Then he dropped to a rocky ledge a good ten feet down, landing with a thud.

"Derrick?"

A tense second ticked by, and her breath stalled in her chest while she waited. Finally, he lifted his head. "Yeah."

"Are you hurt?"

He panted for breath, then sank back against the rock and patted his arms and legs. "I don't think so."

"I'll call Cord!" Ellie yelled.

"No," Derrick shouted. "Just toss me a rope and I'll climb back up."

Indecision shot through Ellie. The sleet was coming down faster now, making conditions more treacherous, the icy crystals clinging to her eyelashes. "We need help," she yelled.

"No time. Tie the rope to a tree, then throw it over."

Jumping into action, Ellie retrieved a rope from her backpack. "All right. Hang on."

Her heart hammered in her chest as she searched for a sturdy tree that would be strong enough to hold Derrick's weight. The live oak was solid and thick. She tied the rope around the trunk, securing it tightly with triple knots, then stretched the rope to the ledge. It wasn't quite long enough to reach Derrick, so she tied a second rope to the end. Thank goodness her father had taught her rope-knotting skills, or she'd be lost right now. The memory teased her conscious. He'd insisted she practice over and over and over until she got it right.

She threw the rope down to Derrick, then leaned over the edge. "Secure it around your waist before you try to climb."

"Got it."

She watched him wind the rope around himself. He gripped it with gloved hands, then planted one foot on the jagged wall and began the climb. He lost his footing once, and she held her breath as he recovered. The rope strained against the wind, threatening to snap, but remained secure until she helped Derrick over the edge.

He collapsed on the ground, then pushed himself up to a sitting position.

"Don't do that to me again," she said, hating the fear that had overcome her at the thought of him falling to his death.

"No," he said, then looked up at her as if he was surprised she cared.

Ignoring the moment, she glanced down at the ravine again.

A tree branch snapped nearby, and was hurled to the ground beside them. They both scurried out of the way. "We need to go," Ellie said. "The storm's gaining strength."

Quickly, she untied the rope from the tree while he removed it from his waist, stowing it in her backpack. After helping him up, together they battled the storm the rest of the way to the holler.

Just as she reached the crest, she peered to the left.

Another cross. Another stone marker.

"There it is!" Ellie slogged through the brush toward the grave, then knelt beside the dirt mound, her chest clenching at the sight of the purple wildflowers covering the small burial spot. Again, a simple cross marked the site along with an etching of an angel on the stone.

This time, the Roman numeral II.

Either the killer had grown tired of the game and wanted the girls to be found, or they were dealing with two different people. One, the killer. The second, someone who'd discovered the bones.

If that was the case, why not go straight to the police?

Derrick made a low sound in his throat as he gently brushed his gloved hand over the cross. The grave looked macabre in contrast to the bright purple flowers.

"Why here?"

"Locals claim the wildflowers on this ridge push through the snow and ice like one of God's miracles, a sign of hope in the face of the evil that lives in the forest." Which meant that the gravedigger knew the area and its significance.

"It's evil all right," Derrick said in a thick voice. "Only a truly sinister person would hurt a child."

Ellie couldn't argue with that.

"I'll call it in." She tried her cell but had no bars, so she used the radio to connect with the ranger station. While she reported the grave and requested the ME and an ERT, Derrick snapped photographs and began searching the area for forensics.

A gust of wind howled from above, and the sleet intensified, fogging her vision. Through the haze of icy precipitation, Ellie thought she spotted a figure moving on the hill above. A long black coat. One of the Shadow People? The person who'd buried the bones? The killer?

She pulled her weapon and scanned the perimeter. Vultures soared above the treetops, their wings flapping.

Derrick paused, brows raised in question.

She hooked her thumb toward the slope and mouthed that she planned to check it out, for him to stay with the grave. Then she crept through the bushes, weapon trained. Sunlight tried to sneak through the trees, but failed, the clouds casting a gray desolateness over the land.

Wind shook rain and sleet from the limbs and pelted her. The plunging temperature made the droplets feel like sharp needles. Ahead, brush shifted. A branch whipped in the wind and slapped her in the face but she kept moving. She stumbled over a tree root and pawed at the air to keep from losing her balance. Her foot skidded on the slippery rock, and dirt and pebbles scattered downward into the holler.

The shadow darted to the east.

Picking up her pace, she dashed through a cluster of pines, taking a shortcut to the top of the hill. Cold slush sucked at her boots.

Her calf muscles strained as the ground grew steeper. She'd almost reached the top when she sensed a presence in the brush behind her.

She swung around, weapon raised, but caught another movement from the opposite direction in her periphery. She pivoted, but before she could decide which direction to go, something slammed against the back of her head.

Stunned by the blow, she grasped for something to hold onto, but her feet slipped, and the world swayed and blurred. Losing control, she went tumbling down the hill, fighting brush, sticks and vines, hands digging at the ground, the rocks, the foliage, anything to stop her descent.

But her fingers grasped at empty air and she fell into the darkness.

CHAPTER FIFTY-SIX

As soon as the ME and ERT arrived, Derrick decided to look for Ellie. He should have followed her, but he'd had to protect the scene.

His baby sister might be buried in this grave.

If not, another little girl was. She'd been abandoned by the monster who killed her. He couldn't abandon her again.

"The forensic anthropologist is analyzing the bones we recovered yesterday," Dr. Whitefeather said. "Hopefully, we'll have an ID by this afternoon."

Derrick's lungs strained for air, and he simply nodded. He wanted answers. Needed them.

So did his mother. She'd tried to be brave when they talked. But fear and grief weakened her voice. So did tears. Tears she tried to hide, but he knew they were there anyway. As a teenager, he'd been tormented by her anguished sobs at night, a sound he'd never forget.

Anxious to see if Ellie had found something, he headed in the direction she'd gone. She should have been back by now. Should have made contact.

Had she found the bastard who'd dug these two graves?

An attempt to contact Ellie on her phone, then the handheld radio she'd given him, yielded nothing.

What if the killer had ambushed her? He'd been at her house the night before. Maybe he'd been watching, following her this morning.

Self-recriminations shouted through his head. He didn't like the worry nagging at him. Or that he'd hugged her the night before. And that it had felt good.

Emotions could cloud his judgement. And he'd worked too damn long to find his sister's abductor to allow anything—especially a woman—to interfere.

Still, he should have provided her with backup. Using his flashlight to illuminate the soggy ground, he followed Ellie's footprints. He wished to hell he knew his way through the woods, but the AT map, with its large scale and details, was worthless.

Broken brush and crushed leaves served as a lead, then he followed more of her muddy boot prints up a steep hill toward another ridge.

Using his binoculars, he searched the forest. Trees swayed. The frosty air bit at his face.

He shouted Ellie's name, but the wind hurled the sound into the depths of the sea of pines and hemlocks. Where the hell was she?

Pausing, he tried the radio again. Static crackled and popped. No Ellie.

Pulse hammering, he climbed to the top of the next hill, then scanned the woods in all directions.

Shit. There she was. Lying face down at the foot of a slope. A noise jerked his attention to the ledge above, and he raised his weapon. McClain stood in the shadows, staring down at her.

Blood stained the rocks, and Ellie wasn't moving.

CHAPTER FIFTY-SEVEN

Sharp, icy pins stabbed Ellie in the face. Someone was calling her name. But pain splintered her head and she didn't want to open her eyes.

"Ellie, talk to me. Are you all right?"

A gentle hand touched her shoulder, but she winced as the throbbing intensified.

"El, wake up," the voice said gruffly.

The hand again. This time brushing over the back of her head. Then slowly rolling her over. A dizziness engulfed her, making bile rise to her throat. She tasted blood. Tried to open her eyes. A sliver of light seeped through the darkness. Too bright, like a flashlight. She blinked against it.

Squeezing her eyes closed again, she swallowed hard to tamp down the nausea.

"El?"

Cord, his gruff voice, soothing, worried. He was here, stooped beside her. His hands roaming over her arms and legs, checking her for injuries.

She pushed him away as jumbled memories of the night before returned. Cord was angry at her. She'd been mad at him.

The dolls… the killer had been at her house.

Her head was throbbing like a mother.

"Look at me," Cord demanded.

Worry mingled with the anger in his voice. Forcing her eyes open, she slowly adjusted to the light. The jagged branches above her looked like ghostly fingers against the gray sky. The wind whistling off the mountain sounded like a banshee.

She shivered and struggled to focus.

Cord's face. Wide Jaw. Scar on his forehead. Smoky eyes darkened and narrowed in concentration.

Footsteps crunched the twigs and brush somewhere nearby. Someone else was coming.

"Ellie?"

The husky, deep voice registered. Special Agent Derrick Fox.

Reality crashed back. The grave they'd found. The shadow on the hill. Running.

She'd almost reached him. Then… he'd snuck up behind her. Caught her off guard.

Dammit. She'd been ambushed like an amateur.

Irritated with herself, especially in front of these two strong men, she pushed to a sitting position. The world spun like she was on a tilt-a-whirl. The trees were falling sideways. The ground opened up to swallow her. Knocked out twice in three days—she'd need a check-up for sure. But not yet.

She dug her fist into the ground and gritted her teeth to steady herself.

"I'll call an ambulance." Derrick speaking.

"No, I'm fine." Ellie would not be carried off the mountain like a damsel in distress. She was tough. She knew the trails and how to survive. She'd taken plenty of falls before. And she'd take more, but she wouldn't let it deter her.

"Let me look at your head." Cord this time, his voice commanding.

She muttered a few choice words but allowed him to part her hair and examine it.

Derrick knelt in front of her. "What happened?"

"I was chasing him and lost him for a moment. Then I saw something." She winced as Cord removed a blood stopper and cleaned the gash with antiseptic. "When I turned, he must have snuck up behind me."

"It's messy," Cord said. "But not too deep. Although you might need a stitch or two."

"Just clean it and put a butterfly bandage on it," Ellie said beneath her breath. "I don't have time to go to the ER."

"Don't be stubborn, Detective," Derrick replied. "You won't be any help if you have a concussion or you're bleeding all over the damn place."

Ellie shot him a seething look. "I told you I'm fine." She snagged Cord's arm. "Just clean it. I have to get back to the gravesite."

Cord went still. "You found another one?"

"In the wildflowers above Hemlock Holler," Ellie said. "I need to look at that marker."

"I can handle it," Derrick insisted. "Go to the hospital."

She shook her head. No way was he going to cut her out of the case. This was hers, and she'd promised herself and the Matthews she'd find Penny.

Cord gripped her arms and forced her to look at him. "You know the drill, El. If you feel dizzy or nauseated or have double vision, get checked out. No questions asked. You should have a CAT scan anyway."

"What I need is to get back to work, not take orders from the two of you." Determined to prove she was capable, she brushed her hands on her pants, wiping away mud and dirt, as she pushed to her feet. But the world tilted again, the ground moving back and forth as rocky as the river current after a thunderstorm.

"Easy now." Derrick steadied her. "Did you get a look at the man's face?"

"No, he stayed in the shadows."

Derrick slanted Cord a suspicious stare. "How did you know Ellie was here?"

Cord straightened. "I heard the call about Hemlock Holler." He gestured toward the ridge where Ellie had fallen. "I was on my way there when I saw Ellie." Cord crossed his arms. "What were *you* doing when Ellie was attacked?"

Derrick's dark brown eyes flared. "Preserving the gravesite until the ERT and ME arrived." His voice turned to ice. "Interesting that you found the first grave, and you're out here alone when Ellie was assaulted. Then again, you're always alone, aren't you?"

Cord started to speak, but Ellie threw up a warning hand to both of them. "Enough with the pissing contest. Let's get back to that gravesite. I want to see if there's an indicator of another grave we should be looking for before this blizzard hits full force."

Yanking her hood up to ward off the icy rainfall, she left them both and headed back down the trail.

CHAPTER FIFTY-EIGHT

As Ellie approached the latest gravesite, the ERT was combing the area for forensics. Another little wooden doll poked through the dirt, mired in the snowy ground with the bones.

Coming to a halt, the world blurred again. Something about those little dolls seemed familiar. But she couldn't put her finger on where she'd seen one. Maybe at a local craft fair?

Perhaps she should check artisans in the area?

Derrick and Cord strode up behind her, both dour-faced and silent.

"A female again?" Derrick asked, his voice raw.

"Yes," Laney murmured. "This one looks as if she suffered from a broken ulna at one time."

Derrick's face paled slightly. "You're sure?"

She gestured toward the markings on the bone. "Looks like the break was treated, but the bone is still crooked."

Derrick walked over to the edge of the holler and looked down at the brown layers of dead brush and hemlocks. He stood so still that he looked as if he was barely breathing.

Cord knelt and examined the grave marker. "The angel again. Could indicate whoever buried the girls is religious."

The angel had been etched on the stone with its finger pointing upward. Above it a carving of a rock with lines trailing down it, like tears.

No, not tears. Blood. Holy hell. It was another landmark.

She angled the picture toward Cord. "Do you see what I see?"

Cord tilted his head and examined it. "Bloody Rock?"

"Right." She stood, hands on her hips. "I'm going to check it out."

Derrick was still staring out into the woods, his expression so full of anguish it took her breath away.

"Derrick?"

"My sister broke her arm riding a bike when she was five."

A heartbeat passed. "It might not be her," Ellie said in a lame attempt to comfort him.

Bleak acceptance flattened his eyes. "But it might."

She wouldn't offer him false hope by arguing. He'd probably been down that road a hundred times.

Instead, she focused on what she could do. "He left another message. There's another grave."

He pivoted towards her. "Where?"

"The etching resembles a place called Bloody Rock. It's about ten miles from here."

"Why doesn't he bury the girls together?" Derrick asked, his voice gravelly. "It's like this is some twisted game. Killing them isn't enough. Now he wants to lead us on a cat and mouse chase to find their bodies."

Ellie shrugged. "Or he needs to keep moving so he doesn't get caught."

CHAPTER FIFTY-NINE

Although Ellie was anxious to head to Bloody Rock, Derrick refused to leave until the bones had been fully recovered. He was adamant they wouldn't separate again. He stood close by, watching, tormented by the possibility that the remains belonged to his sister.

She couldn't imagine the depth of his grief.

Cord checked in with the SAR teams combing the woods for Penny but they had no news, then he had to leave to help rescue a stranded group of hikers. Meanwhile, the ERT processed the scene, taking photographs, searching for forensics in the surrounding area. They carefully collected the cross marker and stone to send to the lab.

"Derrick thinks those remains may belong to his sister," Ellie told Laney. "Can you rush the autopsy?"

"I'll see what I can do," Laney agreed.

Another half hour, and Laney and her team were ready to transport the bones.

It was afternoon now, and the temperature had already dropped well below freezing, the wind chill in the teens. Sleet was turning to snowfall, clinging to the treetops and the frozen ground. "I'm heading to Bloody Rock before the snowstorm worsens," Ellie told Derrick. "If you want to go to the morgue, go."

He shook his head. "There's nothing I can do there. I'm with you."

He gestured for her to lead the way, and she zipped her coat, pulled up her hood and checked her map. The ten-mile hike was a tough uphill climb.

Leading the way, she was more determined than ever to find this monster.

The terrain was rough, overgrown, and they prodded through masses of vines and heavy brush. Derrick kept pace with her as briars and sticks scratched at their legs, and more than once Ellie nearly slipped on the rocks. Snow thickened into thumb-sized flakes, blurring into a white haze.

If Penny was still alive, hypothermia might kill her. Soon, she might need her own grave. The thought made Ellie push on, despite the frigid conditions.

Remembering Derrick's earlier fall when they reached a narrow ridge, she pressed her back against the slab of rock and slowly inched one foot at a time. The drop off was at least seventy-five feet, certain death if she slipped over. Below, creek water rippled, and jagged stones jutted out from the unforgiving mountain wall.

She held her breath until her foot landed on solid ground on the other side, then watched as Derrick maneuvered towards her. His boots occasionally hit loose ground and rock that crumbled, raining over the edge. But he was concentrating and crossed in half the time she did.

As soon as he joined her, they paused to take a breath. "Why is it called Bloody Rock?" Derrick asked.

Ellie wiped snow from her eyelashes with a gloved hand. "A violent battle occurred with Native Americans who lived in these mountains. So much blood was shed that people claim it still shimmers off the rocks at dusk."

Derrick turned pensive. "These areas must have significance to the killer or the gravedigger. But what do they mean to him?"

"We'll ask him that when we find him." Ellie trudged on.

Afternoon shadows fell across the already grisly wilderness as they hiked in silence, and they slowly maneuvered across a makeshift bridge created by logs another hiker had lain across a creek. Icy water gurgled and sloshed over the rocks below.

Three more miles, and they reached a clearing where a giant boulder stood, a familiar landmark that she recognized from trips with her father. They'd collected arrowheads here.

Rubbing her gloved hands together, she visually scoured the area. Her stomach clenched. Another grave was nestled between the trees, protected by the rocks.

Derrick cursed. "Grave number three."

Bending down, Ellie spotted the Roman numeral. Another angel. Another simple wooden cross.

"The angel ushers young ones to the heavens," Derrick said in a pained whisper as he knelt to examine the grave.

Cord had said the same thing.

Something else niggled at the back of Ellie's mind. Her father's notes on another case. He'd mentioned Bloody Rock.

She carefully combed the area, searching for any signs to identify the gravedigger. A hair. Torn piece of clothing. Footprints.

But the snow was accumulating quickly, obliterating tracks. Wind whipped fresh snowflakes around her, and a foreboding feeling filled the air. She raked her hand over the brush and spotted something shiny protruding from the weeds. Reaching out, she pulled the object from where it was caught in the vines.

An antique gold pocket watch. Thumbing it open, her heart stuttered at the sight of the white face with its contrasting black roman numerals.

The watch... it belonged to her father. Her grandfather had passed it to him when he died. Her father always carried it with him. She'd seen it on his belt just the other night.

Which meant that Randall had recently been at Bloody Rock.

CHAPTER SIXTY

Bloody Rock

Derrick brushed snow from the marker as he studied the grave. Ellie had squatted down to examine the neighboring rocks.

The angel… it seemed familiar. Then again, angels, crosses and other religious symbols abounded in cemeteries.

Ellie returned to Derrick's side, her hands in her pockets. "What did you say about the angels?"

Derrick could hear his father's voice. "Angels mark the graves of children and infants and symbolize innocence. The angel ushers the young child into the heavens."

"Where did you hear that?" Ellie asked.

His throat muscles worked as he swallowed. "My father told me that when he described the angel statue his parents put on their daughter's grave. His sister died young."

Ellie's brows puckered together. "How did she die?"

He could sense that Ellie was reading more into his statement. "I don't know. My father didn't like to discuss it."

"How old was she when she died, Derrick?"

Derrick's gaze locked with hers. "Six."

His father's sister had been the same age as Kim when she disappeared.

But he could not let his mind go there. His father would never have hurt his own sister. Or his own daughter, either.

Yet Randall's insinuation that his father could have faked his death teased Derrick's mind. Over the years, he'd sometimes sensed that he saw his father in a crowd, watching him. Or at a park, in the distance. Every year on the anniversary of Kim's disappearance, a white lily appeared on his mother's doorstep with no card or indication who'd left it.

Derrick had suspected whoever had abducted Kim had put it there to torment her.

But none of the other parents whose children had gone missing mentioned receiving flowers of any kind.

Ellie broke the awkward silence. "I'm going to call it in."

He glanced at the darkening sky, the snow falling in a thick sheet. Only an inch of accumulation now, but at this rate and if the meteorologist had predicted correctly, they'd have a foot by midnight. Blizzard conditions.

Too harsh for a little girl out here alone. Was her kidnapper taking care of her, or had he already killed her like these other little ones?

Fresh rage shot through him. Had the girls suffered?

What had sweet little Kim gone through before her death?

CHAPTER SIXTY-ONE

As daylight faded and the storm worsened, they plowed on. The gravestone markings at site three led them to site four, again miles apart. At grave number four there was another Roman numeral, another etching of an angel and another wooden doll. But no sign of Penny. Ellie couldn't shake the horrible feeling that her tactics were all wrong, that they'd wasted a day chasing the dead rather than a girl who might still be alive. As the day wore on, her father's watch also weighed heavily in her jacket pocket, and on her mind. She'd bagged it as evidence, but hadn't mentioned the find to anyone.

The ERT teams were working overtime and battling against the elements to find what evidence they could before the snow buried it. Any clue as to the killer might lead them to save Penny.

Grave number five had been dug beneath an overhang at Blindman's Bluff, a point in the trail so entrenched in the steep ridges it was impossible to see from just around the corner. More wildflowers dotted this grave, the purple buds wilting as snow completely buried them.

Ellie searched the grave marker for a symbol indicating another grave but didn't find one. "There's no marking," she said, frustrated. "But there are more victims. We know that."

"Maybe the bodies were left in the states where they disappeared," said Derrick. "There could be a trail of graves up and down the AT all the way to Virginia."

Ellie pressed her hand over her chest, overwhelmed at the morbid picture. He was probably right. But that meant they might not ever recover the little girls' remains.

The snow was falling so fast now she could hardly see in front of her. Wind gusts intensified, stirring the snow into a blinding haze.

Derrick gently raked snowflakes away from the grave, and another tiny little wooden doll jutted from the ground.

Ellie's chest clenched. There'd been a doll at each grave, in the cave and on her porch... what did they mean?

Shivering, she hunched in her coat, the cold biting all the way to her bones as she glanced across the rows of white-tipped trees and thick, swirling snow. A shadow hovered above on a ridge. But when she blinked, it was gone. A second later, the flap of a long black cape caught her eye. Someone was definitely there. A headache pulsed behind her eyes, as she tried to connect the pieces of the puzzle.

"My father calls the drifters, eccentrics and loners who live in the woods Shadow People," Ellie explained. "They're like ghosts. They hide off the grid, sometimes from the law, sometimes from life itself. There's one he named the Preacher, who is into religious symbols and rituals. He holds sermons in the woods for anyone who wants to come and listen." Her breath formed a white puffy cloud in front of her as she exhaled. "What if he's the one digging these graves?"

"A preacher would fit the profile of the gravedigger," Derrick said. "The religious symbols, the crosses... He etches the angel to help the souls of the victims rise to heaven."

"Maybe Cord could find him. He could have seen something. Or the killer could have come to him for absolution." Anxiety raised goosebumps on her skin. She had to confront her father about that pocket watch.

Another gust of wind hurled dirt and snow in all directions. Derrick suddenly went still, then stooped down.

"What is it?" she asked.

With a muttered curse, Derrick dug a shiny silver object from the ground then brushed dirt and snow away with his fingers.

Ellie's heart hammered. "What is it?"

His face turned ashen as he held it up to the light. "A locket… it's just like the one my mother gave Kim on her birthday. She was wearing it the day she disappeared."

CHAPTER SIXTY-TWO

Blindman's Bluff

Ellie considered herself tough. But the anguish in Derrick's voice tore at her. Although if his sister was buried here, the girl with the broken ulna might not be Kim. Lots of kids broke their arms, so could be a coincidence. "You're sure it was Kim's?"

With shaky fingers, he opened the locket to reveal a photograph of a family. Kim, Derrick as a child, and their parents. Tears welled in Ellie's eyes as Derrick absorbed the shock.

"I knew she couldn't have survived, not without having found a way to contact us. But seeing this..." He swept a shaky hand toward the grave, and she couldn't resist. She squeezed his arm in a comforting gesture.

"I'm sorry," she said softly.

His expression was as forbidding as the desolate sky.

The storm had intensified, the snow coming down in white waves now, the wind so fierce it felt like she could be blown off the mountain. Without a storm, they'd have at least a couple of more hours to search for Penny, but the conditions made that impossible. "We either have to hike back down for the night and come back when the storm lets up or find shelter till morning." Already her toes and fingers were starting to feel numb, her cheeks raw from the cold.

"I'm not leaving," he said, his voice gruff.

It hadn't really been a question. "Then let's cover the grave. I have a tarp in my bag. Then we'll find shelter for the night. Hopefully the ERT can come out tomorrow."

Overnight, the snow would freeze, making conditions even more dangerous. And if it snowed again… She shook herself. She didn't want to imagine how that would affect the situation.

Together they stretched the tarp over the small grave to preserve it. Using the stakes in her bag, they secured the cover, although with the brutal wind, they had to add heavy rocks to keep it in place.

If Kim was the unsub's first kill and this was her grave, it might hold the answer to the killer's identity. But if someone else had buried her here, any evidence might have been lost when she was moved.

Another gust of wind howled through the trees, and Ellie motioned up the hill. Night had fallen, the storm clouds making the skies black, and reminding her too much of the night she'd been lost herself. "Come on. Let's gather wood for a fire and take cover. There's a shelter a little further on."

They radioed in their plans, then together, they worked in silence, hurrying to gather sticks and branches and battling the roaring wind. Finally, they stowed their gear in the back of the shelter, away from the partially open side, stacked the twigs and small limbs in the firepit and lit the kindling. It took several minutes for the wet sticks to light but heat slowly warmed the space. Ellie spread her sleeping bag onto the wood floor, and Derrick followed suit. She pulled a pack of dried soup and a metal tin from her bag, and once they'd heated some water, they had a simple meal.

Derrick watched her with hooded eyes as she handed him a steaming cup. "You're prepared, aren't you?"

"My father taught me survival skills on our camping trips." Memories of their trips blurred with his adamant statement that he was backing Bryce for sheriff. Betrayal cut deep. And how would he explain the pocket watch she'd found near the grave?

Pain strained Derrick's face. She pictured the small grave disappearing underneath a blanket of white. She couldn't imagine the thoughts running through his head.

Restless and agitated, she wiped out the pot and mugs and stowed them in her pack for the night. Silently, they worked together to cover the shelter opening as best they could, tacking the corners so the wind didn't rip it from the doorway.

Grateful she'd worn her thermal underwear and wool socks, she crawled inside the sleeping bag, then leaned against the wall to face Derrick. He poked at the fire with a stick, stirring the embers and keeping the flames alive as he added more kindling.

Slowly the fire warmed her, and the flickering light helped to calm her phobia of the dark. But it was too early to go to sleep. And she was too wired.

"Tell me more about your family," she murmured, needing a distraction and curious about the man with her.

His jaw tightened. "Kim was a funny kid," he said, a small smile tilting his mouth. "She liked the outdoors and followed my father around like a puppy dog. She'd just joined a soccer team, and he was coaching, so they practiced for hours together."

"Sounds like they were close."

"They were. Dad used to do scavenger hunts with us. At Christmas and Easter, we had to follow the clues to find our presents and Easter baskets."

"That sounds like a sweet memory," Ellie said softly.

"It was." His voice grew rough. "He was kind and gentle, a beta guy, Ellie. I never heard him raise his voice to my mother or to us." He warmed his hands over the fire, drawing her attention to his long fingers and wide hands. Not as calloused as Cord's but still masculine, weathered. "That's how I know he'd never have hurt Kim or any other child."

Ellie nodded thoughtfully. "So Kim was a tomboy?"

"Yeah, but she also liked dolls and hairbows. One year all she wanted for her birthday was a pair of red sparkly shoes."

"Dorothy shoes," Ellie said, recalling *The Wizard of Oz*.

"Right. She named her stuffed dog Toto and used to dance up and down the sidewalk chanting 'Follow the Yellow Brick Road'."

"I think I would have liked her," Ellie murmured. "She sounds like a spunky little girl."

"She was. Kim liked to put on impromptu plays. Mom made a special photo album of all the dances and shows she dreamed up."

His voice cracked, and her heart ached for him. "I can't imagine how awful it's been for you and your mother."

Agony flickered in his eyes.

A second later, he shut down. He crawled in his sleeping bag and angled himself to watch the fire, disappearing into his own private world of anger and hurt. Ellie wanted to comfort him, but what could she say?

They had just uncovered five small graves. And there were more. She just prayed they weren't too late for Penny.

CHAPTER SIXTY-THREE

Stony Gap

Judging from the foggy white cloud cover over the mountains, the blizzard was already striking at the higher altitudes but hadn't quite struck the lower areas. Even with it threatening the town of Stony Gap, the stupid residents had carried on the Cornbread Festival.

When he was a teenager and on his own, he'd ventured into town to watch the tourists and locals gathered for the festival, there for the craft fairs, bake sales, pie-eating contests, petting zoo, and garage sales that spanned for miles and miles along the small mountain towns.

Today, cornbread was the focus. The mountain people used any occasion to throw a town celebration.

The smell of spicy chili, turkey legs, and salty boiled peanuts filled the air. Excited chatter over surprising finds at the vendor booths mingled with hushed whispers about the little girl that was missing.

Some paranoid souls clutched their children's hands in a death grip, as if they feared they'd be snatched under their noses. A few even had toddlers on leashes.

Laughter caught in his throat. That nightmare was about to come true for one.

He just had to pick her out.

He'd never taken two girls so close together. Always killed one, then rested for a while or moved around so as not to attract attention.

But excitement stirred inside him at the thought that taking a little girl right in town would throw the cops off and add to his fame.

All the mamas who'd come to the homes where he'd lived like a rat in a cage, to pick over the lot of discarded kids, and then thumbed their noses at him—they would be sorry.

His fingers curled around the newest little doll he'd carved as he maneuvered through the busy streets. So many people with heavy coats and hats, faces scrunched against the blasting wind and hidden by thick wool scarves. It was easy to blend in. Especially with all the tents covering the ground and the storm picking up. Wind banged the flaps of the tents and people scurried from one booth to the next, ducking against the snow, oblivious to each other.

Children squealed from that big hideous bouncy house, and one mother swiped at her little boy's face where he'd smeared marshmallows from his hot chocolate. Wooden decoy ducks, pottery, glass blown bottles, art made out of junk, cornhusk dolls and scrap metal artwork filled the booths. In spite of the inclement weather, one booth handed out fliers for whitewater rafting and guided hikes on the AT.

An entire row was set up for the cornbread tastings and sales. Food trucks sat at one end, selling everything from turkey legs and Brunswick stew to funnel cakes and homemade fudge.

At the corner by the playground, a station had been set up for the kids with make your own sand bottles, henna tattoos, and face painting. Although the crowd was thinning as night began to settle in.

Slipping into the shadows of a live oak, he studied the faces as the children lined up for their turn.

A second later, a couple strolled by. Their little dark-haired girl was in a big puffy lavender coat and a purple snow cap with pom poms on the top. She tugged at the woman's hand.

"I wanna get my face painted, Mommy."

The father veered toward the cornbread tasting station across from the face-painting booth, and the mother smiled at the little girl. "Go ahead and get in line. Daddy and I will be right over there."

The little girl skipped over to pick her design while the parents became absorbed in tasting the different varieties of cornbread.

His pulse quickened. She was perfect.

He pulled the little doll from his pocket and inched closer. While Mama and Daddy were busy stuffing their faces, he'd show her the doll.

And then she would be his.

CHAPTER SIXTY-FOUR

Exhausted and emotionally drained from the day, Ellie fell asleep with images of the dead girls floating through her head. Their angelic spirits were lost, hovering in no man's land between earth and heaven, souls searching for peace and the light.

Then Mae appeared, a ghost of the girl from her childhood.

Mae was playing hide and seek again. "Count to one hundred, Ellie!" Mae ran to hide. Ellie leaned against the tall pine tree, pinecones crunching as she swished her feet around. With one hand, she covered her eyes and began to count. Birds twittered. A dog barked in the distance.

The sweet smell of honeysuckle filled the air. Mae liked to pull the stem off and suck the sweet nectar. Ellie had learned to like it, too.

The air stirred around her. Something brushed her leg. Ellie opened one eye and kept counting as she looked down to make sure a snake wasn't winding around her leg. They always came out in the spring, their babies slithering through the grass and weeds, into the backyard.

But there was nothing there.

"Ninety, ninety-one, ninety-two…" A slight mist chilled the air. Thunder rumbled in the distance. Mama said it was supposed to storm. Not to go far.

"Ninety-nine, one hundred!" Opening her eyes, she turned in a wide arc to peer through the trees. "Ready or not, here I come!"

She glanced to the left then the right, trying to decide which way Mae would go. Toward the creek, or the hills where they liked to hide in the old mine? Or down to the river where they used the rope swing to catapult them into the deep section of the water? Remembering how her daddy followed tracks on the ground, she looked down to study the dirt.

Weeds, grass, moss, leaves, tree stumps… There. A clump of weeds and tree bark were smashed from where someone had stepped on them. She tried to judge where the tip of Mae's shoe was and the bottom to understand the direction she'd gone.

Toward the old mines. Daddy told her not to go inside. Ever. The mines might collapse on top of you.

Ellie shivered. She didn't like small spaces. Especially dark cramped ones.

She followed the footprints up the hill, weaving between the massive trees, around the corner, over the bend.

A shadow moved to the right, and she jerked her head toward the movement. "Mae?"

The wind whistled back, a creepy sound that gave her goosebumps on her arms. But no Mae. Raindrops began to fall, pinging her face and jacket.

"Mae, come back, we have to go home!"

But she didn't answer.

Thunder clapped and lightning zigzagged across the tops of the trees. Rain fell faster.

She ran up the hill toward the mine. "Mae, come on, game over!"

Nothing.

Knowing Mama would be mad that they'd gone so far in the woods, she switched on the little flashlight she'd got in her Christmas stocking and shined it into the opening of the mine shaft. "Mae, we have to get home!"

A twig snapped behind her. She heard breathing. Mae was sneaking up on her. Laughing, thinking it was funny to scare her.

She turned to see, but a big hulking shadow blocked out the light. Then someone pushed her, and she fell into the weeds. She blinked and cried out for Mae.

But when she opened her eyes, Mae was gone. And she was all alone in the darkness.

Ellie jerked awake, her chest heaving for air. The fire had gone out, pitching them into the kind of total darkness that made her body quiver with fear. And the shelter was freezing, the cold seeping through the tarp and thin wooden walls. She blinked against the black, disturbed by the nightmare. It had felt so real, as if it had really happened.

Only her parents hadn't believed her. She still remembered her mother's hateful admonishment.

"Stop, lying, Ellie. Mae is not real. You made her up because you wanted a sister." Eyes disapproving, her mother had shaken her so hard her teeth rattled. "Don't ever go into the woods alone. And no more talk about Mae."

Ellie rubbed her arms to ward off the bitter chill. Too wired to sleep, she crawled over to the firepit, added more sticks, stirred the ashes then relit the kindling. Her nerves settled slightly as she watched the orange and red embers spark back to life and a faint light glow against the darkness. Still, her teeth chattered and she was trembling with cold, her toes and fingers numb.

Derrick must have finally fallen asleep, but he was tossing and turning. He had his own nightmares to contend with. The need to comfort him and erase the horror of the day from her mind seized her, and she couldn't stop herself from curling up next to him. His body shook as he twisted, and she rubbed circles along his back. Seconds later, he suddenly turned over and gripped her arms. His eyes were glazed, his startled look full of questions.

The beard stubble on his jaw made him look rugged, the torment on his face so stark that Ellie couldn't resist. She brushed her thumb across his cheek, then whispered his name. Cocooned from the world, with the firelight flickering across his face, she could almost forget why they were out here. That they were chasing a killer.

Tension simmered between them, charging the air and making the space feel intimate. Hurt flashed in his eyes. Then raw need.

Breath catching, she laid her hand against his cheek. Their gazes locked. He made a low sound in his throat and lowered his mouth to hers.

The cold, fear and sorrow she'd felt during the last few hours were mirrored in the furious, almost desperate way he kissed her. Tension mounted, and she stroked his back then urged him closer.

Firelight danced across his angular face as he growled her name and hunger ignited between them, the world forgotten. Or maybe they both just needed to drown out the horror they'd seen today. The dolls, the shallow graves, the bones…

Banishing the images, she raked her nails across his back. His fingers fumbled with her shirt. She popped the buttons open, then suddenly he was tearing at her clothes and she was pulling at his. Seconds later, they were naked, warmed by the flames.

His hand went to her breast. He toyed with her nipple. Lowered his head to her neck and suckled her skin, then trailed his lips and fingers down her torso. She grabbed his back, felt sweat glistening on his skin.

Their bodies slid together, heat erupting, bare skin stroking bare skin, his thick erection nudging at her sex. She parted her legs, opened for him and lifted her hips in invitation.

Releasing a low growl, he climbed on top of her and thrust his cock inside her. She threw her head back and moaned his name, clinging to his muscled body as she took him in and met him thrust for thrust. Their rhythm built, breathing turned erratic, tingles of pleasure ripping through her as her orgasm rocked through her, fast and dizzying in its intensity.

CHAPTER SIXTY-FIVE

Derrick woke to the sound of the wind roaring and the tarp over the door flapping like mad. The fire had gone out and it was damn cold. When he rolled over, he realized he was intertwined with Ellie. And they were still naked.

Groaning with self-disgust, he balled his hands into fists. What had gotten into him? One minute he'd been dreaming about the day Kim had disappeared, and the next… he'd been on top of Ellie.

Fuck. Fuck. Fuck.

He had no business screwing her. Not when they were working together. And not when he suspected her father of hiding something.

Ellie stirred and rolled over, and he reached for his clothes, which were scattered all over the wood floor. They'd practically torn them off in their passionate haste during the night. Before he could snag his shirt, a knock sounded on the thin frame.

"Ellie, are you in there?"

Shit. McClain.

The man pounded the side of the shelter again, rattling loose boards, and Ellie jerked awake. Her eyes widened as Cord poked his head inside. "El?"

She scrambled to cover herself with the sleeping bag, and Derrick quickly buttoned his shirt. Cord froze. His expression turned as brittle as the icicle dangling from the overhang of the lean-to.

Ellie fingered her disheveled hair but, in Derrick's eyes only managed to make herself look sexier. *Dammit.*

"Cord, what are you doing here?" she asked in a low voice.

"It's nearly seven thirty. ERT is on its way."

"Give me a minute to get myself together," Ellie said. "I'll meet you outside."

Cord glared at Derrick, but he shrugged it off. So, he'd shared a night with Ellie. It wouldn't happen again. He was in Crooked Creek for one reason. When he found the monster who'd abducted Kim and these other little girls, he'd leave this godforsaken wilderness and never look back.

Ellie reached for her long underwear and dragged on the thermal top. It hugged her ample breasts so tightly it made his cock harden.

Get a fucking grip. He turned his back to her as he threw on his clothes, refusing to tempt himself. He heard her scrambling to pull on her boots and repack her bag while he dressed and yanked on his coat.

"About last night," he said, hoping to make certain she understood it was a one-time thing.

"Don't sweat it," she replied, cutting him off. "We were just trying to stay warm in the blizzard. Won't happen again."

Except, dammit, they hadn't used protection. "But no condom."

"I said don't sweat it. I'm on the pill."

He gave a curt nod, relieved she didn't expect more. He had nothing else to give.

Jaw set, he busied himself stirring up the fire enough to make coffee. When he looked up, she was scowling at her phone.

"What's wrong?" he asked.

"Oh, God, Derrick." She looked up at him with an anguished groan. "Another little girl has gone missing."

CHAPTER SIXTY-SIX

"I have to go." Ellie jumped up and grabbed her gear.

"What happened? Where was she taken?"

"The Cornbread Festival," Ellie said. "My captain wants me there ASAP." Outside, she heard more voices and realized the ERT team had arrived. "Stay here and supervise the recovery and crime scene."

A debate warred in his eyes. "I can go with you."

Ellie touched his arm. "No. I can handle it. If you find something indicating another grave, call me." Remembering he'd ridden with her, she gestured outside the shelter. "One of the team or Cord can give you a ride back."

His jaw tightened at the mention of Cord, then he cleared his throat, his voice thick. "Be careful, Ellie. He's watching you."

Ellie nodded. "Let him come after me." She strapped on her gun and holster. "I'll be ready."

Cord's boots crunched snow and frozen ground as he paced outside the shelter door. He looked pissed off, although he had no reason to be.

Except for the fact that she hadn't trusted him. Hell, he should have answered her questions.

You didn't tell him about Mae.

But that was different. She was working a case. Mae was personal.

Cord handed her a mug of coffee, interrupting her reverie. Grateful for it, she warmed her hands with it and took a long sip for fortification. The snow was still falling and was ankle deep, but the wind was dying down enough for the ERT to work.

Penny had been gone nearly four days. Did the fact that he'd taken another child mean she was dead? "I have to go," she told Cord. "Another child went missing."

Cord's thick brows rose. "Out here?"

"From the festival." Which meant the killer had ventured into town again, the night after he'd left her the dolls. "Alert the search teams that we're looking for two children now. I'll update you with the details as soon as I know more."

Cord nodded, his expression distant. "Temperature supposed to reach the high thirties midday. Search teams are starting back in an hour. We sent them home last night during the whiteout conditions."

"Agent Fox will stay here with the grave," Ellie told him. "See if you can find the Preacher and find out if he's seen anything."

"Why do you think he'd know something?"

"The religious symbols on the grave markers." She finished her coffee, needing the burst of caffeine to get her down the mountain. "He'll open up to you before he does me. Maybe he saw something. Or if the killer is living off the grid out here, he could have confessed to him."

CHAPTER SIXTY-SEVEN

Stony Gap

By the time Ellie had braved the weather, the hike and maneuvered the winding roads to Stony Gap, Captain Hale had texted her the name of the missing girl and her family.

As she passed through the town at 10 a.m., fliers of both girls were tacked on storefronts and light posts. Bryce's face also stared back at her, arrogant and full of bravado.

Though the festival had carried on the day before, it had temporarily shut down now. Signs promised activities would resume tomorrow, weather permitting.

Salt trucks and snowplows were working to clear the roads, and snowdrifts a foot high covered the landscape. Heavy winds hurled snow and ice from trees and store awnings. Icicles dangled from windows like crystal knives, and tires churned over patches of black ice.

Vendor tents were abandoned and so were the streets, making it feel like a ghost town. If the weather hadn't been enough to keep people inside, the fact that another child had disappeared would be. People would be in panic mode. No doubt tourists would leave town.

Was the kidnapper one of them or someone in their own backyard?

The WRIX Channel 5 news van was parked in front of her father's office when she arrived. Angelica and her cameraman stood on the steps, with Bryce front and center.

Muttering a curse, she parked, tugged her coat around her, and climbed out. Bryce's voice drifted in the wind as she approached.

"This is Deputy Bryce Waters, candidate for sheriff of Bluff County," he said. "I'm sorry to report that yesterday evening, during the Cornbread Festival, six-year-old Chrissy Larkin disappeared. According to her parents, they left Chrissy at the face-painting booth while they sampled the cornbreads, but minutes later when they returned, she was gone.

"Letty Cantrell, the woman manning the stall, claims she painted a shooting star on Chrissy's cheek, then bent to retrieve more paint and the little girl was gone."

Ellie's stomach roiled. Before, the kidnapper had chosen girls along the trail. This time right in town. He'd never taken two girls so close together.

If they were dealing with the same unsub, he was escalating. Growing bolder.

"Deputy Waters," Angelica said. "What are you doing to find this missing child?"

"As soon as authorities were alerted, we canvassed the area, interviewed people on the streets, all the vendors, managers of the food trucks and staff helping with the festival."

"What about security cameras?"

Ellie gritted her teeth as Bryce explained Stony Gap did not have street cams. "We are asking anyone who may have seen Chrissy or anything suspicious to please call the sheriff's office." He raised his head and stared straight into the camera. "Trust me, as your future sheriff and in conjunction with Sheriff Randall Reeves, we will find the person who took this little girl and Penny Matthews, so our streets and town are once again safe."

Damn him. His voice held just the right amount of concern, compassion and authority. The camera loved him.

Angelica's voice was as smooth as honey. "Deputy Waters, everyone in Bluff County and Crooked Creek are asking the question—is Chrissy's disappearance related to the disappearance of Penny Matthews?" Angelica paused for dramatic effect. "Are we dealing with a serial predator targeting our children?"

Bryce spotted Ellie as she approached but gave nothing away. Instead, he maintained his professional and compassionate persona. "I'm sorry to report that we believe that is the case."

"Do you have any leads?"

Bryce lifted something in his hands and Ellie's breath caught.

"As a matter of fact, we do. The kidnapper, who seems to drift through the woods and town like a ghost, left this tiny hand-carved wooden doll at the face-painting booth where Chrissy was last seen."

"What is the doll's significance?" Angelica asked. "Did it belong to Chrissy?"

Ellie shook her head. *Don't tell*, she mouthed.

But Bryce's expression turned stoic for the camera, and he did.

CHAPTER SIXTY-EIGHT

Rage seethed inside Ellie as she stalked up the steps. Angelica spotted her and started forward, but Ellie shook her head, glared at Bryce, then stormed into the sheriff's office. The wind blew the door shut behind with a slam, but a second later, she felt another blast as it was opened again.

Angelica and her cameraman were on her tail. And Bryce was right behind them.

"Detective Reeves, have you identified the remains of the bodies you found on the trail?" Angelica asked.

She froze, heart hammering so hard she heard the blood roaring in her ears. A quick glance toward her father's office revealed it was empty.

"Detective Reeves," Angelica called.

Before Ellie could respond, a young woman with auburn hair barreled toward her, expression filled with fury.

She grabbed Ellie's arms so tightly that her fingernails dug into Ellie's skin through her jacket sleeve. "This is your fault. If you'd found this maniac by now, he wouldn't have taken my daughter."

Behind her, she heard a gasp, then the door to the office opened and slammed shut again. Footsteps followed, Stan and Susan Matthews storming over to join Chrissy's mother. Deputy Landrum trailed them, frustration lining his face.

"Did you find Penny?" Susan cried.

"Why did you let him take our children?" Stan barked.

"Come on, Stan," Heath said. "Calm down."

Chrissy's mother grabbed Ellie by the elbow. "Don't just stand there. Get someone competent on the job before he kills our babies."

The women's hate-filled words pierced Ellie like a dagger in her heart. Emotions momentarily robbed the air from her lungs. Angelica's cameraman was filming the scene, the silence in the room shattered by the women's tormented sobs.

Bryce brushed past her, and gently touched Mrs. Larkin's arm, murmuring for her to release Ellie. "It's going to be all right," he said softly. "I'll find your little girl and bring her back to you."

Disbelief railed inside Ellie. How could Bryce promise that? Especially when they had no idea who the kidnapper was. And to imply that he could do what Ellie couldn't.

Irritated with herself for allowing Bryce to railroad the situation and grateful Heath had a grip on Stan, she finally found her voice. "Mrs. Larkin, I'm so sorry about Chrissy. Susan, Stan, we haven't given up on finding Penny. All of Bluff County law enforcement, including Crooked Creek and Stony Gap's police departments, along with the FBI, are doing and will do everything within their power to find your daughters. They're out there searching now, while Deputy Waters holds the fort here."

"But you haven't found her and there was a snowstorm last night," Susan shouted. "She could have frozen to death by now."

"What is he doing to them?" Mrs. Larkin cried.

Stan stepped toward her, his hands balled into fists, but Heath held him back. "If our daughter is dead, we're going to hold you personally responsible."

Her father's deputy Shondra Eastwood, who had run over to try and stop the commotion, rubbed Mrs. Larkin's back, then Susan's. "Come on, this is not helping. Let's get some coffee and take a breath."

Ellie shot her friend a look of gratitude as Shondra coaxed the distraught women into the small conference room. Bryce pushed

Heath aside and urged Stan to take a walk, as if they shared a brotherhood bond.

Angelica didn't miss a beat. "Detective Reeves, do you have new information on the case? Any leads on finding Penny or her abductor?"

Still shaken, she decided Bryce had said enough. Shondra was what the mothers needed, not her.

"We are working leads," she said as she faced the camera. "In fact, I need to get to work now."

"Deputy Waters said this predator moves around virtually unseen, like a ghost." Angelica blocked her path before she made it to the door. "Exactly how many children do you think he's taken?"

Ellie simply looked at her. She didn't intend to rouse more panic by answering that.

Instead, she opened the door and rushed outside. The morgue was on her list to visit.

Then she had to see her father about the watch she'd found at Bloody Rock.

CHAPTER SIXTY-NINE

Heath followed Ellie outside. "What can I do?"

Ellie inhaled sharply and forced herself to concentrate on the job. "If this is the same man who took Penny and the other girls, as we suspect, he varied his routine this time. Instead of abducting Chrissy on the trail, he came into town. That means he's getting bolder, escalating, and that maybe he made a mistake. First canvass all the vendors at the festival and anyone else you can find to talk to. Then check into the Larkin family, interview their neighbors and friends. Maybe this time someone saw something."

"On it." Heath shifted and glanced back at the sheriff's office. "They were out of line in there. You're doing all you can."

Ellie's lungs strained for air. What if her best wasn't enough?

She bit back a response though. "Let's get to work. The fact that he's escalated could mean that Penny is already dead."

Tears gathered in her throat at the thought, but she swallowed them back. Heath's face fell, but then he lifted his chin. "Don't give up yet."

"No, one way or the other," she murmured, "we're going to find them. Now I have to get to the morgue."

They parted, and outside she battled her way through the wind and snow. Pulling up her hood, she rushed to her Jeep and drove toward the morgue. But she was still shaken when she went inside.

Laney was working the excavation site with Derrick, but the forensic anthropologist had been analyzing the bones.

Dr. Taylor Wright was tall, with a boxy frame, a prominent nose and purple hair. Her voice sounded like gravel when she spoke.

"I've identified the first two victims from dental and medical records," Dr. Wright said. "One was six-year-old Millie Purcell from Springer Mountain, Georgia. The second, five-year-old Sandy Baines from North Carolina."

"Both were on Special Agent Fox's list," Ellie said. "Cause of death?"

"That's difficult to say. There's no evidence of trauma or foul play except for animal chewing which occurred post-mortem from being left out in the elements. Because lack of trauma or other physical evidence, I'd say the girls were strangled, although the hyoid showed no evidence of trauma either. But that's not uncommon in children as their hyoid components are not fully ossified and are more flexible than in adults."

"How about sexual abuse?"

"Judging from the lack of trauma on the pelvic bones, I would say no."

A small relief. "We're bringing in three more bodies," Ellie continued. "Just a heads up. One of the victims could be Special Agent Fox's sister, Kim. He found a locket that belonged to her. I think she was the first victim."

Dr. Wright shook her head sadly as Ellie said goodbye.

Her father's watch still weighed heavily in her coat pocket as she ducked through falling snow to her Jeep. The flakes clung to her clothes and eyelashes. As she started the engine and exited the parking lot, she prayed Derrick was wrong about her father.

The streets were slick with pockets of black ice, slowing her as she drove toward her parent's house. Snow fell in a thick sheet, and signs advertising the postponement of the Cornbread Festival had been tacked all over town.

Pictures of the two missing girls hung everywhere, mingling with haunting images of the graves in her mind. The unsub had definitely escalated. Did taking Chrissy mean he'd already killed Penny?

The farmhouse loomed ahead, covered in snow, icicles clinging to the tree branches and porch. The picturesque mountains stood behind it, mountains that she'd loved most of her life. Except when they'd terrified her as a child.

Knowing they hid a monster now made them eerier than ever.

Even the house looked less welcoming, sinister, with more ominous winter clouds rolling across the already gray sky.

Ellie parked, trudging through foot deep snow until she reached the brick-paved path. Her father had shoveled it, but still she had to dodge slick patches, and hang onto the handrail to keep from falling as she climbed the porch steps. After kicking snow and slush from her boots on the doormat, she rapped on the door then twisted the knob.

"Mom? Dad?"

The warmth of the furnace inside and sound of the fire crackling from the family room should have felt inviting, but today she sensed a frigid cold inside. "Mom? Dad?" She called her parents' names as she made her way by the staircase. Her father's boots pounded on the wood floors as he walked down the steps.

"Ellie, I didn't know you were stopping by."

"We have to talk."

He joined her at the landing. "I assume you know about the second missing child. Did you find Penny?"

She shook her head. "Let's go into your study."

A frown crinkled his brows, but then he led the way to his office. Typically, he kept his desk neat, aside from the stacks of maps everywhere. But today papers were scattered around, the drawer holding his files was open, and several folders were spread across the oak credenza. The painted paperweight she'd made him out of a river rock sat by his coffee cup, making her heart squeeze.

Three maps lay open on the coffee table in the seating nook, their edges crinkled. An odd look flickered in his eyes, and he quickly swept the folders into a stack and jammed them back in the file drawer.

The hair on the back of her neck prickled. Was he trying to hide them from her?

"Bryce is a loose cannon," she said without preamble. "I told you I could handle the press."

"He's just doing his job," her father said. "You weren't around last night when Chrissy disappeared, and he was."

"He told Angelica about the wooden dolls we found, Dad." Ellie didn't hide the disdain from her tone.

"They were bound to find out."

"But that was an important detail I wanted to hold back, in case we get a confession."

He pinched the bridge of his nose. "I'll talk to him."

"It's too late now," she snapped. "The damage is done."

Her father averted his eyes and sank into his desk chair, a wariness emanating from him that Ellie had never seen before.

"We located five graves," she said, deciding to cut straight to the chase. "We think Kim Fox's remains are among them." She explained to him about the gravestones and the etchings, and Dr. Wright's autopsy.

"You think the killer is burying the bodies?"

"I don't know. Could be someone else discovered the remains and buried them so we'd find them," Ellie said.

Hand trembling, she pulled the pocket watch from her coat. "Dad, I also found your watch by the grave at Bloody Rock." Her breath stalled in her chest.

An angry hiss punctuated the air behind her, and Ellie turned to see Derrick standing in the doorway. Her mother rushed up beside him.

Damn. She hadn't heard him come in.

He shot Ellie an accusatory glare. "You found evidence at the grave and hid it from me?"

Ellie opened her mouth to defend herself, but Derrick strode to the desk, and slapped his palms on the wooden surface.

"I knew you did a shoddy investigation," Derrick snarled. "Now I know the reason."

Ellie touched his arm, but he jerked away.

"I just got word from forensics, Sheriff Reeves," he spat. "Your DNA was on the pocketknife found near where Penny Matthews disappeared."

Ellie gasped. First the pocket watch, now her father's DNA.

"You son of a bitch," Derrick said. "You accused my father and me of hurting my sister, but it was you, wasn't it? You act like some hero, but you killed her. You've been murdering innocent little girls for twenty-five years and no one suspected you."

CHAPTER SEVENTY

Disbelief immobilized Ellie. She expected her father to protest, but guilt streaked his eyes.

"Have you been covering for him, Ellie?" Derrick's tone was as brittle as the wind outside. "Is that what last night was all about?"

His accusation sent a bolt of fury through her. She shot him a look of contempt but didn't bother to respond. Sleeping with him was the least of her worries.

Her father couldn't be a killer. He was the town hero. *Her* hero. Despite everything, he wasn't a monster.

"Dad, say something," she said in a shaky voice.

"No, Randall." Her mother stepped into the room, a pistol clutched in her hand, at odds with her silk blouse and pearls. She didn't realize her mother even knew how to handle a gun. "There's nothing to say," she hissed at Ellie.

Ellie gaped at her. "Mom, what are you doing?"

"Protecting my family," her mother said. "I know you think I'm weak and silly, Ellie. You always have. But I'm not. I've always done what's best for our family, and I will until the day I die."

Ellie shook her head in denial. "Put down the gun, Mom. If Dad wants to explain, then let him." *Please, dear God, let there be an explanation.* One where her father wasn't a child killer.

Randall stood and walked over to Ellie's mother, his expression calm but resigned. "Let me have the gun, Vera. It's over."

Ellie stilled, waiting, hoping her father would deny his connection to the missing girls. But he didn't. "Vera, let me handle this."

He angled his head toward Ellie. "Your mother had nothing to do with this. It's all on me. My choices."

"Stop it, Randall," Vera hissed.

He covered her shaky hand with his. Derrick stood ramrod still, but Ellie sensed that given an opening, he'd pull his gun and shoot her father. Maybe her mother, too, if she didn't back down.

"Please, Mom," Ellie pleaded. "I don't want anyone else to get hurt. Lower the weapon."

Susan Matthews was suffering. So was Mrs. Larkin. And Derrick's mother.

Penny and Chrissy must be terrified. *If* they were still alive.

If her father was a killer, even though her instincts screamed no, she couldn't allow him to keep hunting children.

Her father rubbed her mother's back with one hand, eased the gun from her fingers and placed it on the credenza.

Ellie cleared her throat. "Where are Penny and Chrissy, Dad? Are they still alive?"

"El, I'm sorry," her father said in a pained tone. "This is all a mistake."

Outrage sharpened Derrick's tone. "A mistake? You call killing a dozen children a mistake?"

Her mother stepped toward her, eyes imploring her to listen. "Your father… he's protecting you, protecting me, Ellie, you can't arrest him. He—"

"Be quiet, Vera," Ellie's father growled. "I should have come clean a long time ago."

"Then you admit it?" Derrick barked.

"He's not confessing to anything," Ellie's mother cried. "And you can't arrest him. This town loves Randall."

"Because they don't know the truth about what a monster he is," Derrick said through clenched teeth.

Vera turned to Ellie. "We have to protect the family, honey. Everything we did, we did for you." She suddenly lunged toward the gun.

The crazed expression in her mother's eyes sent a bolt of panic through Ellie. Vera was going to shoot Derrick, and she expected her daughter to cover up his murder.

Ellie dove for the gun, and she and her mother wrestled for it.

"Let go!" Ellie shouted.

Instead of loosening her grip, Vera fought harder. Ellie pushed her with one hand to throw her off balance, and their arms swung upward. Her father vaulted toward them and yanked her mother away. Somehow in the tangle, the gun went off.

The sound of the gunshot echoed in the silence. Ellie's mother screamed. Her father staggered backward with a shocked grunt, one hand flying to his chest.

Blood spattered everywhere. Her father's shirt. The wall.

He collapsed on the floor and a river of red pooled beneath his body.

CHAPTER SEVENTY-ONE

Time stood still for Ellie as she stared at the blood oozing from her father's chest. Her mother screamed and reached for the gun, which had fallen to the floor.

Derrick dove for it at the same time and Vera lunged at him, but Ellie grabbed her around the waist to pull her away.

"Mom, it's over!" Ellie shouted. Her mother shoved her before running to her father and dropping down beside him, sobbing.

Derrick snagged his phone. "I'll call 911."

Ellie nodded numbly.

"If he dies, it's your fault," Vera said to her, her eyes burning with anger.

Hurt seized Ellie so hard she stumbled sideways and had to clutch the wall to keep from falling.

"The ambulance is on its way," Derrick said. "Ellie, bring towels to help stop the bleeding."

His calm order yanked her into motion, and she ran to the kitchen and grabbed a fistful of dry cloths from the drawer. By the time she returned to the study, Derrick had knelt beside her father.

"Leave us alone!" Vera screamed.

"He's trying to help," Ellie said. Derrick ripped open her father's shirt and pressed a towel to the wound, then added another and another, applying pressure.

"Dad?" Ellie whispered.

He blinked, struggling to stay conscious. Finally, his eyes drifted closed and he went limp. Precious seconds ticked by. Her mother's wails intensified. Ellie's heart clenched with fear.

She'd been so angry at her father. But she didn't want him to die.

What about the little girls? Penny? Chrissy? If he knew where they were, he had to tell them…

A siren blared outside. Her mother laid her head on her father's arm and clung to him, crying.

Ellie raced to the door and ushered the paramedics in. "Gunshot wound to the chest. He's losing blood fast and is unconscious."

They hurried into the house with a stretcher. Tears blurred Ellie's eyes as they checked her father's vitals.

"Pulse is low and thready," one of the medics said. They quickly eased her father onto the stretcher. Vera clung to Randall's hand as they carried him to the ambulance.

Ellie raced behind, a fog of terror enveloping her.

"Get in. I'll drive you to the hospital," Derrick said.

His earlier hurtful words echoed in her head. He thought her father was guilty. That she'd seduced him to distract him from the case.

"I'll drive myself." She jogged toward her SUV, jumped in and started the engine. She couldn't be anywhere near Derrick right now.

Her tires skated over the icy drive and onto the highway. Heart pounding, she flipped on her siren and remained close behind the ambulance while Derrick tailed her.

When they reached the hospital, the medics unloaded her father and rushed him into the ER. Her mother hovered by him as they wheeled him to an exam room.

Ellie flashed her badge. "Gunshot wound to the chest," she told the attending physician.

He immediately started barking orders. "Start an IV drip. Let me take a look."

Ellie nodded and stepped to the door of the exam room, but her mother's look of fury made her freeze at the doorway.

If he dies it's your fault.

Ellie leaned against the wall, fear pulsing through her as the nurse cut her father's shirt and the doctor examined the gunshot wound. Derrick appeared, his expression stony.

A minute later, the doctor stepped to the door to talk to her. "The bullet may have hit an artery. We need to get him to surgery ASAP."

"Will he make it?" Ellie said in a choked whisper.

"We'll do everything we can to save him."

Emotions welled in Ellie's throat. She and Derrick stood in silence as they wheeled her father from the exam room and down the hall. Ellie's mother chased behind, an emotional wreck.

When they disappeared around the corner of the corridor, Ellie stood frozen. Derrick's phone rang, the lines beside his eyes deepening as he listened. A second later, he disconnected with a low moan.

"That was the forensic anthropologist," Derrick said quietly. "That last grave… it was Kim."

CHAPTER SEVENTY-TWO

Sympathy for Derrick suffused Ellie. "I'm so sorry," she murmured.

His body went rigid. "I have to make a call. But I'll be back for Randall."

His words felt like a physical blow. Although how could she blame him for how he felt?

Still, the fact that he'd accused her of using him hurt. He didn't really know her at all.

Spinning on his heels, he disappeared down the hall in a cloud of anger and grief. The sound of the medical staff's voices jarred Ellie back to the problem at hand. Keeping her father alive so he could tell her where to find Penny and Chrissy.

The minutes rolled into two agonizing hours as Ellie paced the waiting room. Her mother hovered on the opposite side, wringing her hands together and crying. She must have called Bryce, because he rushed in and dashed to her. Bordering on hysteria, she fell into his arms as if she was a victim and Ellie the enemy. Thankfully, he was sans Angelica this time.

What had her mother told him? Had Bryce known what was going on? Had her father chosen to back Bryce because he knew Bryce would cover for him?

She replayed the conversation with her father in his study, searching for answers. He hadn't actually confessed that he'd kidnapped or hurt the girls. If his fingerprints were on one of the grave markers, maybe he'd found the victims and buried them.

But why wouldn't he have reported it?

That didn't fit with the man she'd grown up with. Her father had been caring. Loving. A man of justice.

He'd bounced her on his knee when she was little and taught her to ride a bike. They'd flown kites together at the park and volunteered at the local pet adoption center. He'd rescued countless lost hikers from the mountains. Had taken her and her friends camping and hiking. He'd been a role model. He was everyone's role model. A hero.

She massaged her temple.

A little after six, Bryce disappeared down the hall, then returned bearing two cups of coffee. After giving her mother one, he crossed the room to Ellie. She accepted the cup with a muttered thanks, but she was in no mood to talk.

Thankfully, the doctor appeared at the doorway and called for the Reeves family, his expression serious. She and her mother rushed to join him, although her mother maintained her distance from Ellie.

"The bullet just missed his aorta, but we removed it," the doctor said. "He lost a lot of blood and is in serious condition in the ICU. The next forty-eight hours are critical."

Vera dabbed at her tears with an embroidered handkerchief. She looked the delicate flower Ellie had known all her life. Not the crazed woman who'd pulled a gun on her and a federal agent.

She was surprised Derrick hadn't arrested her. That still might be coming.

"Can I see him?" Ellie asked.

"I'm his wife, I want to see him first," her mother insisted.

A puzzled look crossed the doctor's face, but he didn't question them. "One visitor at a time. Five minutes at the most. He needs rest."

After the doctor turned to leave, Ellie's mother cornered her. "You heard the doctor. He needs rest, not to be upset."

"I understand that," Ellie snapped. "But two little girls' lives hang in the balance. If he knows where they are, I might be able to save them."

"You keep pressing your father and you'll kill him," Vera spat as she strode down the corridor.

Bryce was watching Ellie with a hooded gaze as her mother disappeared through a set of double doors. "What happened, Ellie? Do you want to talk?"

To him? Not on her life.

Before she could respond, Derrick appeared, a vein throbbing in his neck. "Is he out of surgery?"

Ellie nodded. "In the ICU. My mother just went in to see him."

"I have to talk to him, Detective Reeves."

So now it was *detective*, not Ellie. Any closeness she thought they'd shared had obviously been on her part. He thought she'd slept with him as a distraction. Did he really think she'd stoop that low, or that she'd cover for a child killer?

Steeling her emotions, she spoke curtly. "She'll be out shortly."

Bryce glanced back and forth between them, but neither she nor Derrick bothered to explain. She sipped the bitter sludge from the vending machine, her own strong veneer cracking just like the plaster on the chipped hospital walls.

Five minutes later, she approached the nurses' desk and asked to be admitted to the ICU. As much as she wanted to tell Derrick to stay away, she couldn't deny him access. In spite of what had happened between them and his ugly accusation, they had one thing in common—they wanted to find Penny and Chrissy.

She just hoped they were alive when they did.

CHAPTER SEVENTY-THREE

Together, Ellie and Derrick walked in silence to her father's room in the ICU.

Her mother hovered by the bed, stroking Randall's cheek while he lay as ghostly white as the sheets covering him, tethered to a half-dozen machines that beeped and hummed, keeping him alive for now.

When Vera saw Ellie and Derrick, she shot them venomous looks. Ellie motioned for her mother to step from the room, and Vera reluctantly moved to the doorway, her fingers curled around the edge in a white-knuckled grip.

"Leave him alone, El," her mother hissed.

"I can't, and you know it." She softened her tone. "Talk to me, Mom. Please. Do you know where the missing girls are?"

"Of course not," her mother said, her voice filled with bitterness, as if somehow Ellie had betrayed the family.

Ellie's heart banged in her chest as Derrick handcuffed her father's wrist to the bed.

Vera choked out a pain-filled sound. "You're wrong about Randall. He's a good man. He doesn't deserve what you're doing to him."

"I'm trying to save two little girls," Ellie said, disgusted at her mother's attitude. "If Dad is innocent, why won't you tell me what you're hiding? And why pull a gun and threaten a federal agent? You're lucky Agent Fox doesn't drag you from this room in handcuffs."

"He can't do that," her mother protested. "Your father needs me."

Exasperation made Ellie clench her teeth. "And Penny and Chrissy need you to tell the truth."

Derrick crossed back to them and stopped beside Vera. "Where are the girls?"

"I told you I don't know, and that's the truth."

Derrick stared at her for a long minute, his angry breath hissing in time with the machine pumping air into her father's lungs. Finally, he spoke, a warning on his face. "Don't leave town, Mrs. Reeves. This isn't over."

Her mother's eyes flashed with disdain. "Get out, both of you."

Heart thumping, Ellie brushed past her. When she reached her father's bed, she gripped the rail. "Dad, please, if you know where those little girls are, tell me."

His eyes flickered open, and he groaned. Suddenly his body convulsed, and machine alarms began to trill and beep wildly.

Vera shrieked, and a flurry of nurses and doctors raced into the room.

"You all have to leave." One of the nurses guided Vera away while a team hurried inside with a crash cart.

Ellie's pulse clamored as she stood outside and watched the team try to save her father.

CHAPTER SEVENTY-FOUR

Precious seconds ticked by. Seconds that turned into pain-filled minutes as Ellie waited to see if her father lived or died. Finally, his breathing steadied, and Ellie sent a silent prayer of thanks above that he'd survived.

She still wanted answers, but the doctor insisted everyone leave, everyone except her mother.

"If you or Dad know where Penny and Chrissy are, Mom, please speak up," Ellie pleaded.

"How many times do I have to tell you that I don't? Now leave us alone. I can't lose Randall."

Shoulders knotted with anxiety, Ellie followed Derrick from the ICU. When they reached the waiting room, she had the sudden urge to flee.

Running wouldn't help her find the missing children though.

Still, she needed fresh air. But Bryce cut her off at the exit.

"Talk to me, Ellie." Bryce caught her arm. "Let me help."

"The only way you can help is to tell me where Penny and Chrissy are."

His brows furrowed. "I don't know. But you have to be wrong about Randall. He's the most decent man I've ever met."

Ellie had once believed that with all her heart. Now, she didn't know what to believe. Except he *was* hiding something. "What *do* you know about this?" Ellie asked. "Did he have something to do with these missing girls?"

Bryce shook his head in denial. "I don't believe that. And I don't think you do either."

"What did my mother tell you?"

Bryce clamped his lips tight. "Nothing, just that you have it wrong."

"If I do, then why won't she explain?"

His blank stare indicated he didn't know the answer.

"You got nothing, huh? I thought you had all the answers, Bryce."

Anger flickered in his eyes, then a seed of some emotion she didn't recognize. Did he really care? Or had her father asked him to handle her?

Or maybe he was remembering her retaliation for the rumors he'd spread about her in school. A smile curved her mouth at the thought. After fending off one of the football players who'd gotten pushy with her because of Bryce's rumors, she'd decided to teach Bryce a lesson and had lured him behind the gym. It hadn't been difficult to make him believe that she wanted to be with him. All the girls did. But once she'd had him naked, she'd tied his wrists to the goalpost and left him there alone.

He'd literally become the butt of the football team's jokes, because a girl had gotten the best of him.

Bryce hadn't thought it was funny and had vowed to get back at her one day.

She jerked away from him. "Leave me the hell alone."

Jogging outside, she ran into Angelica Gomez and her cameraman. Just what she needed right now. "Detective Reeves," Angelica said. "We heard Sheriff Reeves was shot during the investigation into the Ghost killer. Can you verify his condition?"

Ellie's instincts screamed that Bryce had called Angelica. *Son of a bitch.*

"How is the sheriff?" Angelica asked.

Ellie did her best to present a calm front. "The only information I can confirm is that Sheriff Reeves is in critical condition and is fighting for his life."

"Do you have a person of interest? Any leads on finding the missing children?"

"I have no comment." Ellie glared at the reporter. "And you'd better be extremely careful with what you report, and not impede our efforts to bring those children back safely."

Angelica's lips thinned into a straight line. Ellie pushed past her and jogged to her SUV, fired up the engine, tires squealing as she peeled from the parking lot. Melting snow and sludge spewed from her tires as she sped toward home, wipers clacking as they scraped at the ice and snow on her windshield.

Her phone buzzed. The captain.

She didn't respond. Couldn't talk right now. But knowing he could have news about the case, she listened to his message on her voicemail.

"*What the hell is going on, Ellie? The mayor wants answers and he wants them now. And what is this about Randall being shot? You'd better fucking call me.*"

She balked at the idea of confiding her suspicions. She couldn't talk to her boss right now. The mayor, the town, even Derrick blamed her. Had she been such a fool that she hadn't seen what her father was doing all this time?

Her tires squealed, rubber gripping at roads that were slick with black ice. Storm clouds began dumping more snow, the wind swirling it into a fog of white that blurred her vision. Despite the heater in the car, she shivered as the frigid cold seeped all the way through her winter clothing.

The storm had definitely caused problems on the highway. Several vehicles had been abandoned, some half-buried in snow. Signs were hardly visible from the accumulation, and tree limbs had broken off and fallen into the road. Slowing as she maneuvered through the icy patches, she passed a fender bender off the side of the road. A quick glance indicated everyone looked okay. Firefighters were already on the scene. No apparent serious injuries.

She kept moving, adrenaline making her hands clammy and her stomach roil. Battling the hazardous road conditions, it took her several extra minutes to reach her house. She parked and hurried inside, fighting the force of the wind to stay on her feet as she climbed the porch steps. Looking down at the floor, she bit back a scream. Another box.

Hands shaking, she picked it up with gloved hands and carried it inside, shoving the door behind her. Kicking off snow from her boots and coat, she set the box on the kitchen counter. The furnace rumbled. A tree limb scraped the window. Falling twigs and sticks pelted the roof.

Senses alert, she pulled her gun and hurriedly searched her house. Nothing looked amiss in the living room. Except… the photograph of her and her parents that sat on the mantle lay face down.

Maybe the storm had rattled the house and knocked it over?

Moving on, she searched the bathroom and her bedroom, but everything appeared as she'd left it.

Satisfied the killer had come and gone, she returned to the kitchen and opened the box. Another doll. One lonely little wooden creature nestled in the midst of a red velvet bed.

A scream of frustration erupted from her, and the tears came, flooding her throat and dripping down her face. Droplets splattered the tiny wooden doll.

"Who made you?" she cried. "Who is he?"

Only silence answered her.

Chest heaving with sobs, she stepped into her bedroom, stripped and threw her clothes in the laundry. *Dammit*, she smelled of sweat and… Derrick's masculine, musky scent.

Self-recriminations screamed in her head. Last night while she'd fucked him, another child was taken. She'd never forgive herself for that.

And now her father lay in the hospital fighting for his life. Raw pain splintered her. A few hours ago, she'd held onto a desperate, naive belief in his goodness.

The realization that he wasn't what she believed was crushing.

Hot water sluiced over her, and she scrubbed her body until her skin hurt. It wasn't enough to cleanse her of the sting of his betrayal.

How could she have been so blind to the fact that he was keeping secrets all these years? That he could be the very monster who'd abducted Penny?

When the water finally grew cold, she stepped out, dried herself then pulled on a pair of sweats. Her stomach rumbled, a reminder she hadn't eaten in hours, so she forced herself to heat a bowl of soup and poured herself a whiskey. Desperate to put images of her father's bloody body and the sound of the gunshot out of her mind, she carried her drink to the window and looked out at the snowy mountains. Shadows hovered and moved, slipping through the forest like the monsters from her childhood nightmares, when she'd played hide and seek with Mae.

Desperate for the burn of alcohol on her throat, she downed the whiskey in one shot. Right now, she didn't want to feel anything.

But she felt it anyway, as images bombarded her. The wilderness she'd always loved was beautiful, yet tainted with the images of the little girls' graves. So many of them.

And the tiny wooden dolls that were scattered among the dead leaves and brittle foliage looked macabre. Clutched in the skeletal hands of the lost little girls who'd died holding them, seeking comfort. Yet the cold wooden dolls gave nothing back.

Frustration at the situation bubbled inside her and she crossed the room to her wall of maps. So many places she and her father had visited. Others of hiking adventures they'd planned for the future.

In a fit of rage, she ripped them from the wall and tore them into pieces. She could never look at them the same way again. Her father had taught her how to navigate the treacherous mountains and survive so she wouldn't get lost.

Had he been preying on children the whole time?

Denial rose again, strong and as steady as her heartbeat, and as ugly and bitter as the taste of rotting food. Grieving what she thought she'd had with her father, she tossed the shredded maps into the trash. She tried to process what she knew and all the unanswered questions rambling through her head.

Her mother insisted she'd misunderstood. What if she had? What if there was another explanation and her father was innocent?

She wanted to believe that. But detective instincts warned she couldn't discount the facts or the evidence staring her in the face.

Hand shaking, she punched the number for the lab. No answer. *Shit, of course not.* They'd have gone home for the night. But she left a message saying she wanted the forensics report from all the items she'd sent to the lab, along with anything they'd found at the Dugan farm.

When she hung up, she poured herself another shot. She downed it, letting the warmth of the alcohol seep into her system, savoring the burn. She tasted the rich hint of caramel as it blended with the saltiness of her own tears. A plan formed in her mind.

She slammed the glass on the table, changed into her weatherproof insulated pants and sweater, then strapped on her gun and holster.

She picked up her phone, called Angelica and asked to meet her at the hospital.

On her way out the door, she grabbed the wooden doll box.

CHAPTER SEVENTY-FIVE

Somewhere on the AT

He handed the new little girl one of the dolls he'd just finished carving, and she clutched it to her chest as if it had the power to save her. Just like the first little girl he'd taken had.

But it hadn't saved her. Just like it hadn't saved Penny.

The woods would soon be crawling with the search teams and cops again. They were calling him the Ghost. That pretty reporter had almost smiled when she'd given him the name, as if she and the other cop were so smart for thinking of it.

He wasn't a ghost though. He was *real*.

Only he had been treated like he was invisible all his life.

Now things were different. People would recognize him. Know his legacy. Make him famous like they had Jeffrey Dahmer and Ted Bundy and the Boston Strangler.

Déjà vu struck him. The new girl looked so much like the first girl he'd taken that he closed his eyes and pretended he was back in time.

She'd been so excited to see the dolls when he'd first shown them to her. He'd thought she'd just want to play with them, but she'd wanted to watch him carve them out of the wood. He'd demonstrated how to shape the head into an oval, then the round body and thin legs and arms. Then the eyes, empty hollow holes like the hearts of the mamas who'd rejected him for the perfect, pretty little girls.

Only the dolls hadn't been enough to make her want to stay. She'd cried and begged to go home.

Don't be a crybaby, he'd told her.

Instead of hushing, she'd thrown dirt at him and called him ugly mean names. He'd grabbed her by the hair and shook her so hard her teeth rattled. Her eyes bulged. Her lips quivered. Snot ran from her nose.

She wasn't so pretty then.

Disgusted, he'd stomped outside and left her alone for a while. She'd learn that being alone was no fun. That it was nice to have someone to play with.

A sibling. That's all he'd wanted. Well, that and a mama who loved him. And maybe a daddy, too.

But he'd had none of those things.

Because they'd chosen the pretty little girls instead.

Disgust tied his belly into a knot, tearing him away from the past. Finally, the mamas were taking notice of him. For once, *they* were suffering.

He gathered the wood chunks he'd stored for doll making and carried them back inside. Whistling the song that played over and over in his head, "Hush little baby, don't say a word," he pulled his knife and dropped the wood at the new little girl's feet.

Her eyes widened when she spotted the knife, and she began to scream.

CHAPTER SEVENTY-SIX

Stony Gap

Before Ellie met Angelica, she called Heath for an update. According to him, none of Mrs. Larkins' friends or neighbors had seen anything suspicious. They claimed she was loving and doted on her daughter Chrissy. No stalkers in the neighborhood or anything suspicious on the family's social media accounts. No enemies.

No leads at all.

The clock ticked away as she drove to her parents' house. If her father had killed the girls, or carved the dolls, there had to be some evidence there to prove it.

Or to prove his innocence.

Before she went live on TV with Angelica, she wanted to be armed with all the information she could get.

The storm was picking up again, the sky as dark and gray as her mood. She trudged through the snow to the front door and used her key to let herself inside.

The sound of the gunshot that had hit her father reverberated through the walls, nearly immobilizing her. Then her mother's scream. And all that blood.

Blinking the image away, she breathed in and out, then forced her feet to move and went straight to her father's office. First, she checked the top of his desk, then his file drawers. There were several filled with old cases, then a folder of newspaper clippings about the disappearances of each of the girls.

Nausea cramped her stomach. Had he kept these as souvenirs, or because he'd recognized the connection and was investigating them himself?

There was no file for Penny though.

Grinding her molars, she checked all the drawers, but found nothing.

Each of the parents had named an item the girls had with them that hadn't been found, but there was no sign of any of the objects inside his desk. Pulse jumping, she searched his bookshelves, opening books for hidden compartments or notes, then found his personal safe.

It was a combination lock, but she didn't know the code. Trying his birthday failed, and so did her mother's. Hers did the trick. Inside, she discovered some bonds he'd bought from the bank, along with his will, but nothing about the missing girls.

She closed the safe, then decided to check the garage, where he did his woodworking. Holding her breath and praying Derrick was wrong about her father, she pushed open the door to his workroom. The space was dark and smelled of pine, oak and cedar. As a child, when she'd wandered out here and found her father building a birdhouse or carving one of his decoy ducks, she'd found the smell comforting. Today, her stomach recoiled.

With the light illuminating the space, she surveyed the room. Scraps of wood stacked and sorted by kind. Pine, oak, cypress, cherry. A shelf lined with crude ducks waiting to be sanded and painted. Another one held the birdfeeders that she'd hung in the trees out back.

Crossing the room, her heart plummeted when she opened the closet door.

Not dolls, thank God.

But there was a dollhouse. A big pretty two-story dollhouse with pink shutters and a string of lights on top.

An empty dollhouse without any dolls inside it.

CHAPTER SEVENTY-SEVEN

The blistering wind hurled snow around Ellie as she rushed from her Jeep to the hospital entrance. Angelica was waiting, with Stan and Sue Matthews and Chrissy's mother hovering beside her.

"Is it true your father has something do with our girls going missing?" Stan shouted.

"Tell us the truth," Mrs. Larkin said.

"Please." Susan's voice was a raw whisper. "Does he know where they are?"

"Are they still alive?" Stan stepped toward her, but suddenly Bryce appeared, sliding deftly between them.

"Detective Reeves is doing her job," Bryce said in a calming tone. "Please stay calm and let her continue. I promise you we're getting closer to finding the girls."

Angelica's cameraman captured the entire scene. Bryce ushered the couple and Chrissy's mother beneath the awning then inside. "Come on, let's get coffee," he urged.

Stan started toward her again, but Bryce caught his arm firmly. "I wouldn't do that, Stan." The man glared at Ellie but conceded, and Bryce escorted them inside the hospital and down the hall toward the cafeteria.

Wrapping her scarf tighter around her neck, Angelica gripped her microphone with gloved hands.

"Do you still want to do this, Detective?"

"More than ever," Ellie said, the parents' pain becoming her own.

Angelica adjusted the microphone, the cameraman counted down from three, and Ellie gave a nod of confirmation that she was ready for the interview.

"This is Angelica Gomez live here with Detective Ellie Reeves, who has been leading the search for two missing children in Bluff County." She gestured toward Ellie. "Detective?"

Ellie stared straight into the camera. "This evening, I'd like to direct my comment to the man who the press has now dubbed the Ghost. I know how many children you've taken and how many families you've destroyed." She held the tiny wooden doll from the latest box in front of the camera for a close up. "I know you were at my house and that you left this for me." Deep-seated anger simmered below the surface of her calm. "Now, it's time to stop with the games." She paused for effect, and to control her voice, which was starting to shake. "Please don't hurt Penny Matthews or Chrissy Larkin. They're innocent children. If you want someone to tell your story, stop hiding in the shadows like a coward and come after me."

Angelica's eyes widened, but Ellie continued.

"Tell me where and I'll meet you. Alone."

Leaving Angelica stunned and speechless, Ellie turned and darted through the hospital entrance. Inside the waiting room, her face appeared on the news segment as the interview aired.

Her mother gaped at her from the corner where she stood. "What in the world has gotten into you?" Vera gasped. "Have you lost your mind, Ellie?"

Ellie steeled herself against her mother's disapproval. "I'm trying to find two missing children and get justice for the other victims. Maybe if you and Dad had talked, I wouldn't have been forced to speak to *him*."

Vera staggered back, as if she'd been punched.

"Are you ready to talk?" Ellie asked.

Sinking down into the chair, Vera dropped her head into her hands and began to pray.

Ellie balled her hands into fists to control her temper. If Penny or Chrissy died because Vera and her father were protecting a killer, no amount of prayer would help them.

Her phone vibrated on her hip. Captain Hale. Knowing he wouldn't be happy with her, she let it go to voicemail and hurried back to the nurses' station.

While she waited on the nurse to come back to the desk, she listened to his message.

"*Are you crazy, Ellie? Mayor Waters and I just saw that blasted interview. You just baited a goddammed killer.*"

Ellie ignored the message.

Better the killer come after her than any more children. She couldn't live with that.

The nurse returned, looking at her warily. "You're going to have to wait to see your father. I already fended off that FBI agent."

Ellie headed to the opposite side of the waiting room, as far away from her mother as she could get.

She'd sit vigil until her father woke up. And she wouldn't leave until he told her everything.

CHAPTER SEVENTY-EIGHT

Somewhere on the AT

Chrissy hugged the little wooden doll to her chest as she curled on her side in the dark. The ratty blanket he'd wrapped around her after he'd snatched her and thrown her in the trunk of his car smelled yucky and was scratchy.

But it was so cold in this dark hole that she burrowed into it.

With the back of her hand, she wiped at her tears. Why had she been so stupid to follow him? Mommy said not to talk to strangers. But she'd just finished getting the shooting star painted on her face when she'd seen the doll on the ground by the booth with the other homemade toys.

A bright purple doll bed was there in the booth, and she'd thought the doll went in the bed. And purple was her favorite color. But when she'd stooped down to pick it up, he'd swooped in. Said he'd build a big dollhouse if she wanted to look at it.

Like a dummy, she'd followed him to the edge of the booth. It was dark then and cold, and she'd suddenly gotten that funny, odd feeling that something was wrong. Just like she did when that meanie Marty pushed her off the swing in kindergarten and stole her lunch.

The sound of his footsteps close by made her stomach hurt. He was singing that lullaby again, the one about the mockingbird. But his voice didn't sound sweet like Mommy's. It sounded evil, just like the look in his eyes was when he'd pulled her from the car trunk and thrown her over his shoulder.

She'd beat his chest and kicked him and screamed for him to let her go, but no one had heard her because they were somewhere in the woods. The fun sounds of the festival were gone. Instead she heard the wind swishing the trees.

Terrified, she turned the little doll up and tried to look at its face, but it was so dark, she couldn't see. She ran her finger over the wood and felt the arms and legs, then the head.

Maybe if she played with the dolls and was nice, he'd let her go.

Why did a big man like him have dolls anyway?

Shivering, she hugged her knees to her chest. The sound of water dripping pinged in the silence. Then nothing. Where was he now? Was he coming back?

He'd told her not to cry, but she couldn't help it. She'd heard some grown-ups talking about a man taking another little girl. They said they hadn't found her.

Someone said she might be dead.

She gulped to keep from crying, but she began to sob into her hands anyway. The dumb doll wouldn't bend or do anything, just lay there stiff and cold in her hand. She didn't want to play with it.

She didn't want to be dead like the other little girls either.

CHAPTER SEVENTY-NINE

Near Atlanta, Georgia

Dread gnawed at Derrick as he knocked on his mother's door. Two hours of anticipation as he'd driven to her condo outside Atlanta had made his stomach curl. But he'd nixed the idea of a phone call, knowing she deserved to hear the news from him in person.

The minute she opened the door, her face fell. But she led him to the living room in silence, and waited until she'd poured him a scotch and made herself a vodka tonic before she turned to him.

Grief clouded her eyes, but her voice was calm. Resigned. "I saw the news. You found her, didn't you?"

Pain and regret nearly choked him, and he nodded. "I'm sorry. So sorry."

He'd half expected her to fall apart. Instead, she wrapped her arms around him. "Thank you for finding her, son. I... know it hasn't been easy."

Tears choked him, and suddenly he was a little boy again, watching Kim run across the yard chasing frogs and squealing as she ran through the sprinkler.

"It was my fault, Mom. I'd give anything if I could go back and change things."

"Shh." She cupped his face between her hands. "Stop blaming yourself, honey. We've both lived a lifetime of regret and sorrow. Now we can give Kim a proper burial and you can finally move on."

He didn't know how to do that. Except to finish the case. Find Kim's killer.

Make him suffer.

The need for revenge festered inside him like a cancer that could only be cured by the bastard's death.

Swallowing back his rage, he squeezed her into a hug. "I have to go back. Find the man who took her and the others."

"I know, Derrick," she said softly. "I saw Detective Reeves on the news a few minutes ago. It sounded like you're setting up a trap for him."

Ellie had been on the news? "What do you mean?"

"She dared the killer to meet her." A frown pinched his mother's face. "Didn't you know?"

"No." A knot seized Derrick's stomach. What the hell was she thinking? And if she'd dared the unsub to come after her, she must not believe that her father was guilty.

An image of Ellie facing this mass murderer alone made his chest clench with panic. "I have to go." He hesitated before starting for the door. "Are you all right, Mom? Should I call someone to come and stay with you?"

Courage flickered in her eyes, and she lifted her chin. "I'm okay, honey. Just go. Find this man and put him away so he can't hurt anyone else."

Derrick gave her another hug, then rushed to the front door. As soon as he started the engine, he phoned Ellie.

Her cell rang and rang, and she didn't answer. *Fuck.* What if he was too late and she'd gone off alone to face this psychopath?

CHAPTER EIGHTY

Day 5 Missing

March 5, 8:00 a.m., Stony Gap

The scent of ammonia, medicine and sick people assaulted Ellie as she stirred awake in the waiting room. Then voices from the nurses' station and the hall.

An incoming text from Heath dinged on her phone.

Maude Hazelnut claims she saw a tall, bulky man in a dark worn coat and black ski cap standing beneath a tree watching children at the kids' corner, then at the face-painting booth.

Ellie's pulse jumped. That man could be the kidnapper. He'd been there stalking Chrissy, hunting for his next victim right in town.

She sent a return text: *Anything else?*

No details. She didn't see his face. I have a couple more folks to interview. No street cams. Keep you posted.

Neither Stony Gap nor Crooked Creek had security cameras, something she wanted to rectify. The mountain towns were quaint, usually not much crime. No need to spend money on security cameras, the town council had said.

Maybe now they'd change their mind.

She had several messages from Derrick, a blistering one about not going off alone to chase the unsub, but she ignored it. She didn't want to talk to him right now. Just to get him off her back, she texted him that she was at the hospital.

A voice on the intercom jolted her. *"Code blue. Requesting Dr. Henry to room 310. Code Blue. Dr. Henry please report to room 310."*

Relieved it wasn't her father's room, Ellie stretched her arms above her head and rolled her shoulders to work out the kinks in her neck. Voices echoed from down the hall. Two women talked in hushed whispers by the coffee machine. Someone was crying.

The nurse walked over and gestured that she could visit her father. "Just a few minutes though," she cautioned.

Ellie followed her through the double doors to the ICU. Machines beeped and medicine carts clanged in the neighboring hallway.

At the sight of her father still tethered to the machines, her stomach twisted. His skin was still so pale he looked like he had one foot in the grave and was barely hanging on to life. The handcuff on his wrist made her feel sick inside.

A nurse who was checking his vitals offered Ellie a sympathetic smile as she crossed the room. Ellie waited until she left before she scooted into the chair by his bed.

For a moment, she watched him sleep, the memories of their camping trips together washing over her and causing a fresh wave of pain. He'd patiently taught her how to pitch a tent and start a fire without matches. How to recognize poisonous plants and which mushrooms and berries she could eat. So many adventures, so many times she'd followed him around, idolized him.

Had he been hiding a sinister side all those years? Loving her and teaching her how to survive in the wilderness while he kidnapped and murdered other innocent little girls?

That thought sobered her. "Dad, can you hear me?"

His breathing grew ragged, then his eyes twitched. "Dad, please wake up and talk to me. I need to know the truth."

He moaned, reaching for her hand. For a brief second, she stared at it. Didn't know if she could touch him. Not if he'd used those hands to kill children.

Get him to talk, Ellie. Do your job. Penny and Chrissy are depending on you.

Stiffening her spine, she inhaled, then clasped his hand. "Dad, I'm here." Slowly he opened his eyes, then blinked. Still foggy from pain and the medications, a glazed expression colored his eyes.

"It's Ellie," she said softly. "Do you remember what happened?"

He searched her face for a moment, then turmoil darkened his eyes. "Shot?"

"Yes, you're in the hospital in ICU."

A muscle ticked in his jaw. "Your mother?"

"Mom's in the waiting room. She's been here all night."

The angular lines of his face softened. He was so devoted to Vera it was touching.

Another memory tickled her conscious—one Christmas when she was seven. She'd snuck into the living room and caught him dressed like Santa Claus as he was putting together her bike.

She had to be wrong about him. She had to be.

"Penny Matthews is still missing, and now a girl called Chrissy Larkin has disappeared," she said softly. "Special Agent Fox thinks you had something to do with it. Either that or you're covering for the killer."

His lips parted as he struggled to breathe, and sweat beaded on his forehead. She had the urge to wipe it away with a cool cloth but restrained herself.

"If you know where the girls are, Dad, or who kidnapped them, please tell me. Their parents are worried sick." Her voice was thick with fear and determination. "Don't let them die."

His hand jerked again, then he mumbled something she couldn't understand before he broke into a cough. She offered him his water cup with the straw and waited while he sipped. When he finished, he choked out a word. "H-Hiram."

Hiram? The name teetered on the edge of her memory.

Her father groaned. "Hiram. Folder… my office, desk."

Recognition hit her. Hiram was one of the Shadow People her father had warned her about. He was dangerous, unstable. *If you see Hiram, run from him and tell me.*

She studied his face. "Did Hiram abduct Penny?"

"I told you not to upset your father," Ellie's mother shrieked from the doorway. "Get out now, Ellie. You've done enough harm already!"

Her father gasped for a breath, and the heart monitor beeped. Her mother raced into the room and shoved Ellie aside. "Leave him alone. You're killing him."

Ellie backed out the door, her gaze locking with her father's. Regret flared in his eyes, and a tear rolled down his cheek. Then he mouthed the word *Go.*

CHAPTER EIGHTY-ONE

The fact that the killer hadn't contacted her after her plea worried Ellie. Although he could be off the grid without access to TV or the news and hadn't even seen her interview.

She pulled into a parking space in front of Stony Gap's sheriff's office, shifted the SUV into park, jumped out and trudged through the snow to the entrance. Bryce's squad car was parked to the side. *Dammit.* She didn't intend to let him stand in her way.

Her phone buzzed as she shoved open the front door. A quick glance told her it was Derrick again. But she ignored it. She had work to do.

Quickly bypassing Bryce, who was on the phone by the coffee counter, she darted into her father's office. Papers were stacked on his desk. She quickly raked across the files. Nothing pertinent to the missing girls—just routine investigations, traffic reports, county ordinances and permitting.

Sinking into her father's desk chair, she attempted to open the file drawer, but it was locked, so she rummaged in the top drawer for the key and snagged it.

"What are you doing?" Bryce barked from the doorway.

Ellie shot him an irritated look. She didn't have time to argue with him. "What does it look like I'm doing?"

Bryce's boots banged against the floor as he crossed the room to her. "You can't search your father's files without a warrant. There's confidential material in there."

"Dad told me to come, Bryce. There's something in here about the missing girls." She unlocked the drawer, then yanked it open.

Bryce grabbed her arm. "You're treating your father like a criminal."

"I'm trying to find a serial killer," Ellie said through gritted teeth. "Now get out of my way, or I'll tell your friend Angelica you refused to help. How will that look for your campaign?"

He jerked his head back as if she'd bitten him. "I don't know what's gotten into you, but you're acting like a crazy woman."

Ignoring his comment, she rifled through the files, her heart racing when she spotted the one labeled HIRAM.

"At least tell me what you're looking for, so I can help," Bryce stammered.

She shook her head. She didn't trust him.

Palms sweating, she opened the file in her lap. A sick feeling stole through her as she spotted a map and unfolded it. Not just any map, but one with detailed markings designating locations where the girls had gone missing over the years.

Using color-coded markers, her father had pinpointed locations where he'd spotted Hiram. Nearly all of the locations were in close proximity to where the different girls disappeared, but one area had been circled in a different color marker to the others.

She rocked back in the chair, her stomach churning. Her father had been working the case all along. Had suspected the disappearances were connected, and that this man called Hiram was abducting the girls.

Why had he kept quiet? Why hadn't he issued an APB for Hiram and plastered his face on the news? And why had he denied the connection when Derrick approached him?

Why hadn't he brought Hiram in himself?

She snatched the map and her father's notes, pushed past Bryce and jogged through the reception area. Bryce trailed her to the door.

"Come on, Ellie. Talk to me. Tell me what's going on."

Why? So, he could cover his ass? No way.

Dismissing him, she jogged to her Jeep and peeled from the parking lot. She had to find Hiram before Penny and Chrissy both wound up in graves like the other little girls.

CHAPTER EIGHTY-TWO

The snowstorm was intensifying again as Ellie made a quick stop at her place. She didn't intend to come back until she found Hiram. And the little girls he'd stolen.

She prayed she'd be bringing them home alive.

Quickly filling her backpack full of emergency supplies, she grabbed extra ammo for her service weapon, and dressed in layers then studied her father's map.

She pinpointed the best entry point to reach the area he'd circled, about ten miles from where they'd discovered the latest grave, and got back in the Jeep.

It was late morning by the time she'd maneuvered the slippery winding roads to the trail entry point. Snow fell in a blinding white sheet again, but she pulled her hood over her head, grabbed her pack and set off on the trail.

This area was deserted, partly due to the weather, partly due to the fact that it wasn't a direct path to the main trail.

Grateful her father had taught her his shorthand markings, Ellie followed the map and hiked north through treacherous terrain and over sharp ridges that, even as a seasoned hiker, made her nervous. Wind battered her body, making it difficult to stand, and the snow hampered visibility.

Miles of steep inclines and twisted paths taxed her calf muscles, and the bitter cold made her bones ache, but she trudged on, searching frantically in case the killer was watching. Finally, two hours into the hike, she spotted a dense cluster of vines and trees.

According to her father's map, an old coal mine had once been active in this area. Using her binoculars, she turned in a wide arc to survey the forest. The branches and vines hugged each other so tightly they formed a natural canopy.

Her pulse jumped. There was a section of vines and branches that looked piled together, unnatural. It had been skillfully done and wouldn't have been noticed by a passing hiker—she'd been looking closely and nearly missed it.

Forcing herself to move quietly, she climbed the hill toward it. When she reached the section, she lifted a branch, then another. Her heart skipped a beat. An ATV was hidden under the mound of branches and limbs.

The area appeared clear, but was secluded. She crossed to where the coal mine shaft was marked on the map. She spotted another clump of branches blocking the opening and peeled them away.

An eerie silence washed over her as she paused at the entrance, the familiar suffocating sensation gripping her. It was almost like an invisible force trying to drag her away from the opening. Tentacles of fear snaked through her just as they had the night she'd been lost in the dark.

Get over it. Penny and Chrissy need you.

Detesting her weakness, she took several deep breaths, then forced herself to focus on the present. She wasn't a child anymore. The only way to destroy her demons was to face them.

Resolve setting in, she crouched over and eased into the shaft. Her senses honed, she pulled her gun at the ready. The interior was as black as the coal that had once been mined here, sending her pulse racing, and she removed her pin light from her pocket and shined it across the flooring.

Dirt and rock, then a tunnel leading to different sections of the mine. At first glance, the space appeared empty.

But a low sound wafted from somewhere in the rear. She froze, heart stuttering. Crying... the sound of a little girl crying. Chrissy?

Fear choked her. Was Penny still alive?

She crept toward the sound, veering to the right when the path split in two directions. Her breathing punctuated the silence, and about a hundred feet in, she came to a more open area and halted. A wooden box sat on the floor, the top open.

Her breath quickened as she shone her flashlight inside. More of the crudely carved dolls. The killer had been here. Had Penny been here? Maybe Chrissy, too?

Fear pounded at her chest. Would she find a body in here?

Using her flashlight to illuminate the interior, she spotted another wooden box.

Dread filled her as she slowly approached it, and she mentally catalogued the contents. A yellow plastic hair bow. Hair ribbons. A small birthstone ring. A miniature teddy bear on a key chain. A pop bead necklace. A pair of pink shoelaces...

Dear God. These were things the little girls had with them when they disappeared. Souvenirs.

The sound again. A child's sob.

She had to keep moving. Go deeper into the mine. At least one of the girls was back there.

She crept deeper into the darkness until she reached another small chamber, big enough for her to stand. An empty mattress lay on the floor in one corner.

The walls and floor were bare. Hoping to find some clue, she holstered her gun and searched around the mattress.

A plain brown shoe box had been stuffed between the mattress and the chamber wall. Ellie yanked it out and opened it. Her stomach clenched at the sight of the photographs. Polaroids of the missing children he'd taken, photos of when he'd stalked them. Photos of when they lay dead, eyes open in terror, tiny fingers clutching the little wooden dolls.

Seconds passed as grief rocked through her, and she pressed her hand to her mouth to stifle a wail of sorrow. Wind whipped through the cold interior. Water dripped, echoing in the hollow emptiness. The darkness surrounded her, closing in on her.

Tears of panic threatened, but she slowly blinked them back and dug through the box again. A divider had been placed at the bottom, as if hiding a secret compartment. She tugged at the edge, lifted it and found another photograph. This one was grainy and old, the color faded.

Not a little girl. A picture of a woman holding an infant swaddled in a blue blanket. She flipped the picture over and found a note Hiram had scribbled on the back—"Me and Mom"—along with a date. Ten years before Ellie had come into the world.

Shock struck her as the woman's face registered. Denial swept in on its heels.

The woman in the photograph was Ellie's mother.

CHAPTER EIGHTY-THREE

Ellie rocked back on her heels, stunned. In the photograph, her mother was holding a baby. A little boy named Hiram. She flipped the picture over and read the date again. Was it the day Hiram was born?

Dear God. Hiram was her mother's son.

Shock robbed her breath. As a little girl, she'd begged her parents for a sister or brother. They'd said they couldn't have more children. That she invented Mae to replace the little sister she'd never had.

But she did have a sibling. Hiram.

Was it true? Why hadn't her parents told her?

Where had he been all this time?

The horrid pieces of the puzzle clicked together in sickening clarity... Hiram had abducted the girls. Hiram was the Ghost.

Had her parents known and covered for him? Was that the big secret they were keeping? The reason her father had closed the case on Kim Fox?

Nauseated, she dropped her head between her knees and breathed in and out to keep from throwing up.

Her mother's words taunted her. *I've always done what's best for our family, and I will until the day I die.*

The room swayed. She was suffocating again, the vise around her throat tightening. Forcing air in and out of her lungs, she fumbled for her phone to call for help. But suddenly the sound of rocks skittering shattered the silence.

Yanking her phone from her pocket, she whipped her head around. A man clad in a big coat and black ski cap barreled toward her with a wooden club. She threw her arm up in a defensive maneuver, but he knocked her phone from her hand, then lunged at her.

Pain splintered her wrist as the wooden club connected with bone. "Stop!" she shouted. "It's over. Where are the girls?"

A knife glinted from where it hung at Hiram's belt. He grabbed her but she fought back, ramming a fist into his gut. Grunting, he swung the club against the side of her head.

Her ears rang. The world tilted and spun. She pawed at the ground, hoping to stay upright, but the darkness beckoned her, and she collapsed.

Ghastly images bombarded her like a bad movie trailer. The graves… the little girls' faces crying for help. Penny… Chrissy…

Her mother holding a baby Ellie had never known about.

Fighting to open her eyes, she realized Hiram was dragging her across the cold hard floor. Rocks and dirt scraped her hands and body. Bile clogged her throat. Fear choked her. Her gun was gone—did Hiram have it?

She had to fight anyway. Wake up and find the girls.

Hoping to slow him down, she remained limp, even as she roused back to life. He was big, with a wooly beard and narrow eyes, slits in his craggy face. He looked weathered, ragged, as if life had worn him down.

His voice came out low and sinister. "I knew I'd find you one day," he muttered. "Knew you'd come back to the trail."

He shoved her against the stone wall, breath wheezing out.

She struggled to see though the darkness. "Where are the girls? Are they still alive?"

Ignoring her question, he yanked her by her hair, but she clawed at his hands to free herself.

"Why did you take Penny and the others?" she cried.

He twisted his hand in her hair, pulling it by the roots. "The fosters. All they wanted were the pretty little girls. Just like Mama. She kept you, but she didn't want me!" he bellowed. "No one did."

Ellie's thoughts raced. Derrick mentioned that at least three of the missing girls had been foster children. Had Hiram known them?

She had to keep him talking. "Mom gave you up for adoption?"

"She tossed me into the system like I was a piece of dirty trash. You… *you* lived the good life with Mama and a daddy, too. You had a family, but I had no one."

"I don't understand. Why didn't you find us? Find me?" Ellie asked, desperate to understand. "Why prey on innocent children?"

A little girl's scream drowned out Hiram's garbled reply.

CHAPTER EIGHTY-FOUR

Stony Gap

Knowing Ellie was at the hospital allowed Derrick to grab a few hours of sleep and a hearty breakfast. He'd also talked to the ME about arrangements to have his sister's remains sent to his mother once she'd completed all the necessary testing for the case.

He strode back into the hospital, determined to talk to Ellie, but she wasn't in the waiting room. Assuming she was visiting her father, he approached the nurses' station.

The nurse buzzed him through to the ICU, and he walked straight to the room where Randall lay in bed, a shell of the strong man who'd interrogated him and his family twenty-five years ago. Mrs. Reeves sat in a recliner beside him, worrying her hands together and wiping at tears.

Ellie was nowhere to be seen.

Vera bolted from the chair. "Randall can't be disturbed."

Derrick barely controlled his temper. "Two mothers want their children back, and if I can save them, I intend to. Now step aside before I arrest you for assaulting and threatening an officer, interfering with a police investigation, and as an accomplice to not just one, but multiple homicides."

Shock glazed Vera's expression, and she sank into the recliner like a wounded animal. He ignored the fresh tears in her eyes as he approached Randall's bed.

"Sheriff Reeves," Derrick said. "I want answers."

Randall moaned before opening his eyes, then panic flared on his face.

"Tell me where the missing girls are," Derrick demanded.

Randall's dark brows crinkled. "I don't know."

"Stop lying," Derrick snapped. "What did you do with them?"

"Not me," Randall said in a raspy whisper.

"Randall." Mrs. Reeves clasped her husband's hand. "Don't…"

The sheriff gave his wife a dark look. "Time to tell the truth. Ellie's gone after him."

Vera gasped. "What? You told Ellie?"

"Not everything," Randall choked out. "Just that it was Hiram."

"Who's Hiram?" Derrick asked.

"He took the girls," Randall said. "I've been trying to track him down."

"Who is he?" Derrick asked, more sharply this time.

"No time to explain," Randall growled. "He'll kill Ellie if you don't stop him."

Derrick curled his hands into fists. "Where do I find him?"

"Ellie… map at my office." His voice warbled. He was fading again. "No, no… she probably took it."

"*Where* is he?" Derrick ground out.

"The trail… Cord. Get Cord. He'll take you."

"The trail is thousands of miles long," Derrick said. "What part of it?"

"North of Falcon's Crest," Randall murmured. "He moves around but I spotted him near there last."

Ellie should have called him. Except that he'd arrested her father, and she was probably trying to prove his innocence.

Only he wasn't completely innocent.

"Go find her," Randall wheezed.

Derrick's first instinct was to go barreling onto the trail with guns blazing. But that was stupid. He'd be lost in minutes. And where would that leave Ellie?

Alone with a madman?

As much as he wanted answers, he didn't want her to die. He'd never be able to forgive himself.

Stepping into the hallway, he phoned her. One ring, two, three, then the voicemail picked up. He cursed, ended the call and tried again. "If you get this, call me, Ellie. I'm coming as backup."

After leaving the message, he called McClain and tapped his boot impatiently as he waited for the ranger to answer. McClain might refuse to help him. Derrick had practically accused him of being complicit in Penny's disappearance.

McClain answered abruptly. "Yeah?"

"Randall Reeves said Ellie is in danger from someone named Hiram. She's gone on the trail to hunt him down."

The ranger cursed. "Which way did she go?"

He relayed the name of the place Randall had mentioned. "I know you don't like me, Ranger McClain, but I need a guide on the trail. There's no time to waste."

"Sending you the GPS for the closest entry point to hike into Falcon's Crest now," McClain said. "I'll meet you there."

"Thanks."

"I'm not doing this for you," Cord said gruffly. "I'm doing it for Ellie."

CHAPTER EIGHTY-FIVE

Falcon's Crest

The sound of the child's scream sent hope bolting through Ellie. At least one of the little girls was alive.

She had to get to her.

Find a way to reach Hiram.

But he looked dazed and disoriented. As if a dark, deep-seated madness had overtaken him. He paced back and forth, dragging one leg behind him, his scarred fingers rubbing the tip of the carving knife he held clutched in one hand.

"You don't have to hurt anyone else," Ellie said. "Especially another child."

His right eye drooped slightly as he scowled at her. "Why should I care about them? No one ever cared about me."

"I'm sorry you feel that way," Ellie said. "But I can help you. We can be friends." She had to keep him talking.

"Friends?" he shouted. "You've been hunting me like a dog." He swung the wooden club back and forth, banging it against the rocky floor. "When I went into town, I saw you on the news telling everyone you'd find me. Calling me a coward." His voice rose to a sinister pitch. "You don't want to be my friend. You want to lock me in a cage."

Like he'd locked up the little girls? "No, I want to get to know you," she said softly. "I didn't realize I had a brother, Hiram. I always wanted a sibling, but Mom never told me about you."

His nostrils flared, eye twitching again. "She loved you, but she got rid of me. She didn't tell you because she was ashamed of me, ashamed I was ever born."

Ellie didn't know the whole story. Didn't know why her mother had kept Hiram a secret. Who Hiram's father was. If her mother knew Hiram was a killer… Or why her father would cover for him…

"We'll sort it all out," Ellie said. "We'll make Mom explain everything to both of us. Why she stopped us from being a family all these years."

She glanced down the mine shaft, toward the part of the tunnel where the little girl's cry came from.

"Please, Hiram, the children have nothing to do with us or Mom," Ellie said softly.

"Yes, they do. They took Mama from me." A crazed look glazed his eyes. "And now you're here, you have to die, too."

He lunged toward her, and she shoved him with both hands, swinging around and kicking him in the chest. He slammed the crudely carved club into her side. Pain shot through her ribs, but she fought back. Kicked him again, this time in one knee. With a guttural groan, he knocked her in the head again.

Pain ricocheted through her temple, and she went down, hands scraping the jagged rocks as she tried to push herself back up. She had to fight. She aimed a kick at his balls but he deflected it, grabbed her hair, jerked her head back and punched her in the face. Stars danced in front of her eyes, then she tasted blood as the abyss swallowed her.

Sometime later, she stirred back to life. But she was falling, falling, sliding deeper into the darkness. A little girl's voice called to her. A voice so familiar. One she'd known as a child. One she'd lost. *Help me. Please help me.*

Mae. It was Mae begging her to come back for her. To drag herself from the shadows and find her.

To remember that once they'd been best friends and built forts in the woods and played hide and seek and pretended the little wooden dolls were real…

Ellie jerked back to the present. Her breathing was shallow, pain ricocheting through her skull and ribs. *For God's sake, Mae isn't here.* But at least one of the girls was. Was Penny dead?

And where was Hiram? A mustiness clogged the air, but his cloying scent was gone for the moment.

A whimpering sound echoed from her right, and she turned her head toward the noise. It was so dark she could barely see an inch in front of her. The haunting fear paralyzed her for a moment, transporting her back to when she'd been lost. She'd dug at the dark hole until her fingers were bloody and raw. Had sweated and thought she was suffocating. Had finally given into the terror and… then what?

She didn't remember anything after that. Not even being rescued.

A shrill cry shattered the stillness around her. She wasn't lost or trapped now. But Penny and Chrissy were.

Squinting against the dark, she finally made out the form of two little girls hunched against the wall. They were clinging to each other, rocking back and forth. Relief rushed through her. They were both alive!

Push past the pain. These children need you.

Gritting her teeth, she rolled to her side. Hard to get up when her feet and hands were bound. She'd work on unraveling the knots once she reached the girls.

Ellie pushed to her knees and crawled, scooted toward them, body trembling. "Penny, Chrissy, it's okay. My name is Ellie."

The cries continued but slowed as Penny lifted her little head. Even in the dark, Ellie could see tears glistening on the child's eyes. Chrissy was sobbing in Penny's arms, her head buried against her.

Rage at Hiram for taking so many lives lit a fire inside her, and she crawled the rest of the way. When she reached the girls, she lifted her bound hands and gently covered Penny's hands with her own.

"I'm Ellie, and I'm with the police," she whispered, forcing a smile. "I've been looking everywhere for you."

"I want Mommy," Penny cried.

Chrissy finally looked up at her with red puffy eyes. "Hey, Chrissy," Ellie said softly. "Your mama sent me to find you."

The little girls fell against her, and she murmured soft reassurances. "Shh, sweet girls. I'm going to get us out of here and take you home."

CHAPTER EIGHTY-SIX

Just as Ellie managed to untie her hands, footsteps shuffled across the rocky floor, and suddenly the space was filled with Hiram's musty odor again.

He was humming, "Hush little baby, don't say a word. Mama's gonna buy you a mockingbird…"

The girls buried themselves against her, their bodies racked with fear.

"All the pretty little girls get chosen," he muttered as his shadow moved toward them. "All the pretty little girls have to die to make the mamas suffer."

Ellie trembled inwardly but put on a brave face for the terrified children. In his twisted mind, Hiram justified his actions. But there was no justification for his cruelty.

Brother or not, she didn't intend to let him kill these sweet girls.

Brushing her hand over the dirt floor, she searched for something to use as a weapon. Something sharp jabbed her fingers. A rock.

Desperate, she closed her fingers around it and gripped the jagged stone between her fingers. Hiram shuffled closer, his awkward gait shattering the silence.

"Stay against the wall," she whispered to the girls. "When I go for him, run past and get out of here. And don't stop running."

Although even if they got out of the mine, how would they survive the brutal storm and wilderness?

She couldn't think about that. There was no other choice.

Cord would keep looking. So would Derrick. She had to believe they'd find them.

"It's time now," Hiram said, venom in his voice. "Time to bury them."

Ellie held her breath until he was closer to her. Then she lunged at him. She punched him in the stomach with all her might, then swung the rock up into his face.

"Run!" she ordered the girls as he staggered backward.

The little girls screamed and jumped up, but Hiram dove for them. Penny shrieked as he grabbed her leg, and Ellie pounced on him, pummeling him with her fists. Howling, he threw her off him. Ellie's head hit the chamber wall and pain splintered her temple.

Before she could recover, he struck her across the face. Once. Twice. Three times. Jerking her by the shoulders, he slammed her head against the rock again. The world swayed and blurred. Pain tore through her skull. A voice inside whispered for her to fight, but he slammed her head against the stone again, and she blacked out.

Monsters chased her through the forest, clawing at her, pulling her so hard she couldn't climb from the dark tunnel. The whisper of a child's voice shattered the deafening silence. A little girl's cry. Slowly, she struggled through the hollow darkness. There had to be light somewhere. She had to reach it. The girls needed her.

Finally rousing herself back to life, she realized Hiram was tying her wrists together. Penny and Chrissy were sobbing from somewhere in the dark.

She kicked at Hiram, but her feet were tied, and he jumped back, dodging the blow.

Then he stomped her in the stomach with his boot and she doubled over in agony. He ran for the girls, sweeping up one terrified child in each arm. The girls screamed and cried, kicking at him and beating at him with their tiny fists, but he seemed unfazed by the blows.

"Don't hurt them!" Ellie shouted.

But his feet shuffled through the tunnel into the darkness, disappearing. Terrified, she crawled after him on her stomach. She reached another chamber, and saw Hiram force the girls into a hole in the ground. Their cries reverberated through the rocky interior.

A second later, he covered the hole with a large wooden board and hammered it into place. Ellie yanked at her bindings, struggling to free her hands. His sinister laugh ripped through the air as he stalked toward her and struck her again. Nausea climbed her throat as he yanked her by her hair and dragged her back through the mine, outside into the frigid cold.

CHAPTER EIGHTY-SEVEN

The sound of wings flapping above the trees broke the silence, the raspy hiss of vultures fighting and grunting like hungry pigs.

Derrick stilled for a moment, trying to discern where they were and praying the birds weren't feasting on a human. Cord pointed east and Derrick followed, fear pulsing through him. Before they'd set off, he'd asked Cord if he had a weapon.

"I thought you didn't trust me," Cord had said in a deep growl.

He didn't know if he did. "Like you said, we're in this together for Ellie."

The ranger had stared at him for a long minute, then gestured toward the knife at his belt. "This is all I need."

It was a serious hunting knife, which raised Derrick's doubts again. But if Cord came upon Hiram first, he didn't want the monster to escape. And he had no doubt Cord would kill the man if he'd hurt Ellie.

Tree limbs sagged and cracked from the weight of the snow and ice as they hiked. Minutes ticked away, a reminder that if Ellie and the girls were still alive, time might be running out for them.

With every step, Derrick's boots sank deeper into the freshly fallen snow, and the fierce winds beat at his body.

The frigid temperatures only intensified his fear, tormenting him with unwanted images of finding Penny and Chrissy dead, as he had Kim.

And Ellie. *Dammit to hell.* He didn't want to care about her. He'd promised himself he would have nothing to do with her when the case was done. That if her father was complicit, and she'd covered for him, he'd lock her up, too.

But… he didn't think she'd known. He'd read the devastation and disbelief on her face. No one could fake that kind of blind shock and sense of betrayal.

She must be desperate to have come out here by herself.

And she was all alone, facing a depraved psycho who would kill her without a second thought.

Of course she didn't call you for backup. You arrested her father and implied she'd slept with you as a distraction.

He'd fucked up big time.

"That way." Cord pointed toward a ridge so steep it would normally make Derrick turn around. Below it, the creek water was rising, threatening to overflow.

He'd never backed down from a killer or a gun aimed at him, and he wouldn't start now. Not with two children's lives at stake.

When they reached Falcon's Crest, Derrick saw a rock formation that looked like the wings of a bird of prey, presumably where the name came from.

Both men started searching the vegetation and trail for signs of footprints, or… blood.

A crushed clump of weeds. Trampled vines. A boot print in the snow. Large, a man's. Then a smaller one.

He and Cord exchanged looks, silently agreeing to follow the prints. The smaller prints were smeared in places, indicating Ellie had slipped. Cord spotted a clump of vines that had been hacked away, and Derrick saw branches and brush tossed into a pile on the ground.

The wind battered the tall pines, sending pine needles, melting snow and ice raining down on them. Derrick moved toward the pile of foliage. Someone had moved it and uncovered the opening of a mineshaft.

Ellie.

He motioned to Cord to stand guard while he checked it out. Derrick pulled his flashlight and held his gun at the ready as he inched inside the mine. Keeping his footfalls light, he paused at every turn and listened for sounds of someone inside.

Nothing. No voices or cries for help.

His stomach clenched. That could mean no one was here. Or they were already dead.

No. He had to find Ellie and the girls alive. Make up for the mess he'd made by letting his emotions get in the way.

Save the girls, because he'd failed to save his sister.

Shining his light along the interior of the space, he searched the floors and walls and found a chamber with a mattress. An open box on the ground was full of pictures of the victims.

Kim's photograph was in there, but he didn't, *couldn't*, take time to dwell on it.

He had to find Hiram and stop him once and for all.

Maneuvering the next few feet of the tunnel, he found another room with a blanket, along with rope and food wrappers in a pile. Ellie's gun lay to the side, indicating she'd been here and lost it. He picked it up, checked the safety then stowed it in his jacket pocket.

It looked like there was another chamber further down the shaft. He moved towards it, but heard Cord call his name. "Agent Fox. Out here!"

He hurried back to the entrance of the mine shaft and saw the ranger peering through binoculars. "Over there. I see something."

CHAPTER EIGHTY-EIGHT

Ellie fought to rouse herself, but her eyes felt heavy, her head was throbbing, and every muscle in her body ached. Where were the girls?

She managed to open one eye. But it was so dark she couldn't see more than an inch in front of her. The suffocating sensation paralyzed her. Breathing grew impossible. She opened her mouth to drag in air, but Hiram had gagged her. Her hands and feet were still bound, the ropes clawing at her wrists. Still, she wriggled, searching for the girls. For an escape.

Although now… she remembered.

The hole… He'd shoved the girls in a hole in the mine floor and covered it with boards.

Then he'd dragged her into the woods. The cold ground beneath her felt soft. Not like the floor of the mine shaft. Dirt. Brush. Snow.

"I like to dig holes," he'd said. "And hide things inside."

She'd screamed at him to release the girls, but he'd stuffed the rag into her mouth and slapped her so hard her head snapped backward. Then she'd passed out again. And now she was outside. Frigid air stung her face and darkness surrounded her.

Get out of here. Penny and Chrissy need you.

She struggled to move. But suddenly something soft and wet hit her in the face again. Then more of the same. Pebbles and dirt. Wet frozen earth and snow. She closed her eyes as it lashed her. Felt the heavy blanket of sludge on her body. Covering her legs and arms. Seeping through her clothes. Icy crystals stinging her cheeks.

A terror-filled breath escaped her as the truth dawned on her.

Oh, God… she wasn't in the mine shaft. She was in the ground. He'd dug a grave and was burying her alive.

CHAPTER EIGHTY-NINE

Derrick crouched low as he inched closer to the area where Cord had spotted a figure. Peering through the tall weeds and vines, he scanned the woods and clearing for Ellie or the girls. He'd never seen so much snow and ice in his life.

But he didn't see Ellie or the girls.

Instead, a man was humming as he shoveled dirt and snow, making a hole.

Fear sliced through him, and he squinted to see if the man had a gun, but it was impossible to tell.

With a flick of his hand, he motioned to Cord that Hiram was straight ahead. The ranger crept to the left while Derrick moved right.

Seconds felt like minutes as they inched closer. Hiram seemed lost in his task and was mumbling something incoherent as he jammed the shovel into the ground, scooped up more of the frost-bitten dirt and tossed it into the hole. *A grave—he's filling a grave.*

Derrick wove through the bushes. Whoever was inside that hole was half-buried already.

Penny? Chrissy? Ellie?

Was he too late?

Focusing on his target, he raised his gun and moved quickly into the clearing. "FBI. Drop the shovel!"

But he'd misjudged—gotten too close. Hiram spun around, swung the shovel at Derrick and knocked the gun from his hand. The gun fired, bullet pinging into the air. Then Hiram lunged toward him.

Determined to stop him, Derrick rammed his head into the man's face. Hiram made an animal sound and stumbled backward, his grip on the shovel loosening. Derrick took advantage, jerked the shovel away from him and punched the creep in the face. Blood spurted from the man's nose, and he shoved at Derrick, but Derrick hit him so hard Hiram's head lolled back. He fell like a tree, knocked cold.

"Ellie!" Cord shouted her name over and over as he dropped to his knees and started digging at the grave. If Ellie was under there and still alive, she could suffocate. A fist-sized knot clogging his throat, Derrick left Hiram and raced to help Cord.

He leaned over the edge of the hole and began to dig away the dirt with his hands. They couldn't risk injuring her with the shovel, but how deep was she? Cord was raking the dirt away as fast as he could, repeatedly yelling Ellie's name.

Ellie could be asphyxiating now. Or already dead.

Sweat beaded on Derrick's neck as he worked, digging away layers of debris. Twigs, wet slush, twigs and fallen leaves. Ice. Snow. Another layer.

"Come on, El!" Cord shouted.

A noise sounded behind Derrick. Brush and leaves crunching. He turned to see Hiram diving at him with a rock in his hand. Derrick rolled sideways to dodge the blow, raised his foot and kicked Hiram in the belly.

Hiram recovered quickly and yanked Derrick backwards, but Derrick kicked him in the face. "Keep digging!" he shouted to Cord.

Hiram came at him again, and they traded blow for blow, rolling across the frozen ground. A hard punch to his stomach made Derrick grunt, but he whipped Hiram backward with another blow to his gut, then another to his face. Blood dripped from the man's nose and cheek. His eyes were wild. Crazed.

The eyes of a killer.

This man had taken Kim's life. His little sister had been innocent and sweet and trusting. Now she was dead.

Years of pent-up rage and grief fueled his temper. He grabbed Hiram's arms and swept his legs, slamming him against the ground. The need for revenge intensified his strength and he straddled Hiram, punching him again and again.

Hiram tried to buck him off, but Derrick pinned him down and continued to beat him. More blood. The man's mouth went slack. His body gave way beneath Derrick. Legs went limp. Arms fell to his sides.

All those innocent children's faces flashed behind Derrick's eyes. Kim's. The futures they had stolen from them by this monster.

Kim might have been married by now. Had a career. A family. His father might still be alive.

So many families destroyed. So many broken hearts and homes. The urge to kill Hiram was so strong, he hit him again. Hiram didn't deserve to live.

He raised his fist to punch the man again, but Cord shouted, "I've got Ellie! Call an ambulance!"

Cord's shout broke through Derrick's tirade. The ranger was lifting Ellie from the grave. Dirt covered her and her body was limp. Derrick's blood turned hot with fury and the need to kill Hiram intensified. But his mother's anguished face flashed behind his eyes. She'd lost Kim. Would she want him to murder Hiram and spend the rest of his life in jail?

No… he couldn't do that to her. If he killed Hiram, he'd be no better than the twisted man who'd taken Kim from them.

Cursing, he pulled himself up. He handcuffed the man, then snagged his phone and called for an ambulance.

By the time he crossed to Cord, the ranger had lain Ellie on the ground and was checking for a pulse.

Derrick held his breath as he waited. Cord's grim expression matched his tone. "She's not breathing. Get a blanket from my backpack." Derrick scrambled to retrieve the blanket while Cord started CPR.

"What about the girls?" Derrick asked.

Cord shook his head. "They weren't in there."

Derrick's pulse jumped. Were they too late to save Penny and Chrissy?

CHAPTER NINETY

"Come on, Ellie, breathe for me."

The sound of Cord's voice drifted through Ellie's mind as she floated up from the darkness. She gasped for a breath and jerked her eyes open to see him hovering over her. His hands were on her chest, but he lifted them and raked her hair from her face. Worry darkened his amber eyes, softening the angry lines.

"You're okay now, El, you're okay," he murmured.

Her mind raced to play catch-up. Memories of the last few hours rolled past in slow motion, jumbled in her head. But slowly she sorted through them. She'd been looking for Hiram. For Penny and Chrissy. Her skin crawled. She tasted dirt. Felt it on her clothes. Her skin. In her hair.

"Hiram," she murmured.

"Hiram's unconscious. Handcuffed." This time it was Derrick speaking. He stood beside her, looking down, his expression filled with anger and other emotions she couldn't read.

"Medics are on the way," Derrick said. "Where are the girls?"

"Oh, God, Penny and Chrissy!" Ellie pushed herself up. "I have to find them."

"They're still alive?" Derrick asked.

"They were when he dragged me out here." She pushed to her feet, swayed slightly, then steadied herself and slogged through the snow toward the mine shaft.

Derrick and Cord chased after her. "Wait, Ellie, let me go!" Derrick shouted.

Cord yelled at her, too. "I'll help."

But Ellie couldn't wait. The girls needed her.

Lungs straining for air, she kept running. Her chest ached as she battled the memory of being buried. The darkness was back. She hated the dark.

Get Penny and Chrissy! Don't give up now.

Determined, she darted into the dark mine shaft. For a brief second, she paused to adjust to the light. To remember where she'd been and where Hiram had taken the girls. She ran down the tunnel, following it until she reached the room where Hiram had first held them. But they weren't there.

Waves of dizziness threatened to bring her to the ground, but she blinked and struggled through it. He'd hit her… knocked her out… then he'd scooped up the girls and carried them deeper into the cave.

Remembering crawling after them, she followed the tunnel toward the next room, shining her flashlight around the interior until she spotted the wooden board on the floor. Dropping to her knees, she yanked at it, but it refused to budge, and splinters jabbed her skin.

"Hang in there, Penny, Chrissy, I'm coming!"

Footsteps pounded toward her. Derrick's voice. "Ellie?"

"Here," she yelled. "I need a tool, something to pry this board loose. Hiram nailed it down."

Derrick rounded the corner then knelt beside her, pulled a knife from his pocket and began to work to loosen the board. She pulled at it as Derrick freed the nails. They removed the cover and exposed a hole the size of a small room. "Penny? Chrissy? It's Ellie."

The little girls whimpered, clinging to each other. A suffocating dizziness overcame Ellie, and she swayed again as she tried to breathe through the claustrophobia.

Derrick laid a hand on her shoulder. "I've got it." He leaned over the edge of the opening. "Penny, can you crawl to me, sweetie."

"No, Ellie," the little girl said in a tiny whisper.

Dammit. Ellie cursed her weakness. She didn't have time to indulge her phobia now. Penny and Chrissy had been traumatized, and they trusted her.

"I can do it," she murmured. She held her breath and leaned into the hole, but suddenly Mae was there. Mae holding the dolls. Calling out to Ellie for help.

Mae huddled in the dark with tears streaking her cheeks. Mae begging her to save her.

The world blurred. Bile burned her throat. She dropped her head into her hands and groaned, blinking away the image.

Derrick's hand squeezed her shoulder. "Ellie, are you okay?"

She nodded, although she wasn't okay. But she had to keep going, so she summoned her courage and lowered herself inside the hole. The scent of dirt and the rotting wood buttresses assaulted her, along with Hiram's musty odor.

Penny whimpered again and Chrissy sobbed, forcing Ellie to stoop down in front of them.

"Come on, girls, it's all right now." She pulled them both into a hug, their little bodies quivering against her. "I'm going to take you back to your mommies."

"What about that big mean man?" Chrissy asked between sobs.

Ellie rubbed their backs. "You don't have to worry about him anymore," she said softly. "Now, just do as I say, and we'll get out of here. Okay?"

"Okay," the girls whispered.

"First you, Penny." Penny wrapped her arms around Ellie's neck, and Ellie lifted her. "I'm going to hoist you up," she told Penny. "The man up there, his name is Derrick. He's my friend, and here to help. He'll pull you up, then I'll lift Chrissy."

Tears trickled down Penny's face, dampening Ellie's clothes, but the little girl looped her arms around Ellie's neck.

"Derrick," Ellie called. "I've got her. I'm going to lift her up."

"Got it." Derrick sprawled onto his stomach and leaned over the edge of the opening, reaching down inside the space.

Still weak from her earlier ordeal, Ellie's muscles strained, pain stabbing her ribs with every breath, as she lifted Penny toward the opening. Derrick clasped the little girl's arms and pulled her up. Pausing for a fortifying breath, Ellie ignored her aching body and lifted Chrissy.

After both girls were up, Derrick helped Ellie from the hole. Then Ellie wrapped her arms around the children.

"I've got you, girls." She brushed her thumb across each of the girls' cheeks. "Now we're going home."

CHAPTER NINETY-ONE

As soon as they made it out of the cave, Cord brought blankets and they wrapped the girls in them. Ellie quickly examined the children to see if they were hurt, but except for scraped fingers and broken nails where they'd probably tried to dig their way out of the hole, neither girl had any visible injuries.

Ellie soothed them with soft words, rocking the girls in her arms as they waited on the medics. "Did he hurt you?" Ellie asked.

Penny shook her head. "I was just scared. He wouldn't take me home."

Chrissy's lower lip quivered. "He was big and smelled bad, and he told me to shut up."

Penny tugged at Ellie's sleeve. "He yelled at me not to be a crybaby."

Ellie's heart clenched. The girls looked physically okay but would need counseling to overcome the ordeal. She prayed that being taken didn't traumatize them for the rest of their lives.

God knows, she understood what it was like to be paralyzed with fear at times.

Cord stood by silently while Derrick made certain Hiram was still handcuffed.

"You'll be home soon," Ellie said in a soft voice. "And that man can't ever get you again. I promise."

"He called me Mae," Penny said. "I told him my name was Penny, but he made me say Mae, that that was my name."

Ellie's heart stuttered. *Mae?*

"He said that to me, too," Chrissy said in a small voice.

Ellie closed her eyes, stunned and confused. Mentally, she tried to piece together the truth about what had happened. Hiram was her mother's son. Her half-brother. He'd called Penny and Chrissy Mae.

Mae was the name of her imaginary friend. When Mae disappeared, Ellie had cried endlessly, had nightmares for months.

What if… what if Mae was real? What if Mae was her best friend or even her sister and Hiram had done something to her? What if Mae was Hiram's first victim?

CHAPTER NINETY-TWO

Stony Gap

On the way to the hospital, Ellie phoned Captain Hale and filled him in on what had happened. They arrived just after 8 p.m. Angelica and her cameraman rushed toward them, capturing their images as the girls were brought into the ER and reunited with their families.

Still shaken and her body aching, Ellie stepped aside for the emotional reunion. Her eye was swelling, her ribs hurting from the beating she'd taken. Her head wound had opened again, and the bruising around her other eye from the Dugan farm was still livid.

"Penny!" Stan and Susan ran toward the little blonde girl and swept her into a hug, the three of them crying as their daughter hugged Toby the teddy to her.

Mr. Larkin enveloped his wife and daughter into his arms.

"My precious Chrissy," Mrs. Larkin sobbed as she closed her arms around Chrissy. "I was so scared, baby."

Out of respect for the parents, Derrick was waiting for the families to go back to the exam rooms before he allowed the medics to bring Hiram in. His face was beaten badly, and he was still unconscious.

Penny's parents looked over at Ellie. "Thank you," Susan said, still clinging to Penny.

Stan looked contrite, tears in his eyes. "Yes, thank you, Detective. You saved our family."

Emotions overwhelmed Ellie, robbing her of her voice.

Mrs. Larkin's eyes were filled with turmoil—she regretted her outburst, but she would do it again. Ellie shrugged it off. If she'd been in the woman's shoes, there was no telling how she would have reacted.

She was just grateful she'd found the girls alive.

Angelica skimmed her gaze over Ellie and seemed shocked at her appearance. Ellie hadn't thought about what she looked like. Her face was bloody, bruised, her clothes wet and damp from being thrown in that hole. Dirt and snow were embedded in her hair, and mud streaked her face and hands.

"Detective Reeves," Angelica said. "Please tell us about the harrowing rescue of Penny Matthews and Chrissy Larkin."

Ellie offered her a tentative smile. Her head and body ached, and as the adrenaline wore off, she felt weak in the knees. She also had more questions that needed answering.

But she couldn't avoid the press forever. Maybe knowing Hiram had been arrested would ease the panic in town. "Today we tracked down the man who adducted both Penny Matthews and Chrissy Larkin. The girls are now being reunited with their parents. We believe the man we have in custody is the person responsible for the kidnappings and deaths of nearly a dozen other children." She heaved a breath. "At the moment, that is all the information I have to share. As soon as I tie up loose ends, have time to question the perpetrator, and analyze forensics, I will make an official statement."

Angelica's gaze met hers, an understanding passing between them. Ellie had promised Angelica an exclusive, and she would give it to her.

The girls were inside now, and the medics wheeled an unconscious Hiram in. His face was bruised and bloody, his clothing torn, and his nose looked broken. In spite of how Derrick must feel about the man, he shielded him from the cameraman.

When Hiram regained consciousness, she planned to interrogate him until he told them where he'd left the other girls' bodies. But she wanted all the facts. If Hiram was her brother, her *mother's* child, she had to verify it.

Angelica lowered the microphone and motioned for the cameraman to put away the camera. "You look like you need to be examined yourself, Detective."

Ellie shook her head. The physical pain she could handle. But she needed the truth. And she was damn well going to find it.

CHAPTER NINETY-THREE

Ellie hurried to the ICU. According to the nurse, her father was in a deep sleep from a fresh injection of pain meds and her mother had gone home to shower.

One of the crime scene investigators had volunteered to drive her SUV home from the trail, so Ellie left the hospital and Ubered to her parents' house. Vera's car was not in the drive when she arrived. The lights outside were off, but a lamp glowed in the den. Her last confrontation with her mother teased her mind. She'd threatened to arrest her.

She still might have to. But first she wanted an explanation.

Why had Hiram talked about Mae when her parents insisted Ellie had invented the little girl?

"Mom?" she called out as she walked through the downstairs. No answer, only a hollow emptiness that mirrored how she felt right now.

If Hiram was her mother's son and Vera had known what he'd been doing all these years, there had to be some evidence to prove her parents' involvement, or their innocence.

If she'd known Hiram was a predator, how could Vera live with herself?

Her earlier search in her father's office and workroom had yielded nothing, so she raced up the steps to her parents' bedroom. She paused at the doorway, the sense she was violating their privacy so overwhelming that for a moment she hesitated. Didn't know if she could go inside.

But hadn't they violated her with their deceit?

Betrayal knifed through her and she pushed through the door. She searched her mother's dresser drawers and closet. Nothing. She noticed a small chest shoved in the back of the closet and tried to open it.

Locked.

She went to her mother's jewelry box and found a key beneath her mother's pearls. She unlocked the chest. Inside, she found a shawl and handmade blanket, then her mother's wedding veil. Emotions thickened her throat, and she started to close the chest, but something in the bottom caught her eye.

Her fingers trembled as she lifted the wedding veil and laid it on the floor, a chilling sense of déjà vu striking again.

A hand carved little wooden doll lay inside the chest. Just like the dolls she'd found in the graves and on her doorstep.

A wave of nausea engulfed her, blurring her vision, and she began to tremble. Mae… she was there. Mae holding the little doll…

Dear God. What was going on?

Pulling herself back together, she inhaled and focused again. An envelope lay below the doll, along with a journal of drawings she recognized. The childhood sketches Ellie had done in therapy. She hadn't realized her mother had kept some of them.

Flipping open the journal, she thumbed through the entries. Her childlike pictures depicted her and Mae playing in the woods, building a fort, having picnics, chasing fireflies. The two of them running hand in hand through the creek. Playing hide and seek. Swinging from the tire swing by the river.

Another showed her standing on their back porch staring into the thicket of trees beyond the house. Her face looked sad and frightened, as if she wanted to go after Mae, but was too terrified of the monsters living in the woods to venture off the porch. Another showed her huddled in a dark cave, her arms around her knees as she fought her fear of the dark. And another—she was combing the tombstones in the graveyard, looking for a marker with Mae's name on it.

The other scenes were of her nightmares. Or had they been memories? She no longer knew what to believe.

Trembling, she opened the envelope and discovered a photograph of a little blonde-haired girl. The picture looked exactly like her.

But when she flipped it over, the name Mae was scribbled on the back.

Dear God. Mae *was* real. A tremble started deep inside her and wouldn't let go. Was Mae her twin sister?

Shock cut through her, sharp and painful. Her parents insisted she'd invented Mae.

They'd forced her to attend counseling, medicated her for depression and hallucinations. Let her think something was wrong with her. That she was crazy.

Reeling with the revelation, she snatched the doll and picture, grabbed the keys to her father's truck in the kitchen, rushed outside and climbed in. More snow pelted the windshield, falling in a sheet of white again. Tiny ice crystals looked like spiderwebs on the glass.

Cranking up the defroster and the wipers, she peeled down the drive toward the hospital.

CHAPTER NINETY-FOUR

Back at the hospital, Ellie found her mother hovering by her father's side. She must have passed her on the road to her parents' house.

"My God, Ellie, you look terrible," her mother gasped.

Ellie shrugged. She didn't care how she looked. She could clean up and rest later.

Her father's coloring looked better, and he was breathing on his own. When he opened his eyes and looked at her, a depth of turmoil and regret lined his pale face.

Her mother started to stand, but Ellie raised a warning hand. "Don't bother to tell me to leave. I'm not going anywhere until I get some answers." She removed the wooden doll from her pocket and twisted it between her fingers. "In case you're wondering, we found the missing little girls."

"I know, Bryce told us," her mother said in a raspy whisper.

"Thank God." Her father heaved.

"We found Hiram, too," Ellie said, grateful her voice didn't crack.

A tense heartbeat passed. Her mother clenched the edge of her chair. "Is he… alive?"

Ellie didn't bother to hide the disdain from her voice. "Banged up, but yeah. He'll be on his way to jail once he's cleaned up in the ER."

Tears filled her mother's eyes. Ellie had no sympathy. There were too many lies. "A wooden doll like this one was found in each grave." Her ribs ached as she released a painful breath. "But I found this one in your bedroom chest, Mom."

Vera made a strangled sound, covering her mouth with her hands.

"Listen, El…" Her father gripped the bed rails to sit up but was so weak he collapsed against the pillow.

"Stop lying to me," Ellie said through gritted teeth. "I found this, too." She pulled out the picture of her mother and Hiram, then the photograph of Mae. "I know Hiram is your son, Mother. He said you gave him up for adoption. That you threw him away and nobody wanted him." She pressed her hand over her heart, disbelief and hurt thickening her throat. "And Mae? You said she wasn't real. You made me feel like I was crazy. You sent me to a therapist for years and gave me drugs to forget her, but she was real. How could you do that to me?"

"It's not what you think," her father rasped.

"Please, Ellie, everything I did was to protect you," her mother choked out.

"Really?" Ellie cried. "Because it seems like you gave Hiram up as a baby, then when he started murdering little girls, you covered it up."

Her mother shook her head in denial, tears flowing now. Her father cleared his throat. "Ellie, please, let us explain."

"Explain why you lied to me my entire life? Why you allowed Hiram to murder nearly a dozen little girls? Why you told me Mae wasn't real when she was?" She slapped the photograph. "Who was she? Was she my sister? My twin? Another sibling you gave away and didn't tell me about?" Horror edged her voice. "Did Hiram kill Mae, too?"

Tension filled the air as her parents exchanged a silent look. "Vera, talk to her," her father wheezed out.

"Tell me the truth about Mae," Ellie demanded. "Is she dead? Was she Hiram's first victim?"

Tears rained down her mother's face. "She was," her mother cried. "But… Mae survived. Your father saved her."

Ellie stared at her mother in disbelief.

"Then where is she?"

CHAPTER NINETY-FIVE

Anxiety pulled at every muscle in Ellie's body. Her head throbbed. Exhaustion mingled with desperation to know the truth.

A sudden calmness seemed to wash over her mother, and she swiped at her eyes. Her lower lip trembled and she averted her gaze.

"Tell me, Mom," Ellie demanded. "I need to know."

A heartbeat of silence passed. Finally, her mother inhaled sharply and looked at her. "Mae is not dead, darling."

Ellie remained still, waiting, her breath frozen in her chest. She was afraid to hear the truth. But she had to know.

"Then who was she?" Her voice rose an octave. "Was she my twin sister? Did Hiram take her?"

Vera shook her head slowly, sorrow darkening her eyes. "Hiram did take her, but not because she was your sister." Her voice broke. "Ellie, Mae was you."

Her mother's words ping-ponged around in Ellie's head. She had to have heard wrong.

"I… wh… what do you mean? *I'm* Mae?"

Her father moaned, then finally found his voice. It was thick with pain, medication and regret, but he began to talk. "It's a long story, Ellie. Your mother gave birth to Hiram long before you were born."

Confusion marred Ellie's mind. What did Mae have to do with Hiram being her mother's son?

Vera sniffed, staring at her hands. Her nails were chipped now, the polish peeling off. "You have to understand what it was like for me. I was only seventeen and my parents were so upset with me. Your grandfather threatened to disown me if I kept the baby. I didn't see how I could raise a child on my own."

"Where was Hiram's father?" Ellie asked. "Who was he?"

Vera made a pained sound. "Just a boy I had a teenage crush on. He ran off once I told him I was pregnant." Tears laced Vera's words. "So, I gave Hiram up for adoption. I… thought it was better for him. That he'd have a better life." She wiped at her tears. "It was the hardest thing I've ever done, Ellie. I couldn't stop thinking about him and wondering where he was and if he was happy. A nurse took that photo for me, and it went with Hiram to the orphanage."

Ellie shifted, struggling for understanding. But she was too shocked and hurt to think about anything other than the fact her parents had lied to her.

"A couple of times I thought about looking for him, but my father forbade it. Then… eventually I figured Dad was right, that Hiram was better off in a stable family with two parents who loved him. Mama kept saying that it was best for him, and best for me. That one day when I was old enough and married, I could have another child, a respectable family." She dabbed at her eyes. "When we brought you home, Ellie, I tried to make up for what I'd done by being a good mother to you."

Shame reddened her mother's cheeks. "Later, Hiram somehow found us. You were five. He saw you playing outside near the woods, and he lured you away with those wooden dolls he was obsessed with making."

Memories flooded Ellie, taking her back to that night she got lost. "He said he had more dolls, and a dollhouse," she whispered. "I crawled into a tunnel with him to see it."

Her father made a strangled sound. "When I realized you were gone, I looked for you for hours. Your mom was hysterical. I followed your tracks and finally found you in that cave the next morning." He wheezed a breath. "You were traumatized when I carried you out, almost catatonic. You didn't speak for days. Wouldn't eat and couldn't sleep. But you kept saying the word Hiram."

"The therapist said you repressed the memory, that it was your way of protecting yourself," her mother said, filling in as her father dragged in a breath.

Vera laid her hand on the bed, and she and her father clasped hands. "After that, you were terrified of the dark," her mother continued with a faraway look on her face. "You had nightmares and cried all the time. Then you kept talking about Mae, saying you saw her in the woods, that you played with her. That you built forts with her and chased fireflies with her and whispered secrets to her in your bed." Her mother's voice caught. "You talked about her as if she was someone else, as if she was your playmate."

All those nightmares she'd had… they were memories, things that had really happened.

"We tried to convince you that you didn't have a playmate named Mae, then one day we found you wandering the cemetery looking for her. That was… horrible," her mother cried. "The counselor said you were so traumatized that you suffered from dissociation. After discussing the situation with her, we decided it was better if you didn't remember. That's when we—"

"Decided to go along with me and tell me Mae wasn't real." Ellie's head swam. "That she was my imaginary friend."

"We thought it was better than telling you that your brother tried to hurt you," her mother said. "That if we hadn't found you, he might have killed you because of what I'd done. We didn't want you to have to live with that fact."

"But that was unethical," Ellie said. "A therapist is supposed to help you deal with the truth, not lie to you."

"She did what we asked to protect you," Vera insisted.

"I searched for Hiram that day he lured you into that cave," her father said. "I chased him, but he got away."

"We were terrified he'd come back to find you," her mother said. "So we moved. Changed our names. Changed yours. That way if he came looking, he'd never know where you were."

Ellie's head hurt. Her heart hurt. She couldn't wrap her mind around it all.

"The next year, when Kim Fox went missing, I wasn't sure it was Hiram, but I did investigate," her father said. "I hit a dead end, though, and the leads didn't pan out. But I never gave up."

Ellie's anger was swiftly followed by pain. "You accused Derrick's father, and then Derrick, of hurting Kim, when all along you suspected Hiram? How could you?"

"We didn't know for sure," her mother said. "Hiram had a way of disappearing, like a—"

"Ghost," Ellie said. "Just like Angelica said."

Her father reached for her hand, but Ellie shook her head. She didn't want to be near her parents and their deceit.

"I kept looking, all this time. That's why I had that file," her father continued. "Why I followed up with the detectives who worked the other girls' disappearances."

"You could have asked for help," Ellie said. "Worked with the FBI. Told them about Hiram. Sent his picture around."

"That's the reason I became sheriff of Bluff County, Ellie," her father went on. "I looked for a small town where we could blend in. I'd been a cop before, and when the sheriff suddenly died in Stony Gap, my superior recommended me as a replacement here. He had connections that helped me set up a new identity, and his sister was on the town council in Stony Gap. She convinced them I could run the county. I did it all to protect you and be privy to any information about cases that might be connected. I wanted to stop him."

"It's also the reason we didn't want you to run for sheriff," her mother said emphatically. "We were afraid if Hiram was looking for you that he'd recognize you in the press."

"And he was looking for me all this time," Ellie argued. "He replaced me with Kim Fox. And the others. He kept killing because he wanted to kill *me*."

"I know, and I'm sorry." Vera laid her hand on her chest. "You were my daughter and I had to protect you. And he was my blood. I had to take care of him, too."

Pain stabbed at Ellie, ripping at her composure, and she slowly backed away. She'd let the police, the FBI, deal with her parents. For now, she had to leave. Couldn't stand to be in the same room with them. To listen to the justification for their lies.

To know that Derrick's sister and all the others had died because of her. That so many families had suffered because her parents had chosen to protect her.

She had to make things right. But how could she? There was no way to bring back those children and give them the life that had been stolen from them.

Sick to her stomach, she jumped up, running from the room. But she bumped into Bryce in the hall. He caught her by the arm. "Ellie?"

She jerked away from him. "Leave me alone."

"Talk to me."

So he could run and tell everything to Angelica? No way. The past few hours had taken their toll. Too many secrets. Too many lies. "Fuck off."

Tears blurred her eyes, and she turned and ran down the hall. She didn't stop until she was outside the hospital.

Then she threw up in the bushes, and let the tears fall.

CHAPTER NINETY-SIX

Five days later

March 10, 4:00 p.m., near Atlanta

Derrick stood beside his mother, his arm around her shoulders as she leaned into him. Someone had placed purple wildflowers on his sister's grave. Ellie's comment about the meaning of the flowers at Hemlock Holler whispered through his mind. The angels were welcoming Kim home.

But who had put the flowers on the grave? Ellie?

Or the same person who'd buried the bones?

The flowers hadn't been here yesterday, when he and his mother had the memorial for his sister. His parents' friends had all shown up, but now it was just the two of them saying their final goodbyes.

His mother traced her fingers along the angel carving on the gray tombstone, engraved with Kim's name, and the words *Loving Daughter and Sister, Gone Too Soon*. Wiping her damp cheeks with a tissue, she knelt and placed Kim's locket on top of the cross.

When she finally turned back to Derrick, a smile softened her face. "Thank you so much for finding her, son. For bringing her back home."

Anguish threatened to overcome him. "It's my fault she's gone."

She cupped his face in her delicate hands. "Don't do that. You loved your sister and Kim knew that. It's time to let go of the guilt."

"I don't know if I can," he admitted gruffly.

"You have to. Kim would want you to be happy, Derrick. To find peace and love in your life."

He hadn't thought about love, hadn't thought he needed it. Or that he deserved it. Had been too focused on unearthing the truth about Kim. And then he'd stumbled on the connections and focused on tracking down a serial killer.

Hiram. He was in jail and would be for the rest of his life. Derrick had finally convinced him to draw a map showing where he'd left the other bodies. Recovery teams had gathered the remains and the families had been notified, hope extinguished—but they had answers, at least.

It was over.

He could leave Bluff County and the Appalachian Trail behind forever.

Just then, a shadowy figure caught his eye across the graveyard, a man in a long coat, his body hunched, a gray beard. He looked… familiar.

A frown pulled at his mouth. The man was watching Derrick's mother. Watching *him*. An eerie sensation engulfed him, and he thought about the bones. The etchings on the grave markers. Hiram and Randall both denied digging the graves and carving the tombstones. Randall had dropped the watch while searching for Penny before the grave had been dug.

The man lifted a handkerchief and dabbed at his eyes, and Randall's suggestion that his father might have faked his death taunted Derrick. Was it possible? Had his father survived? Had he found the bodies and buried them?

If so, why wouldn't he have come back to him and his mother?

He squeezed his mother's arm, telling himself that his father would never abandon them when they needed him most. As he turned, the man disappeared into the shadows.

A brisk wind picked up, and Derrick glanced at the top of the hill to the left.

Ellie stood by a live oak, the wind swirling her hair around her face. She looked small and lost, and he had a sudden pang of longing to go to her and comfort her. He'd torn apart her family, and he couldn't help feeling guilty about that, even though he wouldn't change it.

Although her parents were facing charges, they insisted they hadn't known for certain if Hiram was the Ghost. Randall claimed he'd suspected him and been tracking him for years. He'd almost caught him twice, but the man had managed to escape.

Derrick didn't know whether he believed him or not. It didn't matter. Their silence had cost so many lives.

He wondered how Ellie was dealing.

She met his gaze, and his breath stalled in his chest at the agony in her expression. A second later she turned and fled down the hill toward the parking lot.

The temptation to go to her seized him. But he remained rooted by his mother. Ellie probably hated him. He didn't blame her. He'd given his own family closure, but he'd destroyed hers.

He'd done what he had to do. And if necessary, he'd do it all over again.

So, he watched her walk away. She'd go back to her mountain where she belonged. And he'd go back to his life in Decatur alone.

CHAPTER NINETY-SEVEN

Ellie was broken. Just watching Derrick and his mother at the graveyard hammered home the reality of how much they'd suffered.

That little girls—nearly a dozen—had died because of her.

She pressed the accelerator and sped on to the winding roads and hills that led her back home.

Although she found no solace in the scenery now. And she certainly didn't feel as if she had a home.

Her boss had ordered her to take a leave of absence to heal. They were both dealing with the fallout from her parents' involvement, and the press. Cord had left a message asking about her father, but his voice was terse, and she realized she'd hurt him when she'd questioned him at his house. Still, he'd saved her life.

Even if she wanted to and the public forgave her, how could she return to her job when her family had been embroiled in the worst serial killer case ever on the Appalachian Trail? When guilt suffused every cell in her body?

Who would trust her now?

She didn't even trust herself.

She couldn't bear to see her parents or talk to them. She might never be able to look them in the face again.

Cord was still angry at her, too. She'd broken the fragile trust they'd built. Derrick must hate her and her family. Their twisted secrets had led to so many lost lives.

As she neared town, a Bryce Waters for Sheriff sign waved in the wind. With her father stepping down, Bryce had temporarily taken over the office, and would easily win the election.

Another blow to her gut.

Just as she headed toward a more deserted section where she could drive fast, her phone buzzed. Angelica again. She'd been having a field day with the story. Desperate to avoid her, Ellie let it go to voicemail, then like a glutton for punishment, listened to the message.

"Detective Reeves, you can't run forever. When you're ready to open up about your family, contact me. I'd like to do a tell-all from your perspective. Starting with, 'How does it feel to know your brother was a serial killer?'"

Your brother, your brother, your brother… The words reverberated over and over in Ellie's head at night when she closed her eyes.

Her phone rang again. This time Captain Hale.

Knowing she couldn't avoid him, she answered. "Yeah?"

"Detective, you need to stop by my office. I just got the forensics report back, and I think you're going to want to see it."

"Can't you just tell me what it says over the phone?"

"Trust me, you'll want to look at it in person."

His cryptic comment roused a foreboding feeling inside her. "I'll be there ASAP."

She turned back towards the highway leading to Crooked Creek.

Whatever it was, Captain Hale sounded disturbed. Neither her father nor Hiram had admitted to burying the girls.

What if Hiram had had an accomplice?

CHAPTER NINETY-EIGHT

Crooked Creek

Ellie entered the station with a softball-sized knot in her gut. Heath waved to her from the desk in the corner, where he was on the phone. With her gone, he was working double duty and had risen to the occasion.

Captain Hale motioned her into his office and closed the door behind them. The look on his face as he ran his hand over his bald head made her feel like she was a kid being called to the principal's office.

"What is it?" she asked without preamble.

He gestured for her to sit, so she sank into the chair in front his desk, then he pushed a folder toward her. Nerves tightened her shoulders as she opened it and began to skim the forensics report. Prints on the dolls belonged to Hiram. One of the boot prints confirmed he'd been at the creek where Penny was taken. And his prints had been found at the Dugan farm, meaning he'd been staying there some, and was the one who'd attacked her that night.

No prints on the grave markers though. *Damn.*

"I don't understand," she said as she looked up at the captain.

"Keep reading."

His odd tone made her skin crawl, but she flipped the page and found the lab report for Hiram's DNA. Initially, she didn't know what she was looking at.

Hiram's blood type. Genetic markers.

Then a notation. Hiram's DNA matched her mother's. But not her father's. Just what she expected.

But the next section gave her pause. The comparison to her own blood.

Shock bolted through her, and she studied it again. Her DNA and Hiram's were not a match. Meaning she wasn't biologically related to Hiram.

She rocked back on her heels. How could that possibly be? Her mother had given birth to him. And to her.

Hadn't she?

CHAPTER NINETY-NINE

March 11, 9:00 a.m., Bluff County Jail

The winter storm had passed, but the one in Ellie's life had gained momentum.

Wrangling her emotions as best as she could, she insisted her parents—Randall and Vera—meet her for a chat with Hiram.

Angelica wanted a tell-all. Hell, she wanted a tell-all, but not to feed the reporter. To quiet the disturbing questions in her head.

Her parents were waiting when she arrived at the county jail where Hiram was being held. Both looked haggard and wary. She hadn't spoken to them in days.

Although her father would make a full recovery, he still looked pale and weak and had lost at least ten pounds. Vera's perfect make-up and hair were a mess. Dark circles that no amount of make-up or concealer could hide rimmed her eyes.

"What's this about?" her father asked.

"I thought we should have a family sit-down," Ellie said, struggling to keep her voice even though she wanted to scream at them.

Vera fidgeted, twisting her hands together, then they seated themselves in a small visiting room. Hiram shuffled in, cuffed and shackled, dragging one leg behind him, his eyes darting toward her then Vera. The crazed look of hatred deepened.

Vera looked terrified, a shell of the woman who always dressed in silk pantsuits and pearls. Her father clenched her mother's hand, as if even now he was protecting her from her mistakes.

Ellie laid the folder on the table. "I have forensics and DNA reports here."

Vera gave a small gasp. Hiram showed no reaction. Resignation lined her father's face.

First, she addressed Hiram. "Hiram, it's true that Vera is your mother. But I am not your sister."

A smile tugged at his mouth, as if he'd been anticipating this day for a long time. "I know," he muttered. "Why do you think I despised you so much?" He glared at Vera. "I was her blood son, but she chose you instead."

Ellie's heart cracked. Battling tears, she turned and faced her parents. "Is it true? You didn't give birth to me, Mom?"

Vera bit down on her lower lip, then murmured a pained yes.

CHAPTER ONE HUNDRED

Ellie swallowed against the pain choking her. Disbelief warred with the need to know everything now.

She angled her head toward Hiram. "How did you know?"

Anger blended with his sinister smile. He was enjoying seeing her suffer. "I hacked into the social worker's files on me and found out my mother's name," Hiram said. "Then I started looking for her. But the surprise was on me." He gave Vera a scathing look. "When I found Mommy, she had a little girl. At first, I thought you were my sister, but then I heard Randall say something about adoption. That having you was so wonderful."

"I felt guilty for so long about giving you up," Vera said. "So Randall and I decided to adopt. Then the agency matched us with Ellie."

Hiram grunted. "So you took home pretty little Mae with the blonde curls and big blue eyes and raised her as your child."

Bitterness turned his eyes to molten lava as he turned back to Ellie. "You weren't even her blood, but she spoiled you while she left her own son to rot."

"I tried to find you, but they told me I signed over all rights to you," Vera said. "I thought you'd been adopted into a loving home."

Ellie's mind swirled with emotions. No wonder Hiram had harbored such animosity toward her.

"But I wasn't. I was shuffled around from one bad house to another, carrying my clothes in a trash bag," he hissed. "But once I found out where you lived, I snuck out to see you every chance I got. I watched you with Mae. Watched you dress her up and put bows in her hair and give her dolls." He gestured towards Ellie's father. "And I saw you make that dollhouse for her. She loved it so much that I decided to start carving dolls—"

"You lured me away with the dolls and the promise of another dollhouse with pretty shutters and twirling lights on top," Ellie murmured, her memory returning.

It had worked because she'd loved the dollhouse her father built for her. The one she'd found in her father's workroom…

Her breathing grew unsteady. She had loved dolls once. Until she'd been locked away in that dark hole with the plain wooden doll and its sightless eyes, and its mouth shaped into a silent scream. The one Hiram had given her.

The memory returned in vivid clarity.

Hiram had snuck up at the edge of her yard holding the doll. *"Look, I made this one just for you."* She'd been intrigued that he'd made it himself.

"I built a dollhouse, too. Follow me and I'll show you." And she had. She'd crawled into the cave in the woods to see it, but there had been no dollhouse.

"I'm sorry, Hiram." Regret and shame laced Vera's voice. "I thought I was doing the right thing for you. Thought you'd have a better life than I could give you."

He pounded his cuffed hands on the metal table. "Just stop. You tell yourself you did what's best for me, but you just didn't want me because I wasn't perfect."

"That's not true," Vera cried.

He tried to lurch toward her, but the guard rushed in, yanking Hiram backward. He cursed and growled his rage toward Vera as he was escorted through the thick steel doors.

Silence, thick with tension, vibrated through the room as the door clanged shut.

Vera opened her mouth to say something, then seemed to lose her words as emotions colored her face. Randall reached for Ellie's hand as if to console her, but Ellie jerked it into her lap.

Taking a deep breath, she pinned them with angry eyes. "If you didn't give birth to me, then who did? Who are my birth parents?"

Randall's eyes darkened, and Vera made a choked sound. "We are your parents," her father said. "We loved you and raised you and gave you a life."

"A life built on lies." Ellie shook her head. "Who is my mother?" she asked Vera.

Vera's lower lip quivered. "We honestly don't know, Ellie. You'd been in foster care for almost a year when we learned about you." Her voice softened. "You were so little and frightened looking, and painfully shy that it was heartbreaking. You needed a mother. The minute I saw you, I wanted to take you home. Don't you see how much we loved you?"

Ellie couldn't see anything at the moment, except for the pain of betrayal and secrets.

Unwanted tears threatening, she stood and rushed from the room. Her parents—no, Vera and Randall—called after her, but she didn't stop until she was outside.

Fresh air bathed her face, and as she climbed in her Jeep, she saw her reflection in the mirror. Exhaustion and shock streaked her still-bruised face, a deep lost look permeating her eyes. She had the sudden urge to talk to someone, to call Cord. Or Derrick. But… she couldn't ask them for comfort—or forgiveness—without telling them everything.

And she wasn't ready to do that. First, she had to sort it out herself.

Once, she'd known who she was and had her life all mapped out. She was Randall and Vera Reeves' daughter and planned to take over as sheriff of Bluff County.

But everything she'd known and trusted and loved was based on deceit. Ellie, Mae… she didn't even know her real name.

Or where she was going next.

A LETTER FROM RITA HERRON

Thank you so much for diving into the world I've created with Detective Ellie Reeves in *The Silent Dolls*! If you enjoyed *The Silent Dolls* and would like to keep up with all of my latest releases, you can sign up at the following link. Your email address will never be shared, and you can unsubscribe at any time.

www.bookouture.com/ritaherron

Having grown up with the North Georgia mountains, Appalachian Trail and the Smokies practically in my own backyard, I've always been drawn to stories set in rural small towns. The tall mountain ridges, sharp drop-offs, treacherous terrain, and dangers on the AT are beautiful, but also ripe for murder and mystery and made the perfect backdrop for my new series!

Faced with the dangers of the trail, colorful small-town characters and eccentrics hiding out off the grid, I imagined Ellie Reeves as tough, spunky, and a woman who refuses to back down from anything. She has lived by maps all her life and has her life all mapped out.

But what happens when that plan is derailed? When she must race against time to save a little girl from a serial killer who has been hunting near Ellie's hometown? When everything Ellie thought she knew about herself and her family blows up in her face?

I hope you enjoyed the beginning of Ellie's journey as she faces these questions and tackles the first case in a crime wave sweeping across the AT! If you liked *The Silent Dolls*, I'd appreciate it if you left a short review. As a writer, it means the world to me that you share your feedback with other readers who might be in interested in Ellie's world.

I love to hear from readers, so you can find me on Facebook, my website and Twitter.

Thanks so much for your support. Happy reading!
Rita

 ritaherron

 www.ritaherron.com

 @ritaherron

ACKNOWLEDGMENTS

First of all, a huge thanks to Christina Demosthenous for seeking me out. When she suggested I write a detective series, I had this one in the works and was thrilled to send it over. Her insight from day one, suggestions and edits helped shape it into a much better book with twists I hadn't even dreamed of. I also want to thank the Bookouture team for the great cover and title.

Also, thanks to my agent Jenny Bent for her unfailing support and guidance.

Another thanks to my long-time critique partner and writer friend Stephanie Bond for brainstorming and encouraging me from the get-go with this dark mystery series. And much appreciation to attorney Aaron Rives for answering questions about the law.

Printed in Great Britain
by Amazon

86860659R00192